Praise for T. J. Michaels' *Hatsept Heat*

"Interesting new world. Hot stuff!"

~ *Best selling author, Shelley Bradley aka Shayla Black*

"T.J. Michaels is back again with her exciting third installment in the Vampire Council of Ethics series."

~ *Fallen Angel Reviews*

"This third book in the Vampire Council of Ethics (V.C.O.E.) series is as much fun as the previous two, with some real cliff hangers thrown in for good measure."

~ *Wild On Books*

"I would definitely recommend HatSept Heat to anyone who likes a steamy romance novel to help them get to sleep at night!!!"

~ *Just Erotic Romance Reviews*

Look for these titles by
T. J. Michaels

Now Available:

Vampire Council of Ethics Series
Carinian's Seeker (Book 1)
Serati's Flame (Book 2)
Hatsept Heat (Book 3)

Hatsept Heat

T. J. Michaels

A Samhain Publishing, Ltd. publication.

Samhain Publishing, Ltd.
577 Mulberry Street, Suite 1520
Macon, GA 31201
www.samhainpublishing.com

Hatsept Heat
Copyright © 2009 by T. J. Michaels
Print ISBN: 978-1-60504-284-8
Digital ISBN: 1-60504-079-7

Editing by Jennifer Miller
Cover by Anne Cain

This book is a work of fiction. The names, characters, places, and incidents are products of the writer's imagination or have been used fictitiously and are not to be construed as real. Any resemblance to persons, living or dead, actual events, locale or organizations is entirely coincidental.

All Rights Are Reserved. No part of this book may be used or reproduced in any manner whatsoever without written permission, except in the case of brief quotations embodied in critical articles and reviews.

First Samhain Publishing, Ltd. electronic publication: July 2008
First Samhain Publishing, Ltd. print publication: May 2009

Dedication

To my fabulous future millionaires extraordinaire, I dedicate Kenoe and Shinju's story. Several of the characters in my books are based on you two awesome people who are patient, supportive, the loves of my life with a dash (or a heaping handful, depending on what day it is ;D) of sass and spice—my children. So, Tamara and Michael, YOU RAWK!!!

Chapter One

Maruma Maruyama, Max to those he'd given permission to address him as such, turned to his longtime friend and guard of many years but didn't speak. Not yet. He needed to think for a minute, and thankfully Sasuke was patient.

Shit. Max couldn't believe what a mess he'd gotten the Ooeto clan into. With steady fingers, he calmly dipped a savory Gyoza pork dumpling into a small bowl of ginger soy sauce. He might feel completely unsure of what to do to keep the rival clans from playing hardball, but he sure as hell wouldn't *look* unsure.

After a short stretch of companionable silence, Sasuke broke the ice.

"Max, what do you propose?" Then he simply sipped his wine and waited for an answer.

Placing his chopsticks on their stand next to his plate, Max rested his elbows on the arms of his chair and steepled his fingers.

"When is the contact due to get in touch with you, Sasu?"

"A few days," Sasuke replied. "I received a message that he's on his way back to Japan."

"Now that's a change of plans," Max said, unable to keep his brow from scrunching into a frown.

"I agree. Especially since he gave no indication he was leaving Japan in the first place. He is certainly sneaky for a man who appears so weak."

"Sneaky? Certainly. But brilliant." With a sigh, Max rose from the table. A few steps took him to the wall of glass panes in the living room of his swanky high-rise. Looking down onto one of the many beautiful gardens in Tokyo, he was disappointed that the sight before him did not bring comfort or ease his concerns as it usually did. Just below was one of the most attractive landscaped gardens alongside Tokyo Bay, right across from the futuristic-looking Shiodome. Prime real estate coveted by many. And right now, he just didn't give a damn.

"Sasu, you and I are both proof that he can do exactly what he promised...for a price, of course."

The calm façade that was always plastered on Sasuke's face cracked just a bit. "But we've paid his damned price, and the effects are starting to fade. Max, this fellow is beginning to make me nervous."

"Understandable. Something is certainly more fishy than I care for. I don't think I have any choice but to go see—"

Sasuke cut him off. "Listen, Max, I'd hoped to keep your vampire contacts out of this."

"I know. So did I. But if we're going to stay a step ahead of this guy our options are somewhat limited. So, you know what to do, right?"

"Of course." Sasuke gave a slight bow and headed for the door.

"And Sasu?"

"*Hai?*"

"Keep an even closer eye on my sister, will you?"

"Sure, but not willingly. The last thing I need is an ass

kicking from Shinju because she's mad at you." A smirk accompanied the banter.

"Then don't get caught." Max laughed at the grimace planted firmly on his friend's face.

"Easy for you to say, asshole. You taught her how to catch someone like me."

In the Land of the Rising Sun, the country's namesake had barely climbed into the sky when Kenoe Hatsept walked through the San-Mon gate of the Zenkoji temple. He didn't break stride until he reached the far end of the expansive grounds. His goal—the doors of the Zenkoji Hondo, the main building of the temple compound and his sanctuary while in Nagano.

Thankfully, for the past fourteen hundred years, this place had welcomed people of other places, of different cultures and beliefs. And Kenoe Hatsept was as different as they came. In a country of dark-haired, dark-eyed people, his white locs and ultra-fair skin declared him no native of this island. If his features didn't set him apart, a deadly set of sharpened canines and the arctic barely-blue of his eyes should have. Thankfully no one seemed to notice.

Finally, after weeks of daily meditation and rigorous workouts, his stomach had just begun to loosen its knots. His mind had begun to calm. After years of blood, guts and chasing bad guys, Kenoe felt rested and at peace.

Until this morning.

Suddenly he was back on edge. But there were no problems at home—he'd checked the second the pit of his stomach kicked

into a dance when he'd reached the outer gates of the temple property. There were no assignments awaiting him here in Nagano, and there were still a few more months leave on his calendar. Yet when he'd caught the scent of...*something*, just outside the walls, his nervous system flew into a riot. His fangs twitched, skin itched, blood danced. All because of a barely-there smell in the air? It didn't make a damned bit of sense.

Ducking inside the huge Hondo temple, Kenoe blew a breath of relief from between pursed lips. The incenses and natural wood of the building filled his nostrils and he inhaled deeply. As early as it was, barely a soul stirred. No one saw him slip into the darkness of a corner near an ornate alter at the back of the huge building. His knees hit the floor and his too-full mind immediately cleared as he cloaked himself in a meditative state.

Several minutes, perhaps hours passed in calm bliss. As the crowds grew, the voices of young and old slid over and off of him. Kenoe's breathing remained even, his mind focused on absolutely nothing. No worries about his duties as a Seeker. No concerns about his best friend, Tameth, who was now safely mated and bonded to the man of her dreams. And seeing that the rogue vampires who'd made his life a living hell were safely incarcerated in the bowels of a Council prison, the need for revenge that had spurred him for so many years no longer existed.

There in the darkness of the temple, it was, as his good friend, Dr. Carin, would say, "all good".

Deep breath in, long exhale out. No worries for a good long while, right?

Another deep breath. What? That disconcerting scent slithered into a dim corner of his thoughts and yanked him right out of his carefully cultivated calm.

And though the magnificent cherry blossoms that drew people to this place every year had become clusters of summer fruit hanging heavy on the branches, the gardens were still filled with those who'd come to admire the greenery and say a prayer here in the temple. His keen nose sought out the scent through the crowd. Even keener eyes zeroed in on the source of the fragrance that meddled with his patience. At the same time, a voice laced with sensuality reached out and all but caressed Kenoe. Interesting—the voice and the smell went together. And they both came from a woman he couldn't have missed if he'd tried.

Kenoe rose slowly, so as not to startle anyone who caught his movements, and eased into the light. He leaned against one of the ancient beams that supported the structure, folded his arms across his chest and watched. The woman walked past him and stepped into the stream of light filtering in through the windows, illuminating her features.

His head tilted and his lips parted on a sharp intake of breath. This female stood out from them all. Black mega-wavy hair was pulled back into a short, thick ponytail. Her skin was a deep golden brown with eyes to match. There was a strange familiarity as if he'd seen her, or someone like her, somewhere before. And he wished he had x-ray vision. At all of five-foot nothing, her plain black skirt and white blouse gave not a clue of her waist, hips or legs. Hell, he got barely a glimpse of ankle, yet there was the impression of curves galore. Lips so full and inviting, fine-boned cheeks and the tilt of wide-set eyes gave her a look of innocence with a hint of mischief as she skillfully herded a group of uniformed teenagers towards the main altar.

Just then, one of the young boys in the group kicked up a ruckus, and her voice told yet another story. It seemed much too deep to go with the rest of her. How'd such a sultry, soulful sound come out of such an itty bitty person? The quiet snap of

her words made even Kenoe want to obey.

She'd cast him little more than a glance, but deep down he felt as if he should know her. Know a human female? One that practically screamed raw and wild sensuality, yet appeared contained, solid and grounded? Not likely.

Damn, his chest hurt. He looked down. Well, no bloody wonder—he'd taken a breath in, puffed out his chest, and forgotten to let it out. Instinct had him on the verge of hissing, fangs ready to sink into any and every male of breeding age within thirty feet. Damn, he needed to get the hell out of here.

"Maruyama-*sensei*," called one of the students.

The woman turned, and her natural scent swirled in the air and wrapped around Kenoe's spine as she moved away. The effect it had on him from a distance when he'd caught it back near the outer gates was bad enough. But this close up, it was damned ridiculous.

Maybe he was ill? It was a stupid thought. There was nothing wrong with him, but hell if this kind of reaction to the sound and smell of a woman was anywhere near normal.

He froze as a gentle stroke passed over his thoughts, fleeting and soft as a butterfly wing. And his logical mind fought with biological instinct.

No. It was impossible. The woman couldn't be... Forget about it. He was a Seeker, vampire law enforcement, damn it. He didn't have time for this shit. His fangs disagreed, digging into clamped lips while the rest of his body continued to riot. He turned with a growl, strode down a side aisle and out the front door, grumbling the whole way.

Shinju had spotted the man meditating in a corner the second she and her lively group of high schoolers passed the first row of ancient statues inside the historical building. He'd

seemed oblivious to the stream of people making their way into and out of the temple. Had even ignored all the noise her students made as they toured the site and asked questions.

The words tumbled from her mouth as she explained the importance of the shrine, alter, relics and such, but she had no idea what she was saying. Her attention was on the snow white hair of the man shrouded in shadows. The next thing she knew he was barely two feet away, power radiating from his tall frame. And now that he was more fully in the light, her lungs seized painfully beneath her breasts after just a simple glance. The man was damned gorgeous.

His hair was pulled away from his face and fell in thick braid-looking strands down his back. Shinju was sure that in all her travels she'd never seen anyone with eyes so pale as to be almost white. Nor skin so fair but exquisitely smooth. My goodness, he put her favorite anime character to shame, from his thickly muscled neck and shoulders down to his oh-so-nicely-formed thighs. His expression said "confused", but his stance screamed "ready to pounce".

He shifted his weight and leaned against a pillar. Shinju discreetly eyed the stylish black denim encasing his legs—not too tight, but he did a good job filling it out. Her stomach did a funky little wiggle thing.

A student asked another question. Perfect timing. And reason enough to shake her head and clear it from the pull, the magnetism of the man off to her left. Forcing all her attention to the young lady who'd spoken, Shinju turned her back completely on the man.

But it didn't stop her mind from galloping off on its own, wondering who he was and where he was from. Shinju cocked her head in wonder when, all on their own, her thoughts reached for his, brushed lightly against his awareness. The

unexpected contact produced a delicious shiver that worked its way through her belly and set it to dancing. The second her tummy started doing the samba, the face on Mr. Gorgeous morphed into a fierce frown. As if he'd felt what she had? Nah, that would be too weird.

Instead of dwelling on the strange connection that was no doubt imagined, Shinju watched the man with the snowy locs stiffen, turn and leave the building so fast she wondered how it was possible to not only move with such speed, but to look so damned delicious while doing it.

She was a teacher, a quiet upstanding citizen, and...horny. All from the sight of a stranger? Didn't make a bit of sense.

But no worries. The students and teachers of Shibuya High School were only in Nagano for three days on their annual school trip. Day after tomorrow would see her on the two-hour train ride back to Tokyo. Back to her life.

"Oh joy," she muttered sarcastically.

"Excuse me, Maruyama-*sensei*?"

A blush heated her cheeks as she turned to the girl. "Nothing. Nothing at all. Okay everyone, it's time to go."

A collective "Awwww" from the students was quickly shushed so as not to disturb the other visitors. "Please exit. You may stop at the office for gifts. Please meet at the Mountain Gate where we came in. You have thirty minutes before we board our bus to return to the hotel. Don't worry. This evening you'll all be free to explore the city, have dinner with friends or whatever you like."

Thoughts in a jumble, Shinju turned her class over to the head boy and girl, glad she'd worn a pair of sturdy leather flats today as she hurried out of the main temple and through the compound. There was so much to do. Lessons to prepare. Activities to plan. Men with tight butts to ogle.

"No!" she grumbled to herself, shaking her head on the way to the designated meeting place. "That's just not right, thinking about a strange man's ass like that. Get it together, Shinju. Besides, you can't get wild here. You're back in Japan, a quiet schoolteacher. Now act right, woman."

As she waited for the boys and girls to get their fill of Zenkoji souvenirs and gather at the gate, she didn't see a pair of eyes watching her from a distance.

But she certainly felt them.

Chapter Two

She was right in front of him, give or take a block or two. He'd been dead-on earlier at the temple—her schoolteacher clothes had indeed hidden one curvy little body. The dark slacks and short jacket she wore fit to a tee. Certainly he'd never seen such a perfect ass move under a pair of pants like that.

Kenoe felt a grin tip up the side of his mouth, followed by a chuckle. Here he was, a Seeker for the Vampire Council of Ethics on his first vacation in three years, and instead of enjoying it he was stalking a human who had no idea she was in his sights.

Wait, wait, wait. Back the hell up. He absolutely was *not* stalking a human. He was, uh, simply keeping an eye on the people who were out enjoying the evening. It didn't matter where you were, it was dangerous on the streets at night, and he would protect her, damn it. Didn't matter that it wasn't his job right now.

Kenoe ducked behind a tree as a fellow Seeker passed him by. He kept his mouth closed and head down, pretending to study one of the placards that were common in the city. This one was planted at the base of one of the many trees and told what kind of tree it was and the significance of long ego events that occurred on this very spot.

Moving on, he came to stand in front of a building sporting a huge yellow backlit billboard. Kenoe's sharp eyes sought out his quarry. Quarry? Sigh.

Guess once a cop, always a cop, even when I'm supposed to be relaxing.

Not to mention the woman was nowhere to be seen. Perhaps she'd turned into the soba noodle restaurant up ahead?

And when was the last time he'd lost a person, any person, once he'd put his keen nose to the task of tailing them? He was the best damned tracker in the whole Seeker corps but he couldn't manage to keep up with one female. A human female. He must really be losing it. If it were possible to smack himself in the back of the neck for being so careless, he would have.

Maybe this was for the best. Perhaps he should go back to his hotel and just call it a night. Besides, he'd come here to find himself, not find a woman. He was supposed to be spending his time in meditation, enjoying the clean mountain air and touring the land of the samurai. Letting his inner self heal from all the pain and blood that had been a constant since he was a baby vampire. The same pain that had architected the walls around his heart—walls recently fallen as a result of patience and love from his friends-turned-family.

He wanted the same love and commitment enjoyed by his closest colleagues—Bix and Dr. Carin, Alaan and Tameth. Yet at the same time Kenoe couldn't quite see bringing a woman into his world. It was too damned unstable and unsure.

Thoughts swirling like wind tossed leaves, he stopped down the street a ways under a huge cherry tree right outside a small teashop. Even in the dark the ripening fruit was visible amidst the abundant leaves. Too bad he'd missed viewing the famous cherry blossoms back in April. They were reputed to be so thick

and full, it looked like the trees were covered with snow. But in a few weeks the Toraijin Festival, an international music, food and cultural exchange, would take place here. Perhaps he'd stay long enough for that, then...

The only warning he got was a hint of something exotically sweet with a bit of tropical tang wafting from behind him, a fragrance he recognized—the woman he'd spotted in the temple earlier. The question was, how the hell had she snuck up on him like that?

Before his mind could catch up with his circumstances, Kenoe Hatsept did something he'd never done in his life, even in the presence of a human—he sheathed his fangs.

"Are you following me?" came a voice as soft as down and as smoky as aged whisky. The words were spoken on a whisper from mere inches away.

Without turning to face her, he replied just as softly, "I am not following you." Heat crept up his neck at the total, flat-out lie. Hell, he was an undercover vampire cop, yet he was embarrassed at telling less than the truth to a possible target? No, no, wait. She wasn't a target.

This is new, he thought sarcastically. Pushing his newfound, and currently unwelcome, conscience away, he said, "But since we are both in the same place at the same time, perhaps you would join me for a bite?"

A bite...of her. Now that sounded good. His fangs twitched behind his lips.

No biting, Kenoe. No. Bite. Ting. Keep 'em sheathed, man.

She stepped around his body, eyeing him with an inkling of suspicion. Or was that plain old curiosity? Her stylishly cut hair fell in loose waves. A few strands blew into her face. She raised her head and their gazes met. She gave him a smile. Kenoe's world tilted sideways.

With a simple, "Okay", she turned away, took a few steps and then looked back over her shoulder. "You comin'?"

The irritation at having lost her trail a few moments earlier faded, and Kenoe grinned like a damned fool.

Shinju had known what she was going to do before she'd positioned herself to do it. And it was all her brother's fault. He'd taught her to hold her own with anyone, male or female, since she was old enough to sass him back...and get smacked in the mouth for it. And she'd been training in the martial arts ever since. Without a sound, equipped with a boldness that had always seemed to get her in trouble with her parents, Shinju had stepped back into the shadows and let the beautiful stranger take two steps past her.

Hmm. He hadn't seemed surprised when she'd snuck up behind him and asked him if he was following her. In fact, the twist of his mouth looked like he wanted to say, "Yep, I'm following you", but smoothed into a devastating smile instead.

And now she'd learned his name, and it was as exotic and sexy as the rest of him. Too bad she'd never see him again past tonight.

But in the meantime, they sat in the local soba noodle shop slurping their meals and chatting like old friends.

It was just too weird. Not spooky or uncomfortable, just...weird. Shinju didn't know him from Adam. She'd always been taught never to talk to strangers. Well, not only was she talking to a stranger, she was flirting shamelessly with one she had no intention of seeing again. But damn, not only did she want to see the man, *all* of him, Shinju wanted to kiss those perfectly formed lips, touch those incredibly wide shoulders, play in that mass of silvery silken locs. *Whew.*

"So what does it mean?" he asked.

Shinju looked up. Her brown eyes met his iced blues and something sounded in her soul like a large bell.

"Huh?" Boy, way to use your university vocabulary, she thought.

"Your name, what does it mean?"

"Shinju? It's Japanese for pearl. It means a substance layered upon itself over and over until it is considered precious, like a pearl. And you? I can't say I've heard the name Kenoe before, even in other Asian countries."

"I have no idea." He sipped some tea then set it on the table before picking it up again. She watched the flex of his forearm as he tipped up the small cup with large but graceful fingers. Too bad his shirt sleeves weren't a little shorter so she could catch an eyeful of the biceps pushing against the cloth.

He spoke and her focus shifted back to his lips. They should be outlawed.

"My family is an ancient one. We originate from Egypt, but my name doesn't sound the least bit Egyptian to me."

"Do you think you might be distantly related to the female pharaoh, Hatshepsut?" she asked with a saucy lilt to her words. Then she pretended to lick a bit of sauce from her lower lip. Oh lord, she was flirting.

Kenoe watched her tongue with avid interest, and promptly lost control of his chopsticks. One of them went flying across the table, taking a small piece of noodle with it. It stuck to her sweater like a thick piece of fringe.

The man's sexy lips pressed into a thin line as he caught the remaining chopstick in midair. Shinju laughed. Loudly. Totally unladylike in public, but it simply couldn't be helped considering the man even looked yummy when he was mortified.

While Kenoe cleared his throat, she took a moment to compose herself. Nothing a little biting the inside of her cheek couldn't cure. But just barely.

"So," he coughed, "how is it you speak English without an accent, yet you speak perfect Japanese too?"

Shinju picked the noodle off her clothes and folded it into a napkin, still trying not to smile.

"Learning English from a native speaker means you get ingrained with the English accent instead of a Japanese one. So my family, my brother actually, sent me to international schools when I was younger, then I traveled extensively after attending university. I earned degrees in both the Le Cordon Bleu culinary method and international business management."

"Culinary? Is that what you teach at your school? Shibuya High, right?"

Hmm. He seemed genuinely interested in what she had to say. Not a reaction often received from anyone other than her brother and his right hand man, Sasuke.

"I actually teach English and what you would call Home Economics." A sigh that sounded sad even to herself slipped out before she could catch it. "All I've ever wanted to be was a master chef with my own restaurant. I wanted to learn French methods, Mediterranean cuisine, Italian, and everything else. Not just Japanese cooking. But my family is very traditional and didn't buy into it. Besides, they couldn't afford to send me anyway. So my brother made sure I got into the schools of my choice with no worries, monetary or otherwise."

But once she'd returned home, typical values of society pressed in around her. She was expected to behave, to be circumspect and blend in with everyone else. The nail that stuck out was often pounded down. By all except Max.

"Sounds like a cool brother."

"Uh, yeah, sure. He's the best." Boy did *that* sound convincing.

"Are you sure?" Kenoe asked with a concerned frown etched across his brow.

"Absolutely. It's just that my father's relatives don't really care for what either of us does for a living."

"But you teach English at a local high school in the hippest part of Tokyo. What's wrong with that?"

She snorted. *Geez, woman, you're the epitome of elegance around this guy.* "Well, they'd rather I just get married and be a housewife. Nothing wrong with that. It's just not for me."

"Which part? The wife part or the house part?"

Wooo! He'd laid that question on her real smooth-like with a grin that was too sensual for words. Unbidden, Shinju felt herself reach for him. Not with her body, but her thoughts. Strange. This had never been an inclination with anyone before. And what she got in the exchange was even more unexpected and impossible to explain—a faint sweeping sensation inside her head, like the slightest summer breeze as it barely ruffled the waves of her hair. Yet this was no light wind. It was weird, deep, and just a bit dark. And damned deliciously scary. The man was heating rapidly and becoming more focused on her by the second. Were those words she was picking up as well? No. No way. Impossible.

Shinju laughed at herself this time, brushed the sensation out of her head, then went on to describe the restaurant she wanted—an upscale place that catered to the finest palette.

How would she ever get her dreams off the ground at the rate she was going? Sure, her brother wanted to give her the capital needed to start the venture. Even after she'd refused, he offered to loan it to her. But Max had already done so much, she just couldn't accept the money. She had to do this on her

own.

God, was she being one of those cheesy romance heroines who resisted the help of a man, any man, just because she could? Those books got on her nerves after a while. What the hell was attractive about being stubborn just 'cause?

In her case it simply wasn't a good idea to have the *yakuza* fund her restaurant. She personally didn't care that her brother led a bunch of criminals. They'd always been good to her and seldom engaged in violence. But her parents and the rest of her family minded, and in a big way. If word got out that she was related to the leader of the Ooeto clan, she would be doomed from the gate and bring way too much attention to herself, her school and her brother.

Max had protected her all her life. She'd be damned if she wouldn't return the favor.

Sigh. Enough dwelling on things she couldn't have.

"I've got to go. It's time for bed check for my students." Shinju stood abruptly, snatched a few yen out of her pants pocket and tossed them onto the table. She headed for the door.

Kenoe was practically on her ass.

"And then?" he pressed. The words were gentle, but she detected a bit of edge behind them. Turning slowly away from the door, she faced him.

Those eyes. Those marvelously crystalline white-blues took on a predatory gleam that sent Shinju's feet a step back. Her ass was practically up against the glass of the door.

"Uh," she stumbled. "A-and then what?"

"After the bed check, Shinju. Then what?"

Was that a low growl rumbling in the back of his throat? Barely there, the sound was just loud enough to catch but not clear enough to swear it wasn't something else.

Kenoe stepped closer. Suddenly she felt a gentle brush across her brow, then down the side of her face. That growl grew in volume and intensity in her head. And did it ever make the base of her womb flutter like kite tails caught in the breeze.

But how did he do that? He hadn't touched her. Hadn't said a word. And why the hell wasn't she terrified that another human being actually seemed to jump into her head? She'd never exhibited any kind of psychic or empathic abilities, and her study of the subject was pretty much limited to paranormal romance novels and the SciFi channel. Yet there was an instinctive knowledge of exactly what was happening here. This man with the mesmerizing eyes, the easy body language and feral hunger in his taut facial expression was enticing her. Calling her to him somehow.

Well, it was *so* not going to happen. He was a stranger she'd probably never see again.

Amazed at how quickly she'd fallen into brooding, Shinju shook herself, sucked it up and gave a respectful bow.

"Goodnight, Kenoe. It was very nice to meet you. Enjoy the rest of your time in my country."

God, she could practically feel his gaze burning a hole through the back of her sweater as she edged through the door. With resolve that was quickly melting under his hot stare, Shinju hightailed it the few blocks back to her hotel.

What happened? Had he said something wrong? Did his breath smell like day-old soba noodles? Or had he simply turned her off with his stylish grace with the damned chopsticks?

And what the hell was going on with his lack of control of his fangs? The ache from fighting with the tendons that controlled their movement had given him a fierce headache. As

a Clan Hatsept male, hiding his teeth was a ridiculous notion. Not that he walked around with three-inch fangs of movie proportions or anything so preposterous. God was Bram Stoker overrated. In truth, unless a vampire was agitated, his incisors simply looked a bit sharper and a tad longer than any typical human's, small enough to be hidden by simply keeping one's mouth shut. But being a vampire meant living with his own kind, rarely having to interact much with humans anyway. In fact, Kenoe could probably count the number of times in his whole life he'd actually felt it necessary to sheathe his fangs, and it was never because of a human. Yet something about this woman brought out the need to be a bit more subtle than his usual self.

The urge to protect her from what he was coupled with the need to claim her. Something about the way she smelled, the way she talked. And those barely-there strokes against his thoughts that she probably wasn't even aware of.

Sigh. Well, nothing to be done about it. At least not right now.

Kenoe walked back to the table he'd shared with Shinju and yanked his jacket off the back of his chair. The thing went crashing to the floor and all eyes swung his way. Shit.

He had to remember his chosen clothing was nothing like his typical sturdy Seeker garb. The nylon coat he slipped up his arms had to be several pounds lighter than the tailored leather trench coat—the symbol of his office and status with the Council and his rank in the Seeker corps.

And the weight of his office was especially heavy at times like this. When he had to let yet another woman he was desperately drawn to walk away from him.

Back up, that wasn't altogether true. Tameth had never walked away from him. That female was one of the best Seekers

in the Serati clan, and his best friend for years. God, he'd wanted it to be more between them, but it was his fault for never pursuing her outside of friendship. While he'd always seen her as a woman he could spend his life with, he'd seen himself as Kenoe Hatsept, emotional wreck extraordinaire.

Kenoe's entire will had been bent on revenge. His only focus and determination was to hone his body and reflexes to the point where he could take down or take out any vampire, especially the one who'd made his life a living hell. But that hunt was over and done with now. That particular rogue vamp had been brought gloriously low by Kenoe's own hand.

Kenoe chuckled at the memory of the raid on Lowan Hatsept Shean's stronghold. He'd allowed himself to be apprehended by Lowan's henchmen, effectively leaving a trail for the other Seekers to follow. The bastard also happened to be both his half brother and the rogue who'd killed Alaan's fiancée years before. Or so they'd thought.

While he and Alaan had argued over who would deliver the crippling blow to Lowan, Tameth had stepped forward and simply cut the outlaw with a blade smeared with a bio-agent developed in Dr. Carin's labs. In seconds, Lowan had hit the floor, retching like a sick puppy. Fight over.

But Kenoe was still damaged goods, whether the one who'd done the damage was rotting in prison or not.

He wanted. He didn't want. He wanted...damn it.

Kenoe shook his head at himself and released a pent-up sigh as he wandered along the busy street.

His gaze snapped up from the sidewalk. His nostrils twitched as both brows dove into a frown. A rogue? No doubt about it. There was nothing like the stench of a vampire gone bad. Not wearing his Seeker trench coat was a plus at the moment. If he scented the rogue, then more than likely his own

scent had been picked up as well. But with no identifying Council apparatus, the villain would only smell another vamp. Not a Seeker.

Instantly, the instincts that made him such a good law enforcement officer kicked in. His frown smoothed, breathing evened and stride became slow and easy.

Kenoe stopped at the corner and turned circles, painting on a perfect lost and confused expression.

The stench grew but he didn't see anyone. So Kenoe followed his nose. There, twenty paces ahead, a short, dark-haired, nasty-assed vampire outlaw turned in to a four-star hotel.

Kenoe's fangs slipped free—Shinju's scent also ended here.

Retrieving a small black phone from his jacket pocket, Kenoe began the short walk back to his own hotel. Looked like vacation was well and truly over if a rogue could walk down the streets of busy downtown Nagano with not a single Seeker in sight.

He checked his watch. It was early in the morning back at V.C.O.E. Western territory headquarters. Very early in the morning. But there was nothing to be done for it.

He flipped open his video phone.

"Dial home."

A few clicks and a couple of rings later, he spoke into the phone again.

"Alaan, I think I may have a small problem. Got a minute?"

Chapter Three

"Boss, I've just spotted someone hanging around outside your sister's place."

Sasuke would have been more worried if Shinju was home. But according to Max this was the day her club was scheduled to meet after school. She taught self-defense to the young ladies who attended Shibuya High. *Hah!* He'd love to be a fly on the wall if anyone at that uppity school of hers ever found out how Shinju had come by those skills, courtesy of sparring with *yakuza* since she was a kid.

"Aren't you supposed to be looking after her, Sasuke?" Max thundered.

"Which is why I even see the guy. He's so well hidden, if it weren't for the enhanced vision and hearing I wouldn't know he was here at all. And..."

"And what, damn it?"

"It's the same guy I spotted a couple of times in Nagano."

"So what?"

"At the same time Shinju was there."

"Shit!"

"Indeed. He doesn't dress like one, but he sure moves and acts like a Seeker."

"What the hell would a Seeker, or any vampire for that

matter, be doing snooping around my baby sister? Uuugghhh..."

"Max? Max, what's wrong? Max, are you there?"

The groan became an agonized pant, then shallow breathing with a bit of a rasp.

"Yes, I am here. Sorry, Sasuke, it is becoming more and more difficult to breathe, especially when I get upset."

"Your enhancements are deteriorating, Max, and at an alarming rate considering my health seems to be hanging on."

"Yes, I did notice. Also, the timing of my illness and the arrival of this vampire around my sister couldn't possibly be a coincidence. What does he look like?"

"No worries about that right now. Get some rest."

Just then, the stranger looked around carefully before climbing down from his perch in a huge Gingko tree. Sasuke didn't want to tell his ailing friend that the man appeared to be six feet of packed muscle. Controlled movements screamed deadly grace. Hmm. Sasuke had traveled all over, both in and out of Japan, but had never seen a man quite like this one. Silvery white hair was pulled back into a thick ponytail and fell almost to the middle of his back. From this distance it appeared to be braided. And his skin was so fair as to be almost as white as his hair.

A wheezing cough brought Sasuke's attention back to the cell phone pressed to his ear.

"Listen, Max, I'll contact the rogue leader and see if—"

"No, Sasuke. The rogues are a last resort. It's bad enough they're all over Nagano. I don't want to inadvertently invite them to Tokyo. Call the Ginzu territory leaders. Start there."

Sasuke heard a fond but regretful air in Max's voice that he completely understood. Ginzu district, the main haunt of the

"good" vampires in this prefecture. Calling them meant Max was seriously laying down his pride. The man literally owed those vamps his life, and they would be disappointed indeed to discover what he'd done with his second chance. But Max was right—if anyone knew the identity of Shinju's recent stalker, it would be the Ginzu vampires of Clan Li.

"I don't want you worrying about it. Promise you will let me handle it."

"Thank you, Sasu. Thank you very much, old friend."

After he hung up with Max, it only took a couple of phone calls for Sasuke to confirm what he'd hoped was untrue. A Seeker was tailing Shinju. So why didn't the man dress as befitting his office? No black-on-black clothing. No custom trench coat. The Seekers of Clan Li, the largest vampire clan in Japan, would never be caught dead without their signature sleek leather coats.

And worse, according to the Clan Li vamps, this particular Seeker was a Hatsept. Although there weren't any Hatsepts in Japan, the telltale white hair was a dead giveaway. In fact, the Li contact had immediately identified the man's clan from a simple description. Sasuke knew if he managed to get closer the Seeker's eyes would be practically white as well. Damn it. Why couldn't it be someone else? He'd take anyone over a damned Hatsept. The silver-haired playboys were said to be among the most ruthless and hated clans in the vampire nation, mostly because they managed to get, or take, more than their fair share of females. They were also known to pick fights just for the hell of it, and usually came out on top. Shit.

Sasuke wasn't supposed to know vampires existed, let alone their clan and governmental structures. And in this case, he couldn't even enlist the help—God forbid—of any of the rival *yakuza* to take down this asshole. One, the *yakuza* clans would

probably beat him to a pulp for telling what they would consider an outrageous lie. After all, who the hell believed in vampires? Two, after he'd proven his claims were true, they'd beat him to a pulp to get their hands on the secret of his and Max's enhanced abilities, though Max's were diminishing. And three, they'd beat him to a pulp for creating an unfair advantage over the other clans. If the *yakuza* were anything, they were consistent in their efforts to keep any one clan from dominating the others. And they would definitely see collaborating with vamps as a possible means to that unwanted end.

Sasuke considered following the Hatsept as he left Shinju's house, but decided against it. After all, he wasn't a vampire and had no intention of engaging one. He was simply a human experiment going wrong, just like Max, and the last thing he needed was to be spotted watching a Seeker.

Instead of boarding a plane from Nagano to the next destination on his long-awaited vacation's agenda, Kenoe found himself literally playing around at the top of the Sony building in Tokyo—city of the world's busiest crosswalks and more than its fair share of neon signs and larger-than-life billboards.

Kenoe hadn't been in Tokyo since the hunt for the nasty outlaw vamp, Aleth Sidheon. In the end, the rogue had ended up a big dusty pile on a sandy beach. And his accomplice, a traitor and a former Liaison for the Western territories, currently enjoyed four walls made of silver and titanium bars in a state-of-the-art Council facility in the Mojave Desert. For her folly the bitch would spend the next fifty-seven years in a big vampire cage, followed by some seriously supervised parole. And all without the benefit of silver, sun or any other kind of

allergy meds.

Out of all his service to the Council, that hairy task was the first time Kenoe had been assigned to work directly with the Head Seeker. Now he was an integral part of one of the elite teams in both ass-kicking and on the scientific front, along with Dr. Carin, of course, mate of the Head Seeker himself.

Pride filled Kenoe's heart and his hand stilled on the joystick he'd been absently manipulating. His early years hadn't been filled with much to be proud of. But every goal he'd ever set since then was now accomplished. He stood on his own two feet, made his own way, complete with scars and all. Friends—true friends—surrounded him and wouldn't hesitate to guard his back in the face of danger.

Yet he couldn't have been more alone if he tried.

Last night he'd handed over a small fortune to walk into a large, plush, but very empty apartment when he could have stayed for free in the swanky Council accommodations across town in Roppongi district. As much as he enjoyed that swinging place known as the foreigners' clubbing paradise, staying there would have required checking in at V.C.O.E. Tokyo headquarters. That meant close contact with other vamps. And they were not the ones to whom he wanted to be close.

There were Seekers, Beta Seekers, Iudex Judges and clan members stationed and living in Tokyo just as in every other city with a Council presence. And while he'd seen plenty of his kind here, none of them knew he was a Seeker, and none of them knew his rank, which was higher than every vampire law enforcement officer outside of the Western territories. Rather keep that knowledge quiet. The last thing he wanted was other vampires bowing, scraping and insisting on dragging him sightseeing while he had a woman to catch, a non-vampire woman that he was still trying to convince himself he wasn't

after.

"*Sumimasen, ojisan?* Excuse me, mister."

Kenoe looked down at a shiny-eyed little girl. Yeah, he knew that expression anywhere. He'd seen it often on little Alaina Bixler's face—Bix and Carin's daughter, as precocious a little ball of energy as ever born to vampiredom. The little imp probably waited back home for him just to pull his locs and beg for horsy back rides. And he'd gladly give them.

Kenoe gave a slight but friendly smile, careful to keep his fangs from showing. After all, he didn't want the wee one to run away screaming.

"How can I help you, little one?"

"You are just kind of standing there looking at the screen. May I please play this game?"

With a bow, she gazed up into his face with a grin that proudly displayed a set of deep dimples.

"Of course you may play. Excuse me."

"*Arigato gozaimasu.* Thank you very much," she said in a happy sing-song voice.

"*Ie, zenzen.* No worries." With a polite incline of his own head, Kenoe pushed the reset button, restarted the game for the girl and motioned for her to take over. She was probably better at it than he was anyway.

Kenoe's nose twitched. A frustrated groan contradicted the easy smile spread across his face. Instinctively following the scent, he knew exactly what, or rather who, he'd find at the end of the trail.

At the top of the Sony building a person could get lost among all the games and electronic gadgets, many of which wouldn't be available in the States for a year or better. Definitely not a typical place to find a Seeker, nor a teacher who

was supposed to be instructing self-defense to her female students at Shibuya High.

A little farther down the aisles of robotic pets and games, Kenoe came to a stop. His half-smile edged into a big grin as he eased up behind the female frantically yanking and pulling on a joystick. She played one of the sword-fighting games. Hmm. She was damned good.

He lowered his voice and tossed her words back at her.

"So, are you following me?"

Well before eight this morning, Kenoe had followed this same woman the few blocks past the Tokyo University of Liberal Arts to her own school, Shibuya High. Restless and not in the mood to do the touristy thing, he'd scouted various parts of the city. Very few rogues hung about, and the ones he'd caught sight of had served their sentences and were carefully surveyed while on parole—a good cop always checked up on such things. He wasn't supposed to be working during his vacation but what was the harm in sneaking a couple of quiet phone calls to Tameth when she just happened to be going off duty?

Strange. The criminal element of this city seemed to be human *yakuza*. Some conservative and discreet, others bold, brash and itching for trouble.

Later Kenoe automatically headed back to Shinju's house and made it to his chosen surveillance spot unseen. He'd felt like an idiot after sitting up in that damned tree across from her house for almost half an hour before figuring out she wasn't home yet. But there'd certainly been no expectation to run into her at the top of the Sony building, of all places. And dressed as she was? He'd be lying if he claimed to have a single objection.

Shinju's painted-on jeans and stretchy fitness top almost seemed a disguise, nothing like the outfit she'd worn out of the

house this morning. On her way to school, the woman was the epitome of drab despite her earthy beauty. She'd stepped out her door in a long, dark brown full skirt, matching jacket, a high-neck blouse and flat shoes. Even dressed like the teacher she was, her inner spark had shone through and singed his very soul, far from the plain-Jane female she was obviously trying to get others to see.

But she was *so* busted.

A pair of wide amber eyes turned on him and the woman's shock resonated across the short distance separating them and crashed into the middle of his chest, bringing with it clear insight to her thoughts and emotions.

So, lil' Miss Maruyama thought she'd gotten rid of him after last week's noodle fiasco?

In truth, she *shouldn't* have ever laid eyes on him again, but hell if he could stay away. If the woman found out he'd followed her all the way to Tokyo she'd probably have him arrested as a stalker.

And there went his fangs again. If they twitched any harder his whole body would start vibrating.

The expression in those cat-like eyes of hers went from surprised to pleased to annoyed in mere seconds, and her catapulting emotions went with them. Well, he had just distracted her and caused one of her video game guys to die. When the woman opened her mouth, her voice was laced with perplexity.

"No, I'm not following you. What are you doing in Tokyo, Kenoe? When we had dinner in Nagano, you said you were going to tour the country."

"Isn't this part of the country? And I thought you told me you taught self-defense after school every day."

Feline-shaped eyes went wide. Kenoe smirked—hell, he just

couldn't help it.

Her grumbled "Smartass" had him chuckling as unexpected happiness—no, sheer joy—bubbled right up out of him. *I'm glad for a sarcastic, snarky comment? What the hell is wrong with me?*

Well, when presented with a saucy female, serve her up hot and he'd dive in headfirst. Must be a Hatsept weakness. So he said, "My ass has been called many things, woman, including tight, incredible, even perfect. But never smart."

"Pffftt!"

Curled lip, rolling eyes and all, the woman was a treat. Kenoe laughed outright, hushing himself when several gamers turned to give him the evil eye.

"Well," she said quietly, but with steel behind each word, "I don't think I've paid that much attention to your ass, but if you turn around I'll rectify that right now."

Both snow-white brows flew upward but his smile just got bigger and wider. "Are you sure you're a quiet little schoolteacher?"

"Sure I am. But the words teacher and mouse are not synonymous."

With a fierce yank on the controller, she let out a quiet whoop and watched her score skyrocket. That last move gained her another two lives.

And she wasn't paying attention to him like she should be.

Her head whipped around and she pinned him with a glare. "*What?*"

"What, what?"

"What do you mean I'm not paying attention to you?"

"I, uh, I didn't say anything, Shinju." Not out loud, anyway. So how had she done that? The woman had just waltzed right

into his thoughts? It was no small feat given he was one of the stronger telepaths in the Seeker corps and kept his thoughts protected at all times when away from home. And the little spitfire was too upset to even be afraid of how they were communicating.

"Damn it!" she snarled aloud. The video lives she'd just gained were history. "Stop distracting me."

Kenoe stepped back without a word, quieted his mind and eyed her from head to toe.

"That's *so* not helping," she tossed over her shoulder. Her loose dark waves brushed the back of her neck. A very inviting, very smooth neck.

"But I'm not distracting you. I haven't said anything." But he sure as hell was thinking it, and totally against his will. In fact, images of her neck bared to him flitted through his mind, followed by a perusal of how her stretchy sports jacket molded to her shoulders and down her back to her waist. And that ass! My God today!

She hissed at him while the most delicious blush turned her skin to a burnished caramel. "Stop looking at me like that, damn it. It's just as distracting as...as talking."

"You want me to stop looking at you?" He stood behind her. How did she know he was looking? Shaking away the disconcerting questions, he asked, "A gorgeous, perfectly put together woman wants me to stop admiring her?"

He knew he'd made it sound ridiculous because, well, it was. Time to up the ante.

He stepped within a hair's breadth of her back and hovered. The woman didn't move away, keeping her gaze glued to the video screen. But he clearly heard the quickening of her heart and the pulsing of her blood. The scent of the light sheen of sweat coating her skin filled his nostrils as it made its way up

through her pores. God, it was almost as if he'd wrapped himself in her essence. "All right, I'll stop looking at you. If..."

"If what?" Breathless anticipation shimmered in the air, wafting from both of them until it swirled together and filled the space between them.

"If you play me at one of these games."

"Are you serious?"

Hmm. Was that a hint of disappointment seeping from her? But she wouldn't back down now. Kenoe didn't know how he knew such a thing, he simply...did.

"I'm totally serious. Choose your poison, gorgeous."

Now it was her turn to raise a questioning brow.

"Fine. Twin Dragons. I go first."

Kenoe almost smiled like a loon without a worry in the world. It didn't take long. Three furious rounds of Twin Dragons were played with all his heart and soul. It wouldn't have been fair to do less than his best. Seeker's code and personal honor wouldn't allow it.

And she kicked his ass up one side of the screen and down the other. The "Game Over" banner flashed, displaying a score several thousand points higher than his. Kenoe held out his hand.

Shinju took it in a firm grip and shook it.

"Congratulations, gorgeous. You win. You may now take me to dinner."

The smirk fell off her face. God, he wished he had a camera.

"What! You said you'd back off if I played you at one of these games."

"I never said that. I said I'd stop looking at you if you played me at one of these games. But I'm so awful at them you

should have asked the stakes."

"The stakes?"

"Absolutely. The stakes were if you beat me I could look all I want and get dinner in the offing. If I won, I'd leave you alone."

"What the hell kind of backwards-assed bet is that?" Ooooh. The woman was hissing and spitting mad. And it turned him on like a fucking light switch until he practically glowed with it.

"It's *my* kind of bet. I'm no good at any of these damned video games. Why in the world would I ever gamble on the off chance I'd do well against you after watching you hit high score after high score? I'm no fool, lovely." Lowering his mouth to the shell of her ear, he whispered, "You may as well know now that I always play to win, even if it's pretty much assured that I'm going to lose."

"And how can I be sure you're not lying?" She was still as stone, back ramrod straight as the words slipped from her lips with a mixture of amusement and anxiety.

"What would be the point? Considering we seem to be so in tune with each other, you'd surely catch me. Besides, it's not my style." He might keep a few secrets, but flat-out lie to her? He didn't think he could pull it off, undercover vampire law dog or not.

"All right, Mr. Hatsept—"

"Kenoe to you," he said with a flourish of a bow.

"Fine, Kenoe. Dinner it is. Of my choosing."

"Of course. But no McDonald's. That's where I draw the line."

She snorted. "McDonald's?" Her laugh set his insides dancing. "I do have some class, sir."

Chapter Four

The anticipation of being in Kenoe's presence alone had Shinju's hands shaking. Amazing how a man so fair could be so hot. And not just plain old hot, but Kenoe-is-my-favorite-cajun-dish hot. Shinju hadn't inherited the darker skin tones of her Louisiana grandmother—a woman who'd turned Japan on its ear when she'd married into a traditional Japanese family back in the day—but she had the woman's hips, lips and attitude in abundance. Then there was Grammy's gumbo and shrimp creole recipes, which Shinju had mastered. Maybe that was the true reason for the hips.

Shinju still couldn't believe that of all the times to run into Kenoe Hunkin' Hatsept, it had to be the day she'd decided to cancel her afternoon club at the last minute and play hooky while getting her fix of video games. Amazing. Having dreamed about the tall, white-haired handsome hunk since Nagano, it was almost as if she'd conjured him.

Her head snapped up at the sound of a chime. The doorbell.

Seven o'clock. Right on time.

Shinju set the ginger salad on the table, wiped her hands on her apron and hurried to open the door. And cursed a blue streak.

"Sasuke? What the hell are you doing here? I thought you

were in Osaka taking care of Ooeto clan stuff. Is it Max? Is something wrong?"

"No, Max is fine. I'm in town on business and thought I'd check in on you."

What fucked-up timing. And why would he check in on her? Both he and her brother knew exactly how she felt about being babysat. Not to mention the risk to her career and Max's less-than-savory lifestyle being exposed if either of them were seen anywhere near her house, damn it.

"Sasuke, you know good and well I don't like to be checked on, as you put it. And your timing is totally shit."

"Watch your mouth. I am still your elder."

"Yeah, and I'm still a grown-up. And I have a date in, like, right now."

"Really? Perhaps I can meet him?"

He went to step inside. Uninvited? Oh, don't think so. His big toe met up with the edge of the door. Damn, that had to hurt. Too bad.

"No, you can't meet him. Will you get lost already?"

"I don't think I will ever get used to your Westernized language, Shin-*chan*."

"We can discuss my language later. Good night, Sasuke. I'll call Max later to say hello." Though she'd just talked to him yesterday and he hadn't said a thing about Sasuke being in town. Something was going on here and she'd get to the bottom of it. Later. Right now, she had a handsome *so*-not-from-around-here man to entice, er, entertain.

She grabbed Sasuke by the front of his shirt, and pulled him forward for a quick peck on the cheek, shoved him out the door and closed it with a quiet snap. Before Shinju could take five steps toward the kitchen a knock sounded. She snatched

the door open.

"Damn it, Sasuke. I told you I—" *Gulp.* "Kenoe..." she gasped, hand flying to the base of her throat. And the man looked just as good under the dim light right outside her door as he did while losing badly at a video game.

"Hi, handsome." Shinju flashed a grin that felt goofy even to her own lips, then tilted her head to the side wondering when she'd become such a flirt. He just seemed to bring it right out of her. "Ready for something to eat?"

The answering look from those beautifully unusual eyes of his made her kneecaps tickle. Amazing how a gaze could crackle like ice and smolder with heat all at the same time.

Kenoe hung his jacket on the little coat rack just inside the door. Then he removed his boots and walked inside like he owned the place. Hell, she should have been offended, but couldn't take her eyes off the way his backside filled out his—whoa, back up a step—perfectly creased designer jeans.

And that crease ran into a perfect ass? Absolutely.

He turned and winked and her belly did a sexy little twirl. God, he was so out of her league. Then again, maybe he wasn't out of her league and she was just out of her mind.

They sat down to an informal but tasty meal of miso soup, curry rice, meat and potato croquets and pickled *ume* plums. During dinner she learned he lived in a small town in Montana, something to do with his job. A typical man, one of his hobbies was obviously working out, which she could tell from the bulge of muscle peeking out from underneath his form-fitting fitness tee. He also enjoyed golf—yawn and double yuck—traveling, football and, not surprisingly, all things Japan. He even had the language and etiquette down pat.

"That was a delicious meal, Shinju. Thank you for winning and not taking me to McDonald's."

Her chuckle lodged in her throat when Kenoe laughed. The man sounded like sin on a cracker. Suddenly the expression in those iced blue eyes of his had her wanting to wrap him in a tortilla made out of her six hundred thread-count sheets.

But she didn't actually blush like a schoolgirl until Kenoe insisted on helping her clear the dining table and put the cushions away. Handsome, sexy and thoughtful? All in one package? God, this couldn't be real.

By the time they'd stuffed the cushions into the little bins up in the linen closet, then put away the traditional low table and all the dishes, her back was killing her. Kenoe noticed. Then again, the loud "ungh" as her hand pressed to the small of her spine may have given it away.

Both hands raised in a non-threatening manner, Kenoe motioned towards the source of her pain. "May I?"

"Huh?"

"Your back. I promise I'm not trying to cop a feel."

He wanted to rub her back? Good lord, had she made a totally off judgment call regarding this guy not being a weirdo? What man offered to rub a woman's back after dinner? She didn't know any. But there was no helping being flattered at the awkward request.

"Just lean forward a little and put your hands on the countertop," he instructed.

He stepped up behind her and the tummy jiggle thing showed up again, then intensified when boiling warmth coursed off of him and into her...head? And damn, it was bad enough to feel the heat of his hands seep through the material of her blouse, but when a heat of equal fervor coursed through her brain it was almost too much. Okay, now this mind thing with him was happening a little too often to be a coincid...oh never mind. With the pressure of the man's strong fingers so expertly

applied, thinking just wasn't going to happen just now. It felt so good. In fact, it was heavenly after a long day of standing on her feet teaching, beating him at video games and cooking.

So why the hell wasn't she afraid of this big, surely bad, intense-expressioned, long-haired, absolutely beautiful man?

"Mmm, that feels wonderful. How do you know how to do that?"

Someone she'd only met twice was in her kitchen rubbing her back—perilously close to her ass, at that—and she was letting him. Kenoe's low-pitched words were soft with a sexy growl tossed in. It obviously did funny things to her common sense because she didn't seem to have any right now. And if Max ever found out she had a stranger in her house with her bent over the counter, he'd have her committed.

"Well, here at the base of your spine." He accented the explanation with a little extra pressure in just the right spot. Ooohooo. Nice. "Several ligaments attach to your sacrum. When your muscles get stressed they tend to pull the sacrum out of position. The key is to gently reposition the bone and hold it there until the ligaments figure out that's where they should be anyway. The tension releases as they settle into their correct position. Better?"

Oh lord yes! It was better, and she was hot and beginning to sweat in a place that hadn't seen heat in a while. But she couldn't scream at the man to jump her. So instead, she asked, "Are you a doctor or something?"

"No. Actually, I used to give my best friend massages. She had the same issue with her shoulders."

Well that was a stalling, half-assed explanation if she'd ever heard one. *She*, eh? So who was this *she* who'd experienced the pleasure of Kenoe's hands on her—back, shoulders or otherwise? Grrrr.

"Massaging your friend gave you such definite knowledge of sacral ligaments?"

"I happen to have a degree in anatomy and physiology, with emphasis on genetics."

Okay, back to the point. "Soooo, are you a doctor, Kenoe?"

"No, not exactly. I, uh, I'm...in law enforcement," he said hesitantly.

Oh, no. The last thing she needed was a cop in her apartment when one of Tokyo's most well-connected mob underbosses had just been standing in her doorway. Damned Sasuke.

"Did I hurt you? Your back got all tight again."

"Uh, no, not at all," she hedged, wanting to pop herself in the forehead. "Just hit a nerve is all. It's a bit sore." Well, she was telling the truth. But it was Max who'd hit a nerve by sending Sasuke here. Why did he have to show up today of all damned days?

But Kenoe seemed to sense her mood and backed off big time.

Taking her hand in an easy grip, he guided her to the futon in the living room.

"So," he asked playfully as they settled side by side on the low, comfy couch. "What movie are we watching? Something naughty or nice?"

The giggle wiggled right up out of her, like one of her female students when they were being flirted with by a cutie pie at school. "Who said we were watching a movie?"

"Well, the bet was only for dinner, but I haven't gotten to do any looking at you yet. And—" he leaned so close the mass of silver locs swung forward and brushed her shoulder, "—you know you want to."

Arrogant-assed man. Sigh. And he was so right—it was totally wrong on too many levels. When had she become so ridiculously horny, er, *friendly*, toward someone she didn't really know? Try the day she'd spotted Kenoe scowling at her in the Zenkoji temple a week ago...and every single day ever since.

"Fine," Shinju grumbled and motioned him toward a pile of DVDs stacked next to the television. She was pissed and didn't appreciate him just bogarting her into a movie...so why the hell was she grinning like a lunatic?

He'd picked an action film purchased weeks ago that had never been opened. Sometime during the shocks and surprises of the film, Shinju's jumpy "Oh my Gods" managed to scoot her hip to hip with her guest. Kenoe's arm settled around her. Her head flopped back against his shoulder the second his fingers made contact with her skin, and the movie was all but forgotten. Surely her lungs would explode if she breathed any deeper. Kenoe's long legs sprawled out in front of him made him appear relaxed, at ease, yet an air of danger lurked just below the surface. Ropey, cut tendons were a mere ripple of movement with every subtle movement of his wrist and forearm. The brush of his fingers over and down the bare skin of her biceps sent a shiver dipping below the skin. And that shiver worked its way from arms to breastbone and clear down to her nipples. The taut tips seemed more sensitive than usual, and actually tingled until they stung.

Note to self—never wear a tank top in Kenoe's presence.

His skin, cast in a pearly gray from the television screen, seemed absolutely flawless—no five o'clock shadow, no scars, simply perfect. Long, silky locs were pulled over one shoulder in a thick fall of tempting silver strands. When had he taken the tie out of his hair? Normally a man with long hair turned her

off, but those damned locs were the sexiest thing she'd ever seen on a man. It didn't even bother her that Kenoe's hair was longer than her own by a good stretch. Clenching her fists until the knuckles cracked, she spoke to herself in a mantra.

I am not going to play in the man's hair. I am not going there!

God, so gorgeous.

Just then he turned and gazed down at her and her tongue stuck to the roof of her mouth. Eyes so infused with a frosty hue. Strong jaw, high cheekbones and a smile that could light up the darkest night. Framing that smile was a pair of lips just full enough to be perfect for kissing.

The moment the thought formed, Kenoe was giving her exactly what she wanted—his mouth on hers. Gently coaxing at first, then taking and finally demanding.

Suddenly, Shinju found herself sitting sideways on Kenoe's lap across a pair of solid thighs. And solid...other things.

He moved with a speed that caught her totally off guard, yet when their bodies met there was no jarring. He had so much control over his strength, yet he, the man inside, was as off-balance as a teeter totter.

So, just how did she know all this? There was no way she should intuitively understand this level of emotional detail about someone she'd met mere days ago. Hell, even her brother, whom she knew inside and out, didn't come through so loud and clear.

Shinju found herself wondering yet again about this connection, this zing, between them. But when he let his fingers play at the base of her skull, curiosity became wonder. Wonder at how a simple kiss could feel so good. How a single touch could make her skin so hot it practically smoldered the cotton of her tank top. And his taste? Dear God, it was addictive. The

natural flavor of this man was better than sex dipped in chocolate and drizzled over her favorite ice cream. French vanilla. Exact same color as his skin. His Adam's apple bobbed in the hollow of his throat. Suddenly she wanted to lick it. Would it be as satisfying as soft serve in a sugar cone, or a strawberry-flavored shaved ice on a summer day? She had to find out.

Shinju parted her lips, let her tongue tease his skin and was immediately rewarded. Oooh, the man had the sexiest damned sigh she'd ever heard. It urged her to more direct action and sent her exploring. He looked like he had it all together, calm, cool and relaxed. Could she change that? Find all the little spots that sent him soaring?

Her lips latched onto the pulse just beside the bulge of well-developed neck muscle. Kenoe's entire body stiffened with a chest-deep groan. Then, just as suddenly, the dam unleashed and he completely took over.

Kenoe leaned Shinju backward until her spine touched the cushion of the futon while her legs draped over his hard thighs. A wide, strong hand, trembling with restrained strength, cupped the swell of her breast as a lone thumb teased just out of reach of a straining nipple. Oh, how she wanted him to touch her there. But all she could do was grab his biceps and hold on for dear life.

The sting gathering in her nipples became a throb. And that throb slithered through her entire body, her entire being.

Shinju's head fell back and Kenoe dove in for the feast, nipping the tender skin of her throat clear down to the scoop neck of her top.

"Mmm, I like that." God, she was lost. How could this happen, and so quickly? On the other hand, who the hell cared? All that mattered at the moment was, "More. Please."

And then Kenoe's thoughts followed her own, sending his hands down her body to more firmly caress her swelling breasts. The thin little bra underneath may as well have not been there. She gulped wildly as Kenoe eased the fabric up to bunch just above the aching mounds. Cool air whooshed over bare skin. She'd been so wrapped up in the maddening sensations of longing and lust, she'd forgotten the air conditioner was on.

The lips that had stolen her breath in a delicious kiss and then nibbled their way down her throat were now wrapped around a stiff, swollen peak and sucking viciously.

"Oh, yes," she hissed, holding his head to her flesh. "Harder." The thoughts folded in on themselves until her whole body was into the dance. The next thing Shinju knew, her breath came in deep gasps and her ass wriggled against the obvious bulge at the juncture of Kenoe's thighs. And she wasn't talkin' little-breakfast-sausage bulge either.

He wanted her just as badly as her out-of-control self wanted him. And it was more than just a swollen cock that told her so. No, it was the thoughts that swirled around and down into her head before sinking into her brain.

"Shinju, you feel so good against me. God, it's been so long..."

His mouth was plastered against her skin yet his words were loud and clear.

"And you taste even better." Kenoe's hands, lips, teeth and tongue were all in play now. Oh, good gracious. That nip he'd given just above her nipple was sharp, but felt oh so good.

"I like the nip of your teeth. Bite me again, harder." The words came out a whispered plea. Something inside of her craved it. Needed it. Reached for it.

In a snap, the warm, sensual caress swirling around her

consciousness went ice cold. Simply shut off. As if someone had closed her out of a bank vault. A deep bong, like a two-foot-thick wall of metal clanged heavily in her soul. It shut and shut tight, keeping out everything that gave life—air, light, sound. Love. Like a vacuum. And Kenoe was on the other side of that door.

She fucking *felt* his withdrawal, experienced it profoundly. It was no different than if she'd thrown up her own emotional walls and ran smack into them. So the attachment she'd thought was there as they sat and talked at the restaurant in Nagano wasn't just her imagination. The ease of conversation over dinner tonight had been so much more than comfortable. It had *felt* right, literally.

In a blink her bra and tank were rearranged and Kenoe was up and off the couch, headed for the coat rack at the door. The man snatched his jacket off the rack so hard the thing rocked back and forth, threatening to clatter to the floor.

Reaching for him, Shinju flinched at the invisible glimpse of so much pain and uncertainty.

Kenoe, a wounded man? Yes. In mere seconds she'd experienced enough of his emotions to reveal his torment. So alone and shut off from everything, everyone. Shinju's insides instinctively reached for him again, wanting to take up her sword and break him out of his self-imposed prison. And perhaps free herself in the offing. After all, she kept her own secrets close to hr heart.

His name should be Naoru instead of Kenoe. It fit him perfectly. It meant "to be mended". Definitely something this man needed. But could she give herself to him? Though he seemed to already be a part of her, he was still a virtual stranger. If he knew who she really was, would he look down on her rather than accept the restoration of his soul that was so

freely and unexpectedly offered? And who the hell was she to think she could help him in the first place?

He turned, stepped close to her, then backed away again, jamming his arms into his jacket sleeves with a force that should have torn the fabric.

"I'm sorry, Shinju. I had no right to touch you that way. But damn if I don't want to again."

"I'm not offended, Naoru," she said softly. The words came out solid, confident

Oh sure, she could talk a good game, could skin and grin with the best of them. The only time she showed half her true colors was while teaching or counseling her students. Even then she kept a part of herself hidden.

Then common sense intruded—he was a law enforcement officer. She didn't even know who he worked for or what he, obviously a foreigner, was doing in Japan. He claimed he was on vacation, which added another fly in the ointment. Vacation meant he'd eventually be going home. Without her.

Sigh. Perhaps she should just make the best of having such an intensely attractive man after her, even if it was only for a few days or a few weeks. When was the last time she'd enjoyed such delicious company? Hell, try never.

Take the money and run, Shinju. Even if you spend it all in one night. It was a risk, messing around with a cop. Keeping Max and Sasuke from snooping would be even more important now.

Not to mention the small investment she'd have to make in handkerchiefs when Kenoe finally left the country for home as she cried her eyes out. But the man seemed so worth it.

Even if short-lived, this thing with Kenoe would require the opening of her own doors, facing her own fears.

But not today.

He opened the door, then stopped long enough to ask, "You called me Naoru? What does it mean?"

Slipping her arms around his waist in what she hoped was a reassuring squeeze, Shinju hugged him tight and said, "I'll tell you another time, handsome."

Returning her embrace, Kenoe smiled and warm relief flooded Shinju's mind. Then he was cut off again as if he'd caught himself doing something he shouldn't.

Hmm.

She promised to lock the door behind him as his sweet kiss landed softly in the middle of her forehead. Every inch of skin his fingers had teased was a-tingle as she watched him depart. Strong, long legs flexed with each step. A broad back spread from east to west beneath his light jacket. Everything about the man was larger than life and chiseled to perfection. She not only saw it, but felt it beneath her own hands as they'd explored each other on her futon.

And there was no denying that when Kenoe touched her, every nerve ending torched and flamed. *To be mended. To be mended.* The words tumbled around in her head then took root. Well, if she could stand in the midst of the heat of Kenoe Hatsept, then a little sewing would be a snap, right? Besides, she'd always been good at mending things.

Her mind made up, Shinju snatched up the little piece of semi-crumpled paper Kenoe had pushed into her hand as he'd left. After a quick shower, she dug her PDA out of her schoolbag and keyed the digits into its memory.

Kenoe stalked down the block and crossed the street, headed away from Shinju's house, grumbling. Without his permission his mind replayed how sweet Shinju had been in his

arms. The rapid rise and fall of her chest had only pushed his lust higher. With each pant came a small cry, with each cry came a ragged intake of breath. And each breath she took stole one of his own, yanked it out of his soul until they were a single beating heart, a single set of lungs. And the words that came out of that woman's mouth—dear God, how would he ever survive the raw erotic sight, sound and feel of her body beneath him? And only she touched him this way, was the only female who'd ever made him *want* to be out of control. While his need for blood was under wraps, thanks to a healthy diet and suppression meds, Shinju still aroused the urge to nip, bite and suck. And the woman walked right into his head regardless of the fact that he could block just about anyone out of his thoughts.

Then she had to go and mention biting.

After that it was all he could do to keep his fangs in their sheaths at all. But he would never take her blood without her permission and that was something he simply couldn't seek right now. At least not without revealing who, or rather what, he really was. No way in hell would he scare her away, not when his mind and body screamed for this woman. Wanted to touch her while pouring himself into her, then opening up to be refilled with her sweet yet fiery essence. Hell, it didn't make any sense, and he hadn't cared until losing command of his fangs moved from a possibility to a reality.

He hadn't wanted to leave her but knew getting the hell out of there fast was his only recourse. Now, out in the evening air, Kenoe sucked in a deep breath and allowed himself a tight-lipped grin. The taste of his own blood hit his tongue. But Shinju said she'd explain what *Naoru* meant "next time", so who cared he'd practically bitten through his lip when the woman all but guaranteed they would see each other again?

Moving off into the darkness, he started to leap up into the

thick, towering tree that he'd taken to watching over her house from.

A prickle danced across the skin on the back of his neck. A feeling so strong, he half expected his thick hair to stand up on end. He stilled and let his keen senses open up to the night. And there it was—the sound of a man's footsteps. They were close, too close to Shinju's house for comfort, especially at this time of night. His nose caught the scent of nothing and no one, only the familiar humid smell of gathering rain clouds. His eyes saw...he wasn't sure what the hell he was seeing, only that whatever it was certainly shouldn't be walking the streets of Shibuya district in Tokyo or any other "yo".

Chapter Five

Kenoe silently flipped open his vid phone, slipped the ear bud in so he could have his hands free, and whispered into the tiny microphone.

"Dial home." His words formed as mist in the cool early summer air. The line rang two, three, four times. Relief left his chest in a huff when someone answered.

"Serati here. This better be fucking good."

"Alaan, it's Kenoe. Something is wrong in Japan, and I mean more than just the number of rogues in Nagano. I'm in Tokyo—"

"Tokyo? What the hell are you doing there?"

"Changed my itinerary. As I was saying—" Kenoe rushed on before Alaan could question him further, "—I'm in Shibuya district and I've just seen the weirdest damned thing. I'm not sure I can describe it."

"Spill it already, Hatsept. I'm in bed, so get to the point."

Alaan was his usual charming self. Kenoe couldn't blame him. It was barely morning back home while the night was young and the parties were just getting started in the clubs not far from where he stood.

In the background came a female voice.

"Who is it, Alaan?"

Alaan answered his mate on a yawn. "It's Kenoe."

"Really? Give me the phone." Tameth, as bossy as ever. Kenoe smiled thinking of his best friend.

"No. Roll over and go back to sleep."

"We weren't sleeping anyway, asshole. Now give me the damned phone."

"Careful, woman," Alaan snapped. "Behave or I'll cut down your weekly quota of cock."

Alaan Serati—the only man Kenoe knew who could make a bass-filled growl sound playful. And Tameth was one of very few females who could handle the big blond brute. They were perfect for each other.

"Oh, please. You'd never survive." She laughed. Then Tam's voice filled the line. "Kenoe, you okay? What's going on?"

Funny. Her voice had always gotten under his skin. But now, it slid over his consciousness like a soothing balm rather than a stimulating liqueur. But the blood-firing effect did happen with Shinju, hell almost ten times worse than Tameth had ever affected him and... Oh *shit*. Could Shinju be the one? His bondmate? Nah, no way. Impossible.

"Kenoe?"

"Huh?" *Come on, Hatscpt, get your shit together.* "I mean, yes, I'm fine. I just happened to be leaving dinner when I saw something...someone."

"So?"

"It was a man, a human with no scent of vampire origin. But he moved like one of us, there one moment and gone the next. And if I'm not mistaken, I've caught a glimpse of him before."

"But that doesn't make any sense, Key. You're the best damned tracker of all the elite Seekers. How could you not be

sure whether you've scented him before or not?"

"Like I said, he carries no vampire scent. In fact, he has no scent at all. You know I never forget a smell, but this guy doesn't seem to have one. I swear, he moved so fast I almost missed him."

"That is strange," Tameth said in confusion. "But even still, if he's a human why do you care?"

"I have my reasons."

"Hold on, let me conference Carin in. This sounds like some stuff you two should discuss. It worries me that a human moves like a vamp, but doesn't smell like vamp, rogue, or...anything."

"Exactly. In fact, I'll just call her directly."

"No way," Alaan said with a raised voice in the background. The man always had exceptional hearing. "I want to hear what the hell is going on too."

A few moments later a sleepy and none-too-happy Bix picked up the line.

"Head Seeker here, goddammit."

Tameth put her phone on speaker and relayed what Kenoe had told them. Bix roused Carin, who was instantly awake after hearing their concerns.

"That worries me," Carin rasped, voice scratchy and thick with congestion.

"What the hell's wrong with you?" Kenoe wondered quietly. His brow pulled down into a frown as he watched the shadow of the man creeping around Shinju's house. Seeker instinct went full tilt and he was ready to drop the phone, jump out of that tree and take off at a dead run to aid his woman.

Whoa. Hold the door. *His* woman? Aw, hell.

"Cold. First one in three years." Carin croaked while trying

to clear her throat.

"How? We don't get sick."

"Out playing in the rain with Alaina. Took my new vampire DNA for granted and got kicked in the ass by the human genes behind it. I'll be fine by morning."

"Damn, I hope so. Anyway, why does this guy I'm watching concern you? What are you thinking?" Kenoe asked on a whisper.

"I'm thinking about facts," Carin said, followed by a huge sneeze and Bix's quiet "ewww" in the background.

"Oh shut up," Carin mumbled to her mate. "Make yourself useful and grab that box of tissue on the nightstand, will ya?" After a pause and a few totally unladylike snorts and sniffles, Carin continued. "Anyway, the facts are that the only way a human can be enhanced with vampire traits is by ingesting large quantities of blood or exchanging bodily fluids via lots of sex with a vampire—a full-fledged, natural-born vampire—over a long period of time. But that kind of contact leaves an imprint on human and vampire alike."

Kenoe cut in. "Basically, scent."

"Right. But you said this guy doesn't have any vampire scent. Even I, an altered human, can smell the subtle differences between vampire and human. So for this guy to have *no* scent at all is just not normal in either of our worlds."

"So what do you think is going on?"

"Kenoe, I just don't know, sweet pea. I'll have to think about it."

Bix added, "In the meantime, looks like pseudo-duty, Seeker. Just watch this guy, get a visual and send us the digital. But you're not assigned to him, nor on real duty, so no other investigation. You're still on vacation, understand? We'll

see what we can find on him. If he's dirty, we'll put somebody else on him while you get your downtime in. We do have some good agents planted inside the human government over there. We'll find something. Check in with Alaan in a day or two."

"Yes, sir. Oh, wait, Dr. Carin, can you and Tam stay on the line for a minute?"

"Sure. Whatcha need?" they asked almost in unison. He loved his friends so much. Always there for him no matter what. And the two biggest damned mother hens he'd ever known.

"I figured I'd ask you two since you're female, but now that I have you on the line I'm thinking I should have gotten a guy's point of view."

"Well, it's not like we aren't listening."

Bix. And the bastard was laughing at him. Kenoe laughed back and then let it all hang out.

"I've met someone. A human. But I'm way out of my element here. I can't say I've ever experienced anything like it. I smell her everywhere and the sight and scent of this female sends me on a fucking trip."

Four voices echoed across the phone line as they all started talking at once. "What? Really? Do you think she's the one? What does she look like? Have you approached her yet?"

With his eyes still plastered on the shadow near Shinju's home, the doubts Kenoe had about the woman's place in his life began to fade. The urge to strangle the possible threat had him snarling into the phone.

"Kenoe? What the hell are you growling at?" Tameth snapped.

"Sorry. I'm watching her house and...shit, this is driving me crazy."

"If you feel so strongly, she could very well be your mate.

Or maybe even a bondmate." Carin sniffled. "I'm human, yet Bix and I went nuts after we met. Not to mention that psychic-link-bond-zing thing we had going. It was insane."

Hmm. It would certainly explain his tumultuous emotions. God, he was horny and protective, afraid and bold, certain and unsure. All at the same damned time.

"I think...hell, I don't know what to think," he pushed out forcefully, even though he knew Carin was right. And from the thoughts and feelings seeping through what must be a true newly forming bond, Shinju was all over the map right along with him. He couldn't quite hear her thoughts yet from this distance, but her emotions were pounding at him like a sledgehammer against a concrete wall.

"Then what's the problem?" Carin asked impatiently. Her tone was the same as she used when trying to reason with her three-year-old daughter. "You know how weirded out you prime males get when you try to resist the mating call. God, I remember when Bix and I first met. He hardly played fair once he decided I was the one. Pulled the most underhanded tactics out of the hat..."

"Underhanded tactics? Like what?" Kenoe had never heard this part of the story.

"One day we were in my lab—in fact, it was only the second time I'd ever seen him. He decided to pull some junk...and he was successful. The underhanded part is this—Bix knew I was an empath. I'd never really looked into how to use my gift, but I could sense something zinging between us."

"Yeah, I know what you mean."

"It's there with...what's her name?"

"Shinju. Shinju Maruyama. And yes, it's there. She just waltzes right into my head and I don't even think she realizes it. It's like she isn't aware she has any psychic skill but is using it

just the same."

"Hmm. That's different. Anyway, I was supposed to be mad at Bix and he was determined that he'd rather have me horny. So as he left my lab he sent the nastiest, most lust-inducing images into my head, and at the same time he made me actually *feel* his hands on me. It was the wildest, weirdest sensation I'd ever experienced. Something only he could do because we were meant to be together as bondmates."

Kenoe's eyebrows practically flew off of his face. So he could send images into Shinju's head? But only if she was "the one"?

"Now I can talk to Bix and send images to him too. And he's the only one I can't block because we're bonded."

"Key?" Tameth chimed in. "If she's it, go for it. Besides, you've already seen the outcome of two of the most bullheaded men you know try to outrun their females. And vice versa."

"Yeah, tell me about it." Kenoe chuckled. "But I just don't know."

"Well, I do know," Tameth snapped into the phone with a tone that bordered on pissed off. "You think you don't deserve it."

"What the hell are you talking—"

"Hush, you. You think that because of what you went through at the hands of that asshole brother of yours that you're tainted or something." It wasn't a question, but a heated, mad-as-hell accusation. And it hit the mark pretty damned close. "Well, listen, Kenoe Hatsept, you're one of the best men I've ever known. A perfect mix of sensitive and badass. Whoever this woman is, she'll be lucky to have found a man like you."

Kenoe did something he hadn't done since learning how to pleasure a woman at a young age in the harem from hell—he blushed. Not sure what to say, he let the first thing he could

think of slip past his lips.

"What is this, some kind of psychobabble?"

"Cut the shit, Kenoe. This is serious."

Great. Now it was Carin's turn to chime in. May as well prepare for the shredding he knew was coming. Thank God they had his best interests at heart.

"We're talking about your life here, stud," Carin gubbed through her stuffy nose.

"But what if I can't...I mean, what if I can't love her like she deserves?"

"What about what you deserve, damn it? If this woman is the one for you, it's because she's meant to be. She'll complete you in a way you'll never understand unless you go for it. Everything you've worked for since the day you fled your brother's harem has brought you to where you are today. But that's over, Kenoe. It's done. Lowan is history. Now it's time for you to live for yourself. And that's all I got to say about it. Now don't make me and Tam have to fly all the way to Japan to kick some vampire sense into your ass."

"Yes, ma'am." Kenoe couldn't keep the grin out of his voice, nor the unfamiliar flutter out of his stomach. Blushing? Butterflies? Geesh, he was turning into a girl! "I'll catch you guys later."

Tameth chimed in. "All right. Hey, remind me to tell you about the new jet we just got. Fill you in later?"

"Yep."

"Love you, Key." And in the background he heard Alaan's deep bass echo, "Yeah. I love you too, Hatsept pipsqueak."

With a balancing breath, he thanked his friends, disconnected the call, then watched the shadow settle down in a crouch on the far side of Shinju's little house.

Kenoe waited, still as stone, but inside he was barely leashed.

So this is what it felt like to stumble upon a mate? To be intoxicated with the inexplicable yearning to crawl inside of another? And with the psychic awareness between him and Shinju, she was probably his bondmate as well. When Bix and Alaan tried to explain what it'd felt like when they'd met their bondmates, Kenoe hadn't understood why it had been so difficult for the two men to articulate the experience. Now that he'd met Shinju, he had no idea how Bix and Alaan ever found the words. How did one describe fire in the blood, or the existence of someone else's presence constantly caressing your soul, finding its place in a little corner of your mind? Or the strength of an unseen force practically moving your feet in the direction of the one your spirit, soul and body craved like…like what? There was nothing in Kenoe's vocabulary that even came close.

And they'd only kissed once. God help him after they made love for the first time.

"Fuck. Now what?" Moving only his eyes, Kenoe surveyed the area. He didn't see anyone other than the scentless man. But he certainly caught something on the wind. And whatever it was didn't smell friendly. Rogue.

Dan hung up the phone, tucked it in his pocket and pulled back the drapes. Surveying the city around him through the wall of glass with a huff, he watched the nightlife of Tokyo light up below him. The clubs didn't close until five a.m. here. The night was young…but there was no way in hell he was stepping out into it. Not with the news he'd just received.

There was a Seeker, definitely not a local, hanging around the sister of Max Maruyama. Dan wondered if it was one of the huge bastards that had almost made him pee his pants on the streets of San Diego three years ago. In fact, it had been three years, eight months and fourteen days since the night he'd never forget, nor forgive. Fucking vampires. A mean-assed Aleth Sidheon had marched into Idac Pharmaceuticals where Dan worked as a scientist. Part of what he'd loved about his job was working on the same floor as Dr. Carinian Derrickson. But that crazed bloodsucker had gotten Dan tangled up in a mess that cost him his dreams, his job and almost his life. And all because the freaky vamp couldn't keep his dick in his pants where Dr. Carin was concerned. Well, that and a need to bring the entire vampire nation to its knees if they didn't kiss his ass. Needless to say, it backfired in a major way. But Dan had escaped with his skin intact and fled to the east. As far east as he could get.

Dan stood and looked twenty stories down at the tiny bodies swarming through the crosswalks at specific intervals. Animated ads marched across gigantic billboards hawking everything from soft drinks to music to television shows. His brow furrowed as his head filled with thoughts of another time and place.

Oh, what a mouse he'd been back then, letting that Sidheon idiot pull his strings and make him dance to his tune. But those days were long past. Dan was a bit rougher around the edges than he'd been the night he believed he'd never draw another breath. Two Seekers, one dark as night, the other a platinum blond, had shaken him like a rag doll and threatened to literally peel his hide if he didn't hand over the information to help them get to Dr. Carin in time to save her life. In fact Dan had never been so happy to pass out cold than he had upon waking on the chilled concrete sidewalk.

Later, he'd learned the dark-headed one was Head Seeker for the Vampire Council of Ethics. And that Seeker was Jon Bixler—just the mention of that name caused every vampire he'd met since then to cut him a wary glance or flat-out refuse to do business with him. Dan had later discovered why. Jon Bixler, now Dr. Carin's husband, was the meanest, baddest, most feared fang-bearing bastard with a badge. In short, the Head of the Seeker Corps, and those like him, were known for kicking butt, taking names and asking questions later. And the Seekers' favorite prey was rogue vampires, the very scoundrels Dan needed to make his schemes pay off. Then there was the blond refrigerator that worked with the Bixler asshole, Alaan Serati who served as second-in-command. And Dan had no intention of ever tangling with either of them again in all his natural-born days.

So he'd dealt with rogue vampires instead. Here in Tokyo they tended to remain underground—not literally, but they flew well under the radar. Every vamp declared rogue was a criminal in one way or another and had done something to get himself excommunicated from the ten clans of the vampire nations. Only a fool would deliberately bring himself to the attention of the Seeker Corps.

The rogue vamps also knew that in order to gain territory they'd have to fight not only the ruthless Clan Li Seekers, but the human *yakuza* clans too. And those tattoo-wearing mobsters were more cutthroat, if not more dangerous, than the vampires. In fact the only difference between the two factions' modus operandi was the vamps just kicked ass with a little more class and flair.

Yep, self-preservation rated high on these boys' list of important things in life, so they specialized in smuggling black-market-type stuff. Simple things like firearms, ammunition and good old-fashioned pornography, which were all illegal in this

country. Now, thanks to Dan, they peddled those things along with special biotech agents, like the physical strength enhancers that emulated vampire traits in humans.

That Dr. Carin was a true genius.

In fact, just after that little run-in with Jon Bixler and Alaan Serati, the two vamps left him unconscious on the sidewalk and rushed to Dr. Carin's home. And Dan had taken off out of San Diego like a man with the hounds of hell on his ass, but not before breaking into Dr. Carin's labs to borrow some of her research. Sidheon was in the middle of ripping her throat out on the other side of town while Dan shook and trembled as he tucked a few vials of samples and compounds into his pants pocket. He'd actually cried as he quickly and carefully went through her files and specimen carts. Afterward, he made sure to put everything exactly the way he found it, though he doubted Carin would ever be back in that lab again.

The grimace on his face from recalling the unpleasant memories morphed into a small smile as he thought on the day he'd received news on Dr. Carin. Dan had always liked her and had been glad to learn a year after her terrible ordeal that the two men, vamps rather, who'd jacked him up had been able to save her. It would have been a shame to see such genius snuffed out.

After Dan had a chance to really examine the items he'd snatched helter-skelter from Dr. Carin's labs, he'd discovered that the woman had quietly developed a compound that, when given in the proper doses and intervals, produced agility, speed and unusual strength in humans. Basically, vampires without the fangs or the need for blood. Only one problem—the formula was incomplete and Dan hadn't been able to perfect the serum. The end result was the human trial participants, as he liked to call them, had all become deathly ill after several months. In the end it was as if the enhancements not only reversed

themselves, but did so with a vengeance, practically nuking the specimens' immune systems. They'd have been better off with AIDS than the side effects of his treatment.

Since then he'd managed to tweak the formulation enough to stretch the deterioration time out to a year, which was plenty of time for Dan to do business, get the hell out of wherever he'd temporarily set up shop, and head somewhere else. And he'd keep right on milking that cow until it dried up altogether.

And dry might be coming up soon with a Seeker skulking around the home of one of the relatives of a human who should be approaching the illness stage of the enhancements.

Did the Seeker know about the flawed treatments? Worse, was Max Maruyama working with the Seekers to get revenge on Dan for giving him a short-lived treatment? Never mind the fact that Dan hadn't bothered to reveal the side effects. Maybe the ghosts of his past had come to haunt him, come to take him to task for the punishment he'd escaped three years ago the night Aleth Sidheon had attacked the innocent Dr. Carin.

A deep tremble seeped into the core of each limb, as if his old cowardly self was clawing to get out and run for the hills. For a moment, terror gripped his chest and sped toward his heart. His lungs seemed to have a fierce determination to hyperventilate.

He forced his logical mind to the forefront.

"No!" he yelled to no one. "I refuse to be the victim ever again. This time I am in control. This time, I'm the perpetrator. I'm the savant, damn it." And he refused to ever go back down the hill he'd fled up so long ago.

Come on man, think, think, think. Thumb and forefinger squeezed desperately over the bridge of his nose as Dan pulled in deep, fortifying breaths.

"Okay, Dan, relax. It was only a sighting of a stranger who

happens to be a Seeker." A Seeker who his sources claimed was dressed like a common man and hadn't bothered to speak with any of the territory leaders in regard to his arrival. Just because a vampire cop was sneaking around didn't mean anyone was on to him. Besides, Dan never stayed in one place long enough to get caught by humans, and could only be reached through the rogues he'd brought into his employ. And not even they always knew where he'd be at any given time.

He'd escaped before. He could do it again. And this time, he was a whole lot wiser, richer and could at least be comfortable while on the run. Shaking himself out of the cadaverous grasp of the old specters, Dan pulled up his resolve and began to plan.

Angry at himself for allowing fear to send him pacing through his living room—well, his living room *this* month—he forced himself away from the windows and commanded the muscles in his thighs to relax enough to sit.

Settled in a comfortable chair, he put his feet up on a settee and picked up the remote control. Perhaps there was something good on the science channel tonight. With a snap of his fingers, his companion of the moment, a beautiful little human female, all dark hair, dark eyes and dark lashes, scurried into the room and knelt at his feet. In her hands was a silver tray with four of his favorite drinks and a few snacks displayed to his satisfaction.

God, he was tired of sushi, sake and soba noodles. What he wouldn't give for a piece of southern fried chicken, mashed potatoes, biscuits and gravy.

Sipping a dark brown liquid from one of the glasses, Dan sucked in a breath as the liquor burned a path down his throat, leaving behind a hint of mint and lime.

He turned his lip up at the whitetail sashimi but ate it

anyway, then chased it down with the next glass of alcohol—grape liqueur and sake.

Perhaps recent events were a sign that it was time to head for greener pastures...pastures with more unhealthy food. But first, there was a manufacturing facility to clean up and a *yakuza* clan war to start to cover his tracks.

Chapter Six

Kenoe had obtained the digital of the man he'd spotted scouting Shinju's house and sent it off to Bix hours ago. Duty done. Now what? Well, he could use a new suit. He'd always enjoyed shopping for the designer purple label that adorned the best custom-fit jackets and slacks, but right now it simply held no appeal, though no Hatsept worth his salt would ever admit to such. Perhaps he'd work out with his blades? Please. Even a Seeker had to admit when he was distracted. And distracted was an understatement. Hell, he couldn't even pretend he'd wandered around the shopping district only to find himself across the street from Shinju's school with no idea of how his feet managed to carry him there.

Pffft. Some Seeker you are. You can't even keep your mind on where you're supposed to be going. Just then his phone rang. Kenoe yanked it out of his inside jacket pocket and flipped it open so fast it went flying into the air to land with a loud crack on the sidewalk.

"Shit. They should make these damned things big enough for a man's hands," he grumbled, retrieving it and trying yet again to flip it open to answer the call. "Hatsept here."

"Naoru? It's Shinju. Busy?"

Kenoe almost sat down right where he was...which happened to be in the middle of the street.

Shinju's call came at exactly two-thirty in the afternoon. About damned time. He'd only looked at his phone six hundred and forty-two times to make sure he hadn't missed her, was getting a decent signal, and that the battery hadn't died.

The steel-belted knot he hadn't realized was rooted in his gut loosened after a few minutes of amicable conversation. So she hadn't called to tell him to take a flying leap for pawing her, or jab at him for practically running out of her house after such a fabulous evening.

"So what are you doing?" he asked with genuine curiosity.

"Getting ready for my next class. I'm in the teacher's lounge for a short break. After school I have club, so…"

"Aw hell, not now," he snarled to his fangs. Would the damned things always twitch and hum just from the sound of her voice?

"What's wrong? Is this a bad time?"

"Uh, no. Nothing's wrong. It's fine. Timing's perfect." And now he was babbling. God, what next?

Demanding the sharp canines to withdraw and sheathe, Kenoe licked his lips and put himself out there. After all, he'd never been accused of being subtle. He might run like hell when an itty bitty woman asked to be bitten, and take off to keep from jumping her bones…but none of that was normal for him, so bump the small talk. It was time to get down to business.

"So, lovely, when can I see you again?"

"Well, you don't waste any time, do you?"

He could tell she was smiling. "No, I don't. What would be the point?"

She snorted. Kenoe could imagine her with a hand on her hip, rolling her gaze up toward the ceiling while curling one side of her mouth into a sassy smirk. And he couldn't wipe the grin

off his face to save his life. Damned woman.

The conversation was short and sweet, just like Shinju. And when Kenoe flipped the phone shut, he stood in the middle of a dim alley and turned circles like a damned girl getting her first piece of real jewelry from her equally first boyfriend. And she'd called him Naoru again—a name that resonated in his soul, caressed the very depths of his being like a warm hand sliding over his psyche. Yep, he was a goner.

Later that night, showered, changed and scowling at the butterflies that wouldn't stop dive-bombing the base of his spine, Kenoe made his way to their meeting place. *Damn it, Kenoe, she's only one woman.* In response, the winged insects moved around to the front of his stomach to play there. Oh well. Guess there was no fooling the damned things into believing Shinju had no effect on him.

Kenoe didn't like the idea of meeting at the train station, but the second his, yes *his*, woman stepped into view, he was glad they were nowhere near her house or his apartment. She looked so edible even a eunuch would be tempted to snatch her up, settle her on his face and feast to his heart's content. Kenoe wanted to run his hands over her smooth-looking skin, then suck her essence off his fingers.

Curvy little hips were sheathed in a delicious cream leather miniskirt. A short-cut jacket in a complementing shade of light purple buttoned at the bottom and hugged her waist. The rest of the coat lay open to reveal the sexiest little sheer white top Kenoe had laid eyes on in all his days. Not that he'd never seen head-rush-inducing clothes on beautiful women before, but Shinju made every experience he'd ever had pale until it was nothing but a vague recollection.

The psychic shields he always kept in place fell like

boulders, opening to her. Unadulterated fierce attraction hummed along their fragile bond. And now that he was pretty sure of what she was to him, mate and bondmate, the next time they were alone would certainly turn out differently. He wouldn't freeze up at the mention of biting, that was for sure. There was now a new goal—to gently touch, tease and taste until she wanted him so badly she fairly crackled with it...just like he did for her right now.

With a femininely calculated tilt of her head, she lowered her eyes and watched his approach through her lashes while easing her coat down her arms and off. Making a smooth little twirl, she showed off her outfit. Teasing peeks of cinnamon skin were visible under what turned out to be a sheer tank top with a little cropped shirt under it to cover her breasts. The skin of her neck and arms shimmered slightly. He wondered what she'd smoothed over it to make it glisten like that.

Artfully applied, the eyeshadow above her slanted almond-shaped eyes brought to mind stormy seas. And her full lips were lined with a berry gloss he wanted to lick and nibble until there was nothing left but her own unique taste. A flavor he hadn't nearly gotten his fill of the last time they were together.

Kenoe walked right up to the woman and towered over her smaller frame. Shinju refused to take a single step back. Instead, she looked up at him with those lovely chocolate brown eyes as they stood practically toe-to-toe and the tips of his boots were flush against the tips of her...holy shit. Those shoes!

My God, I'll never make it to the end of the night.

The woman wore a pair of side-zip, high-heeled ankle boots that sent his balls scrambling for his throat. So sexy and perfectly fit, they hugged her little ankles, bringing attention to a pair of legs that would stop traffic anywhere.

When they'd embraced on her couch with her lovely ass

nestled against his groin, Kenoe had enjoyed skimming his hands over her body, feeling the play of muscle underneath her jeans, but he hadn't gotten a good look. Tonight that was no longer an issue. He got an eyeful, all right, would have to be blind not to. In fact, several other men were getting a good fucking look too. And Kenoe pierced each and every one of them with a stare as cold as a Montana winter, knowing the bluish whites were beginning to take on an eerie silvery hue.

The popular movie myths about vampires with glowing red eyes were total hooey, but, like many of his genetic human cousins, Kenoe's eyes did in fact change color with his mood. And right now he teetered between flat-out lust and unreasonable fury.

His thoughts turned to gutting one of the staring men—a stocky fellow with one too many piercings and such a dumb-as-a-stump expression Kenoe almost felt sorry for the fellow. But another lecher wore a leer so telling it made Kenoe's gums twitch hotly with revulsion.

A gentle touch eased down the side of his face, bringing him out of unpleasant musing. A single finger smoothed an errant loc back behind his ear.

"Down, Naoru. Besides, there are just as many women looking at you as there are men looking at me, and I'm not growling and staring daggers."

He shot a thought her way.

"When are you going to tell me what Naoru means?"

She hesitated a second, as if deciding whether to trip out that he so easily communicated with her this way. Maybe she hadn't realized.

Then a saucy smile spread across those glossy lips as the woman winked, backed up a step and responded, "I think you scuffed my boots."

Kenoe's foul mood was immediately wiped away by her cheeky response. So she wasn't telling yet, eh? He wouldn't mention that he'd already looked it up. Instead, he pretended a sneeze and barked the word "bullshit" behind his hand, discreetly taking the opportunity to sheathe his errant fangs while Shinju laughed.

Slipping an arm around her shoulder, Kenoe steered her toward the oncoming train without another word, though his step was considerably lighter.

Upon arrival at their destination station, Shinju found herself floundering for surer footing as the automated attendant's voice rang through the car.

"We have now arrived at Roppongi Hills."

Damn it, damn it, damn it! Why in hell hadn't she entertained the idea that he might want to come to this district?

A taxi waited outside the train station and he still wouldn't tell her exactly where they were going. She'd poked and prodded, but the man was as stubborn as her.

"But why Roppongi Hills? It's a club scene for foreigners."

"Well, I kind of fall into the foreigner category, don't you think? What's the matter, lovely, can't you dance?"

"Asshole."

"Yeah, I know. But this asshole is very keen on showing you a good time."

Sigh. That grin got her every time.

Settled in the backseat of a cab with her jacket covering her legs, Shinju still could have kicked herself. Why hadn't she asked the man where they were going dancing before she'd agreed? Some of Max's Ooeto clan members tended to hang out in Roppongi district when they weren't running merchandise for

their businesses. And the last thing she wanted was to be recognized while out with a man, foreign or otherwise.

Her mind shot back to the last phone conversation she'd had with her brother. He'd actually had the nerve to ask questions about Kenoe. Max had caught her so totally by surprise it took Shinju a minute to even think of a snarky retort. That call ended with a promise: "If you don't back the hell up and tell Sasuke to lay off, I swear I'll skin your balls, Max." And she'd meant it.

Shinju had no doubt Kenoe could handle himself—the man's stance alone screamed confidence, ability and kickassivity. However, it was rare that a clan member ventured out clubbing alone, which meant she'd possibly have several annoying Ooeto men on her hands. She simply wasn't dressed to jump into a fray and lay the smackdown on guys who'd looked out for her most of her life. Or more like, kept her single most of her life with all their overprotective nonsense. Neither did she want to go all bad-girl in front of Kenoe. The man was no idiot. What law enforcement officer wouldn't put two and two together—being attacked by *yakuza* for hanging out with Shinju Maruyama, a woman who happened to be able to fight like a man? Surely he'd figure out there was more to it than them just wanting to protect the virtue of a female.

By the time she'd reasoned through half of the possibilities of things going wrong, Kenoe was steering her into Valdarre, the largest high-class, but no less wild, club in the area.

After shooing away a small party of Goth wannabes, an impeccably dressed attendant nodded at Kenoe and opened the front door. A fast medley of techno mixed with hip hop spilled out onto the street. The thump, thump of the deep bass tickled her spine. Her feet wanted to move to the beat. But regardless of the fact that a serene smile and perfectly calm façade were plastered on her face, Shinju stood frozen in the doorway.

Kenoe picked up on her distress and moved in close, instinctively comforting her in the alcove of his body.

"What is it? What's wrong?"

"Uh, nothing. Let's go in," she said much too brightly, putting a little bit of distance between them. Kenoe wouldn't quite let her escape.

"First off, I don't believe you. No, don't get upset, I can feel your anxiety. If you want to leave, we can."

"Not!" There was no way she'd chicken out. This was her first date in ages, and with a man she actually *wanted* to enjoy. She refused to let the mere possibility of running into some of her brother's associates keep her from reveling in a night out. She took his arm and beamed. "Let's get it on, handsome."

The attendants took their jackets, and they jumped right into the fray.

By the time a slow song came on, Shinju's slinky little tank top stuck to her back like a second skin. Sweat poured down her neck and left a trail between her breasts. And Kenoe eyed those lines of liquid as if he wanted to roll around in them.

He stepped close and eased his arms around her. Shinju locked her knees to keep from swooning into a puddle of wooed woman when the man began to sing along with the words of the song. Right into her head.

Sexy and sultry described his perfectly pitched voice. She'd heard this song a million times, a soulful ballad by a stateside artist. But boy did she have a new appreciation for the lyrics tonight. Shinju looked up and watched Kenoe's tongue travel across his biteable lower lip as he tilted his head and eyed her appreciatively. Oh. My. God.

When he dipped his head, she instinctively eased away, then wished her sense of propriety had stayed home.

"What's wrong?" Kenoe whispered.

"We're in public," Shinju hissed through clenched teeth.

"What does that have to do with anything?"

"It's just that, well, we don't touch or neck in public. It's a cultural thing." She felt the features of her face morph into something between mortified and hungry. Must be because she really wanted to let her tongue take the same path across his mouth his had only seconds ago. God, she could have kicked herself for falling back on old behavior.

While her African-American grandmother encouraged Shinju to live her life as she chose, her grandma on her father's side had always frowned on Shinju's independent nature. The woman insisted on teaching her and her cousins proper public etiquette. Unfortunately those childhood lessons, which included a huge dose of "good girls don't", seemed to stick just now.

"And if we were visiting your relatives in the States, would there be any issues with PDA?" he asked, sweeping her back into the crowd. The bodies were thick on this particular patch of dance floor.

"PDA? You mean public displays of affection? Of course not. It's just not done here." Which was one of the reasons Shinju always looked forward to her yearly summer trips to visit her stateside cousins. Once her feet hit the city streets of Atlanta, all bets were off. She didn't sleep around, but she certainly did her share of ass shaking in the clubs, along with the occasional kiss or two from whatever beau her cousins set her up with for the duration of the trip. As a result she'd gathered quite a few pen pals over the years.

In fact she was due to meet up with her kin in a couple of weeks. Strangely enough, the expected thrill of a bit of freedom from the strictures of Japanese life didn't appeal. It meant

leaving Kenoe behind.

"So it's a Japanese thing?" he asked, leaning in close. God, he smelled good. Like musk, hot sex and dangerous man.

"Duh." She snuffled, batting playfully at the hands trying to pinch her ass.

"Fine, as long as it's not an 'I-really-don't-want-to-be-seen-with-Kenoe' thing."

"Oh don't get your boxers in a twist. It's nothing personal."

"We'll see. Later."

"Oh yeah? What's going to happen later?"

"Well, my beautiful Shinju, I love that you're a lady when on the street." He lightly ran a single finger down her cheek, leaving a path in the sweat. It sent a shiver clear to her baby toes. "But I want a freak in my bed."

"And who says I'll end up in your bed?"

Kenoe moved in for the kill as the words of Locutus of Borg, the alter ego of Jean Luc Picard of the Starship Enterprise, played in his mind—*resistance is futile.*

Now what was it Carin said about Bix sending pictures into her head when they'd first met? Was it possible for him to do the same with Shinju? After all, what better way to explain what he meant than by showing her...explicitly?

Kenoe concentrated on the woman dancing so sexily in front of him and fixed her image in his mind. Then slowly peeled the clothes off that image, baring her lovely skin a bit at a time. Next, he put himself in the picture with her, naked as the day he was born and his cock gloriously hard. Next, came the raunchiest positions he could think of—Shinju on her knees with her ass up in the air as he pushed into her body, Shinju on her back with her strong, lovely legs and those sexy-assed boots wrapped around his waist, Shinju arching against him as

he stood behind her with one hand caressing a full, achy breast while the other slipped between her thighs and stroked until she writhed and shifted her weight from one foot to the other, calling his name, begging to be stuffed full. Whew, lord!

And when he thought his head would explode with the sensual imagery he'd created, he imagined a lifeline from his heart to hers, and sent every thought streaking along their special connection until she had to be practically drowning in not only his lust, but her own as well.

A startled feminine gasp gave a clue that his little experiment was working. The woman's breathing hitched up a notch, then two. The air left her chest in loud, harsh pants and was barely drowned out by the music.

"Oh, dear Lord, what the hell are you...? How are you...?" She gasped, eyes wide. Her skin was flushed and dewy. And Kenoe breathed it all in and held it close until his cock filled and ached. Maneuvering her off to the side and out of sight in a shadowed alcove at the edge of the dance floor, Kenoe pulled her close and fit his groin into the hollow of her belly.

Her eyes slid closed at the same time her lips parted on a husky sigh.

"Oh. My. Freaking. God."

"Freaking? Not yet, gorgeous. But we will."

"Holy shit..."

"Watch your mouth, young lady", preceded an imaginary but wicked nip to the slim, muscled column on the left side of her neck.

So not only could the man fill her head with the most wickedly sensual images, but he could make her feel his mouth moving over bare skin when he was actually touching her with

nothing more than one hand...and a cock that felt a mile wide straining against his pants.

Shinju didn't know what to say or do. All she seemed capable of was feeling, and damn, it all *felt* so good. Kenoe's deep-throated chuckle sounded in her head and did naughty things to the nerves that ran along the inside of her thighs.

"Naoru...Na...Kenoe, we have to leave. Right now."

"Really?" Oh lord, he was doing that purr-growl thing again right into her head.

"This is insane, but I absolutely, totally need you." She should have been embarrassed to admit such a thing, especially on a barely-there gasp. But instead of mortification, she simply burned alive. Surely there was a fire extinguisher in the place? Preferably the thick and no doubt ready one between Kenoe's legs. "Can we go now?"

Speaking while trying desperately to yank him toward the door, Shinju grit her teeth when that big, gorgeous body didn't move. He stood there and just held her in a gentle and seemingly appropriate embrace for a slow song. But the sexual melee in her mind was another story. The man was torturing her, damn it.

He leaned in, buried his nose in her hair and inhaled. Very slowly. She started to correct him, tell him to step back. Aw, to hell with propriety.

"Kenoe, I'm ready to go, handsome. Mmm, God I want you."

"Say the magic words." The demand vibrated on the inside of her skull.

"Please," she murmured, almost salivating from the thought of what he'd taste like.

"Wrong one."

Another image flooded her brain. It had her cheeks burning

and her head swimming. Immediately, the so-called magic words became as clear as the intent etched across Mr. Torturer's face.

"*Say it*" was followed by a psychic caress of her left ass cheek.

After several deep breaths Shinju squeaked out what he wanted to hear.

"Spank me."

"Your wish is my command." Then Kenoe hauled her to his side and all but flew to the front door. They retrieved their belongings, stepped out into the evening air and hailed a taxi.

God, it would be the longest, nastiest, most luscious ride of her life.

By the time they actually got back to her place, Shinju wasn't sure she wanted Kenoe to come inside, or anything else for that matter. After leaving the club, she'd gotten her bearings, scooted away from the questing fingers tormenting her in the backseat of the taxi and talked him into stopping for a late dinner then a walk in the gardens near her house. And all the way home he'd been an overbearing ass. Almost as bad as her brother and that damned Sasuke, who she suspected was lurking somewhere nearby.

At her door she rounded on him, not bothering to school her features or hide her irritation.

"Look, Kenoe, I really like you, but I'm not sure I want you to come in tonight." If she hadn't been so pissed off she would have giggled at his crestfallen expression. Silvery brows knit together on a scrunched frown. But the man pulled it together quickly and rocked her back on her heels.

"Shinju, I know I've upset you. You're an independent

woman. You do what you want, when you want. But let's just cut to the chase. I want you, lovely. And what's mine I protect, even from stupid males who are reckless enough to look too long."

"You can't snarl and growl at every man that looks at me."

"Why not?"

The man was serious! How the hell was she supposed to answer such a question? It was, after all, a dumb question, but Shinju felt even more stupid for not having an answer to it. As her mouth glubbed open and closed like a goldfish out of water, Kenoe took her lapse in mouthy-ness as a signal to keep talking.

"Look, Shin, I know you sense something special between us. We share a unique connection, a link. Just reach out a little bit, lovely, explore my emotions and you'll know that I don't wish to control you. But I'm so out of this world when I'm with you, all I want is to dive into you and drown, baby. And I don't want to share you with anyone, even in their imagination. I'm sure I'll relax about it all...but not tonight."

With that, he swooped down and laid a liplock on her that saw her pushed up against her door. A dam burst inside the man, and just as he said, all his longing and fierce need to keep her safe and happy poured out of him. Shinju let it fill her up until it made her drunk on the passion that beat against the inside of his skin, aching to get to her. It was beyond a physical attraction, beyond Kenoe just thinking she was pretty. This was something deeply profound and unexplainable. She'd have been at a loss if he'd asked her to articulate it.

All she could think about, focus on, was Kenoe's strong hands gently kneading the small of her back. Kenoe's breath warm against her ear. Kenoe walking around in her head like a caged animal that couldn't wait to get to its...mate?

"Yes, lovely. Mate."

The swirling depth of feeling when he thought the word made it clear there was more to it than a simple lay. It seemed endlessly precious, but she couldn't quite put it together.

Not now. Not with the heat between her legs flaring like a glass-melting Japanese torch. He broke the kiss. Shinju held on to the front of his jacket and whispered, "Wow."

"Open the door, lovely. I don't know how much longer I can go without having those sexy ankle boots wrapped around my waist."

"I don't wear shoes inside the house."

"Indulge me, sweetness." He bent down, loosened the ties on his boots and toed them off. "Better yet, I'll make it easy for you." With that, he lifted her off her feet, a thigh firmly in each hand, and urged her legs around his waist.

When the hell had she ever been completely at a loss for words? She could remember being sort of speechless, once. But absolutely unable to form a coherent sentence? In all her years she couldn't remember...wait, how old was she again?

Okay, she was definitely losing it.

Two steps over the threshold and Shinju was once again pressed up against a door for the second time in as many minutes. And lovin' it.

Kenoe wedged his knee against the solid wood and lowered her over his thigh.

"Ride it, lovely."

And ah, God, she did. Angling her hips so they canted forward, Shinju met his ferocious kiss with equal fervor, grinding her overheated pussy against his hard body.

Holding on with both her hands full of Kenoe's long silvery locs, Shinju fed the fierce hunger gnawing at her insides with

the sweetness of his mouth. With lips and tongue tingling from dueling with Kenoe's, Shinju gasped as he eased her down to the floor and stepped back.

Instinctively, Shinju unsnapped his pants and let down the zipper. Silk light blue boxers the same color as his eyes. Nice, she thought as she reached inside, grabbed him by the cock and gently pulled, making a beeline for the bedroom.

Kenoe laughed.

"What?" she asked airily, only halfway looking where she was going.

"Gives a whole new meaning to being led around by the balls."

They grunted together as Shinju ran into a wall then bumped her shoulder on the bedroom door, causing a slight tug on Kenoe's swollen jewels.

Kenoe plopped down on the edge of the bed with Shinju straddled over his thighs. She reached back to unzip her boots but a hand shot out to still her fingers.

"No. Leave them on," he murmured silkily.

Shinju almost toppled over backwards when the man wasted no time diving into the valley between her breasts. His warm breath heated her body, ignited the pores of her skin.

Then his fingers joined in the dance and skimmed over her flesh, tempting the mounds to rise up to meet them.

"Mmm, yes, touch me, Naoru."

"Tell me what Naoru means."

"Not...ooh, possible."

"Why?" He licked a wet path from her collarbone down to a straining nipple, worrying it between his teeth through the fabric of her top and barely-there bra.

"Because I can't think right now."

She felt one side of his mouth lift around her nipple and knew his devastating grin was firmly in place. But she had no problem giving the man his props. Considering she was quickly approaching overload and it was all his fault, he deserved any accolades coming his way. Also, she'd never had sex on the second date—the man was setting all kinds of records.

The filmy top was yanked up, off and sent flying across the small room to land at the foot of the dresser. Her bra joined it just before Kenoe eased her skirt up over her hips. The air conditioner was on, but she was so hot and ready, the cool air that should have soothed overheated skin simply evaporated. Leather bunched up around her waist. Kenoe grabbed both her butt cheeks in his hands and kneaded them against the hard lengthening bulge at his groin, causing her to ride his cock. From grinding her core shamelessly, Shinju's soaked thong rolled off to the side, and she was so wet her own honeyed juices left a slick trail over his zipper.

Finally, she couldn't wait another second. Shinju sat practically naked while Kenoe wasn't even close to being undressed. And she didn't give a damn. Obviously neither did he.

She reached down and pressed gently against the soft sac of his balls. Kenoe fell backward with a ragged groan. His beautiful hair lay like a waterfall of silver spread behind him, contrasting against the dark blue fabric of her comforter. With one hand he eased her forward to lick and nibble just underneath her jaw as a single finger played along her slippery folds. When a lone digit slipped inside to tickle her slick flesh, Shinju emitted a sound she was sure she'd never made before. A high pitched, out-of-control-with-longing squeal.

Oh yes, finally! Finally he would lay some pipe her way and

put out her forest fire. Thank God. In fact, thank all of them—her mother's Baptist God and her father's Shinto and Buddhist ones too!

With her sitting fully astride him, Kenoe lifted his hips at the same time his finger eased in a bit more. A welcome sound echoed in her ears—the rustle of fabric sliding down his legs. Then true desert heat seared her flesh, compliments of the velvety skin of his cock, so hot, so smooth.

"Now, again. Say the magic words."

With no hesitation, no shame, she yelled, "Spank me!"

Kenoe was sure he'd never experienced, or even dreamed of, anything as addictive as the sopping wet folds of Shinju's fragrant pussy. Jasmine and spice, and it was all his. He knew she would fit him like a hand in a custom-made glove.

The head of his cock was so beyond ready for her, it seemed to reach for the creaming channel hanging suspended above it. The second the plum-shaped tip touched her flesh it throbbed, engorged to the point of pain. Ooooh, damn.

Flexing his hips, he began to ease into her willing body. He wanted to go slowly to give her time to adjust to him being inside, yet wanted to impale her at the same time. He was barely in an inch and already she scalded him. He breathed in raggedly and caught something in the air.

His hackles rose. Hatsept rogue. A rogue was in Shinju's house. Not the one he'd scented before, but a vampire criminal just the same. Shit. Shit! *Shit!*

Kenoe went perfectly still at the same time Shinju did. Had she sensed the same thing as he? Well, of course. She must have felt his surprise and anger flash through the bond. But then she put her fingers to his lips to signal silence at the same time his fingertips met her lips for the same purpose. What?

Without a sound she eased up and off of his body. They both planted their feet firmly on the floor. He signaled for her to stay put. A single brown brow rose and she pinned him with a no-way-in-hell glare.

Rising together, they silently eased toward the open bedroom door. And there in the threshold Kenoe came face to face with the one woman he'd gladly condemn to the fucking depths of hell and roast marshmallows over her burning ass. Hell, he'd even make s'mores and hot chocolate if the flames lasted long enough.

No doubt she was beautiful—slanted whiskey brown eyes, lovely caramel brown skin and a body so fit and tight you could bounce a quarter off her ass and it would fly into the air and do somersaults. The woman looked a bit like Shinju, only Shin's hair was longer, and her eyes darker while the tone of her skin was a shade lighter. Well, he'd seen enough of this female while on the last hunt in London. And right now he wanted her to go the fuck away.

Instead she looked him up and down like a cat eyeing a fat, juicy mouse, then dragged her gaze away to stare at Shinju.

"Hi Shin, how are you? And Kenoe Hatsept? What a surprise."

"What the hell are you doing here?" Kenoe thundered in unison with Shinju. His woman jerked her neck back and looked at him like he was crazy.

"Don't yell at my cousin!"

Now it was Kenoe's turn to be shocked.

"Your cousin? You couldn't possibly be related to her."

"Yeah, my cousin. And how the hell do you know each other anyway?"

Kenoe didn't, could in no way, answer that question. His

skin crawled with disgust as the female he would have no problem never seeing again stared at his cock. And that was certainly one part of his body that never wanted to experience her again. Kenoe's lip curled involuntarily. She still smelled like Lowan Hatsept-Shean.

"Kimora, what are you doing here? You're supposed to be in London for at least another month. And stop staring at Naoru's cock!" Shinju snapped, easing her skirt down before leaning over to snatch a clean T-shirt out of a laundry basket.

Kenoe turned away from Kimora, tucked himself back into his pants and zipped them up. When he faced her again she was staring at his ass. Good grief.

"Well, cuz," Kimora practically purred. "I got ill in London."

Kenoe snorted. Ill was right. She'd lost her fucking mind and practically tortured him senseless, and all on the orders of a rogue vampire.

"So I figured I'd come here early instead of going home to Atlanta. And it's so nice to—" she licked her lips, "—see you again, Kenoe."

Shinju scowled, cutting her cousin a scathing glance.

"We met in London a few weeks ago, Shin. Never expected the man to turn up here," Kimora said.

Kenoe wanted to strangle Kimora for looking at him as if something significant had gone on between them.

"What do you mean, turn up here?" Shinju growled.

Aw, hell. Now she'd aimed that scowl at him. Great.

"Well, we didn't talk much in London. So I had no idea he was coming to Japan after such an interesting, uh, vacation."

Kenoe sucked in a deep breath and painted on a semblance of control. Kimora might be hinting at something more intimate between them, but at least she wasn't going to rat him out. She

might make him look like a two-timing dog, but it didn't appear that she planned to reveal either of their connections to The Vampire Council of Ethics. Thank God.

After Shinju shooed Kimora out of the bedroom, she turned eyes on him. Kenoe inwardly winced as she looked him up and down, then stormed out. Practically on the woman's heels, Kenoe caught her arm when she almost fell over the mountain of luggage her cousin had left piled in the middle of the floor. Guess Kimora was here to stay. Damn. So much for spending the evening making love.

Kimora settled on the futon in front of the television and a frosty Shinju headed straight to the kitchen and began bustling about, completely ignoring him.

"Kimmie, are you hungry?" she called to a seemingly oblivious Kimora. "I'm sure they didn't feed you worth a damn on the plane."

"I could do with a little something. Nothing too heavy, though. It's pretty late," Kimora replied without even looking up. And Shinju went right about her business as if nothing had happened. Frost rolled off of her in waves, but underneath, a vat of anger and suspicion smoldered like hot coals.

Guess the thrill was gone.

One thing he'd learned over the years watching Bix's and Alaan's relationships with their wives, was when to back the hell off. Pushing Shinju right now was the farthest thing from wise that he could do. The only true choice was to let her cool off.

"Uh, Shinju, I think I should go. Call you soon?" He leaned in to kiss her on the cheek. Back stiff and lips pressed into a tight line, she stood there and let his lips make contact with her face, but in no way moved to return his little peck or hug him back when his arms came around her. Shit.

All she did was mumble an unconvincing, "Yeah. Sure."

Well, she didn't sound sure so he tried to speak to her silently. And ran into a brick wall, blocked out of her head completely. It was like running full speed at a huge tree. Kenoe almost grinned, knowing that once their mating and bonding was done, she wouldn't be able to keep him out, period.

Kenoe was tempted to present a few choice images of what they'd been doing before Kimora showed up. Nope, better not. The thunderheads forming on Shinju's face told him not to push his luck. So he settled for sending a soft, reassuring caress and another easy brush instead.

He knew she'd felt it when her head swiveled around on her neck and cat-shaped eyes pinned him with an astonished, then skeptical glower.

"See you later?"

"Uh huh." A smile spread across her lips that said all was well, but the ice coating their forming bond told a different story.

Kenoe stepped out into the night and the door closed firmly behind him with a definitive-sounding snap.

Damn.

Chapter Seven

This just wasn't happening. Yep, he'd wake up any minute and find himself in his apartment, tangled up in his sheets and covered in a cold sweat. There was just no way his luck could possibly be this bad that Kimora, of all people, would show up at the home of a woman he was eager to sink into and stay put for the rest of his days.

God, please, please let a bad guy cross my path right now. The need to hit something, anything, was so strong Kenoe clenched his teeth and shoved his hands into his pockets as far as they would go. He'd already had his love play interrupted. The last thing he needed was for someone to see him knock a hole into a wall and call the police to take him to the crazy house.

The moist, cool evening air sank through his jacket and into his skin, adding a chill to his already morbid mood. A soft breeze brought the scent of cherry, birch and Japanese pear, all so prolific in this country at this time of year. In the distance, the low-hanging clouds were lit up by the profusion of lights and signs typical of the city's nightlife.

Kenoe's keen hearing picked up the sounds of one of Shibuya's main drags a few streets over. Auto and foot traffic, crowds congregating, discos, bars, coffee houses. Young and old, it was all about fun at night in this district. Surely everyone

was enjoying what was left of the evening...everyone except him. And it was all that damned Kimora's fault.

Kenoe had made it six steps from Shinju's front door when his body slammed to a screeching halt. Instincts on full tilt, he picked up a slight, almost silent rustle off to his left. *Aha.* Just what he needed. Right there in front of him crouched behind a bush was the man he'd seen tailing Shinju before. The same one he'd sent a digital photo of to Bix this afternoon. And Kenoe was in the perfect mood to do a little interrogation. Too bad he didn't have his tainted blade on him. Kenoe liked to call the film on his katana the Dr. Carin Vampire Puke Serum. One cut with the stuff and a full-blooded vamp would fall to his knees in seconds, hurling up his guts. Took the fight right out of 'em and made the scum that Seekers spent their time chasing a whole lot more cooperative.

Then again, this man moved like a vampire but didn't smell like one. Would the serum smeared on Kenoe's blade even affect him?

Well, since Kenoe wasn't on duty and had left his gear behind in his apartment, his fists would just have to do. He eased up on the man without a sound, extended one hand and lifted him right up off the ground by the back of his collar.

The man responded by kicking backward with his heel to land a blow to Kenoe's solar plexus. Even a vampire had to flinch at that one. Might even have a bruise in the morning, and the pain was just enough to piss Kenoe off some more. Dropping the guy to the ground, he moved in swiftly. Granted, the man got in a few good punches, but even with vamp speed he was no match for a full-blooded male Seeker in his prime. So Kenoe proceeded to kick his vampire-moving-but-no-smelling ass all over the front of Shinju's porch. Finished playing with his prey, he'd just cocked his fist back to deliver a knockout blow when the door opened and a blur that looked like an

enraged woman flew at him. Followed by a knee to the balls.

He went down like a ton of bricks.

Well, at least he wasn't alone. Shinju's talented knee made contact with his opponent's balls too—a man who happened to be a hell of a lot more bruised up than Kenoe was at the moment. Well, except for his now-purple balls.

"Kenoe, what the fuck are you doing? No, never mind, don't answer that. I can see what you're doing," she yelled, then rounded on the other man doubled over on the ground next to him.

"What are you doing here, Sasuke?"

"I was just coming to visit. I'd hoped to get some of that cake I saw on your table yesterday." Each word was a gasped groan. "Damn it, Shinju, my balls were just fine where they were."

"Mine too," Kenoe rasped, then wished he'd kept his mouth shut when the crazy woman smacked him and the Sasuke guy in the back of the neck like they were little kids. Here he was, a Seeker for cripes sake, groveling at the feet of a five-foot-nothing human female. God, he hoped no one ever got wind of this 'cause he'd never hear the end of it.

Shinju stepped back, practically snarling. "Do you really think I'm buying that, Sasuke? Max has you here spying on me. Well you tell my brother that this is the last time he is to send anyone to babysit me, damn it."

"He's only concerned for you, Shinju," Sasuke wheezed.

Kenoe lifted his head and growled, "What the hell are you talking about? She's my woman and mine to protect."

Sasuke's head swiveled around to pin Kenoe with a puffy-eyed stare. The man's eyes were already swelling shut and the bruises forming into an interesting pattern across his face. Boy,

that was going to hurt in the morning. Not to mention the cuts oozing blood from his brow, lips and cheeks. Still, he was able to talk shit.

"Says who, you fucking long-haired, pasty-faced, white-haired..."

"Oh shut up, both of you. You both need Plexiglas bellybuttons," Shinju fumed.

"Huh?" Sasuke and Kenoe both gurgled, hands jammed between their legs. Kenoe, for one, wondered if he'd ever get the feeling back in his testicles. He almost grinned when he saw Sasuke in the same sorry shape.

Shinju hissed, "You need a Plexiglas bellybutton so you can see when you've got your head up your ass. Now get the hell off my property."

Kenoe made to step up on the stoop. Her arm shot out and landed dead center in his gut. Damn, the woman was strong.

"Both of you. Besides, I don't have anything else to say to you. You're street fighting? I don't believe it. You're supposed to be a cop. And as for whatever's going on with Kimora, I don't even want to hear it. Go away."

For the second time tonight the door closed in his face. And his woman had just bested two grown men—one a vampire and the other with vampire traits. Kenoe and Sasuke both flopped down on the front steps to catch their breath.

"Is she always like that?" Kenoe panted, one hand holding his stomach, the other his sore sac.

"You have no idea. I'm Sasuke, by the way." He wheezed just as hard, partly from the exertion of keeping his head attached to his body, which Kenoe had seemed pretty keen on removing, and partly from the swift kick to the nuts, compliments of Shinju.

"So, you're not tailing her for any ill purpose. That much is clear," Kenoe stated flatly.

"Glad you figured it out. I'd hate to have to finish the fight Shinju broke up. That woman."

"So you're a friend of her brother's?"

"Something like that, yes. He worries about her but can't always be here. Since he's my boss, and Shinju is like a little sister to me, I sometimes take it upon myself to keep an eye on her."

"She seems to be able to take care of herself."

"For the most part, yes. But her brother is a very important man and the last thing he wants is for her to be threatened because of it."

Kenoe understood all too well. Alaan had cut himself off from just about every female in the vampire nation because his position in the clans would put any female he chose to mate in terrible danger.

"It's not unheard of...ow!" Kenoe's leg smarted and throbbed. When had that happened? He'd have to check himself over thoroughly when he got back to his apartment. "As I was saying, it's not unheard of for some to use family members for ransom and extortion. What does Shinju's brother do that would make her a target?"

With a sigh, the man rose shakily to his feet.

"Nice to meet you, Kenoe." Sasuke's hand reached out, grabbed Kenoe's and pumped it up and down quickly. Then he walked daintily to a black-on-black motorcycle parked in front of the house next door. Easing himself onto the crotch rocket, he started the bike and took off.

On the way home, all Kenoe could think about was the

possibility of Shinju in danger. After a quick shower he eased into bed with an ice pack over his balls and called Bix to share what he'd learned tonight. The man, Sasuke, did indeed have a few vampire traits. But more importantly, during their fight, he'd caught the scent of a rogue vampire near Shinju's house for the second time in as many days. Something foul was afoot, and he had a feeling he needed to get to the bottom of it. And quickly.

Raiden had been a member of Clan Vigee before being exiled as a rogue. If he hadn't earned his conviction by The Council when it was first handed down, he certainly had by now. Over the years he'd seen and done unspeakable things, but the silent ruckus heating up before him wasn't among any of his experiences thus far. In fact, Raiden wasn't sure what the hell he was seeing, but his curiosity wasn't strong enough to make him move any closer to the scene unfolding down the quiet street from where he stood. With a whisper barely louder than the breeze floating through the rows of trees lining the sidewalks, he flipped open his phone and dialed the one called Dan the Mouse.

"I'm not far from Max Maruyama's sister's house and I swear there's a Seeker kicking the shit out of Max's right hand, Sasuke."

"What? A Seeker? Same one you spotted before?"

The rogue winced at the quiet menace behind the words. Many of Raiden's associates thought the mousy-looking four-eyed scientist on the other end of the phone line was simply a nerd way out of his league. But he'd personally seen what the little brainiac could do with his serums, potions and gadgets.

Dan could make a vampire fall to his knees and beg for mercy as he crumbled into a pile of blackened nothing. Or make him so strong he could reach through the rib-protected chest of his enemy and yank his heart out. Raiden shivered in disgust.

"I'm not sure, but I'm keeping my distance. I don't want him to pick up my scent. This guy's not dressed like a Seeker, but he's a Hatsept. I can tell by that clan's telltale white hair. I bet he's the same one Shibuya is buzzing about."

"What makes you say so?" came the bored words through the earpiece. Raiden wasn't fooled in the least.

"What are the chances of more than one Hatsept with hair braided down his back like that being seen in this district, and hanging around Max's sister's house at the same time?"

"I see your point," Dan said on a long, drawn-out breath. "Just keep watching the house. Don't follow him."

Hell, he might have been stupid enough to throw his lot in with the enemies of the vampire nations and end up exiled as a rogue by the V.C.O.E., but he wasn't idiot enough to follow a Seeker. He had no intention of getting anywhere near the vampire. His speed alone told enough of the story.

Clicking the phone shut, Raiden backed up silently, slipped into the shadows cast by the frame of a small house down the street, and disappeared into the night. No way in hell was he sticking around to see the outcome of the fight between what was obviously a Hatsept and the little human, Sasuke.

Besides, he and his fellow rogues had survived this long by remaining on the down low, operating behind the scenes and staying off the radar of the Seekers in this area. He'd heard rumors that the rogues in Nagano and Nagoya were unwisely starting to rise up and take control of their territories. Stupid, stupid, stupid. That sort of thing was exactly what caused a blip on the Seeker radar.

So why had they become so reckless? The word on the street was that those rogues were making huge purchases from Dan, the same human scientist-turned-vamp-businessman he'd just hung up the phone with. Dan promised his customers an edge over their competition. But Raiden knew what those drug-buying idiots didn't—they were getting a short-lived high. But by the time they figured it out, Dan would be long gone. It was his M.O.

And since Raiden was the one who'd introduced Dan to the rogue bosses in this area, he'd have a pack of vampire no-goods after him, along with the Seeker Corps, while Dan had his feet up relaxing in some tiki hut somewhere out of reach. And God help him if they sent in the big guns, like the Head Seeker, Jon Bixler, and his tank of a Second, Alaan Serati. And their women were just as ruthless and dangerous.

Thankfully not every rogue faction in Tokyo was hooked up with Dan. Perhaps it was time to rethink his association with the human bookworm and cut his losses.

Max would have laughed harder if he had the energy. He and Sasuke made one hell of a pair. Max's name was known not only on the northern island of Japan, but also by their affiliates in the States and Australia, while Sasuke was his underboss responsible for one of the most powerful and feared organized crime clans.

And they were both laid up like old women.

With painful effort, Max turned his head toward his best friend and Second sitting—or rather lying—on the couch on the other side of the coffee table in the living room. A gurgle rumbled up from Max's diaphragm and ended in a laugh so

consuming, he was bent over double in near exhaustion when he was through.

"What?" Sasuke hissed with a scowl.

"Look at us. Me, Max Maruyama, leader of Clan Ooeto, practically in need of a nurse. And you, my Second, covered with bruises like you've taken the beating of your life."

"I did take the beating of my life, damn it. Then your sister made it worse by practically removing my ability to ever bear children. And stop laughing, you fucking sadist."

Max laughed harder until his chuckles became struggling wheezes. After several long minutes of just trying to breathe, he turned back to Sasuke and spoke.

"So, tell me about the man who managed to turn you such interesting shades of purple and blue. And, uh, yellow? Is that yellow, or green?"

"Oh shut it, already. Kikiyo!" Sasuke called as loud as he was able. A stocky man in a stylish gray suit eased the door open. "Bring me some more ice packs, man. And some tea for Max."

With a simple "*Hai*" and a slight bow, the man disappeared and returned shortly with several ice packs to replace the ones Sasuke had already used.

All the while, Sasuke's grumbles turned the air blue. "Fucking pasty-faced, white-haired vampire. Damned pretty boy Seeker. Muscle bound clod of a ..."

"All right, already," Max wheezed. "Stop whining and tell me what happened."

"You'd think...ah, God that hurts. You'd think it was obvious, Max. I got a call from one of our men who spotted your sister on the dance floor at Valdarre. I went to her house and waited for her, scoping it out, keeping an eye on her. Or so I

thought."

"Valdarre? Shinju went to Valdarre?"

"Yeah, Shinju and that damned long-haired fellow I told you I'd seen before. By the way, I contacted your friend in Clan Li and described the man. He confirmed our suspicions. The guy with Shinju is indeed a Seeker. And not just any Seeker, but what they call an elite. I'm not up on all their hierarchy, but the Clan Li vamp certainly seemed concerned for me while at the same time saying the guy was vamp law enforcement. A good guy. Anyway, they showed up at her house. I wanted to shoot the idiot."

"Since when do you refer to Shinju as an idiot?"

"Not Shinju, damn it, Kenoe."

"Who...?"

"Am I telling the story or not?"

"I think getting your ass kicked has made you cranky."

"Fuck you." Sasuke made to scoot up a bit higher on the pillows piled behind his head. A deep frown and annoyed-sounding grunt said his efforts were rewarded with some obvious aches and pains. Max watched until Sasuke's head settled back on the arm of the couch.

"Great," Sasuke grumbled. "Now my temples are throbbing in time with everything else on my body."

At Sasuke's grimaces and hisses of pain, Max bit the inside of his cheek to keep from cracking up again.

"So anyway," Sasuke continued, "Kenoe, it turns out, is the name of the Seeker on Shinju's ass. Literally."

"What the hell do you mean?" Max thundered. Well, it actually felt more like a dull poof than a thundering bellow given how tight his lungs felt these days.

"He kissed her like they were old lovers right there outside

her door before they went inside. After about twenty minutes I started to kick her door in, then Kimora showed up."

"Kimora? What the hell is she doing in Tokyo? She's supposed to be in London. And isn't Shinju supposed to visit her family in America next month?"

"That's what I thought. In fact the last time I spoke with your mother, she said Shinju was to come visit her and your aunt right at the beginning of summer vacation, as soon as school was out. She was trying to get me to talk you into joining them."

"Well, she's been working on me slowly but surely ever since she moved to America. But at least she's got Kimora's mother to keep her company and out of trouble."

Sasuke replaced the ice pack on his thigh, another on his lower stomach, secured one to his shoulder and yet another over his left eye. "Your mother? Stay out of trouble? The woman is a man-magnet, even at her age, and speaks her mind no matter what. Of course she'll always be in the middle of one thing or another."

Sasuke was so right. But it was typical for the women in his family. Ever since Max's grandfather showed up in Tokyo with his grandma so many years ago, it seemed to be a family tradition for the Maruyama men to go abroad to study or work, and bring home a dark-skinned, saucy, beautifully smart female as a wife. Kimora's father, and his own, had been no different. Kimmie's parents lived in Atlanta and welcomed his own mother into their home after Max's father died. Max didn't have the darker skin tones of his mother, but he had her fire and attitude—the two main reasons he'd risen up through the ranks of the Ooeto clan, taken it over, and expanded their territories—all without bloodshed.

"That Kenoe bastard beat me up one side and down the

other. My enhanced speed and strength made no difference. Even after I pulled a blade on him, it didn't matter. The man just dodged each strike while landing every punch he threw at me. And the asshole grinned the whole time. Fucking fangs gave me the creeps."

"And then?"

"And then Shinju came outside and broke it up. After kicking us both in the nuts, she told me to tell you that she didn't need, and I quote, 'a fucking babysitter'. I was lucky she didn't have a katana on her or she'd have shaved my balls. Then she bit the loc-wearing vampire's head off and told him that she didn't date thugs who were intimate with her cousin. What she meant by that I have no idea. But then she turned around and left us on our knees. And that damned cousin of yours stood in the doorway laughing. Bitch."

"Do you think Shin knows the Seeker is a vampire?"

"No, I don't think so. He sheathed his fangs quick when she came flying out of the door while he held me six inches off the ground. Asshole."

A crippling pain wrapped around Max's lungs, bringing about a gasp when he would have rather guffawed at his friend.

Then a chill crept into his intestines at the thought of a Seeker sniffing after his sister. It was bad enough when they thought he was simply following her. Based on what Sasuke said, this Kenoe guy had done more than watch Shinju. The bastard had touched her, kissed her. Then hurt her feelings in some way. And what did Kimora have to do with any of this?

With this Kenoe vamp and all the other strangers seen hanging around Shinju's house lately, it seemed she was the center of some unwanted attention, even if she wasn't aware of it.

There was no way Max would leave his sister unprotected.

No way in hell, even if he had to die and come back as a ghost that haunted every asshole who dared get near her. With his health deteriorating at an alarming rate, it was even more imperative that they locate the source of all their troubles—Dan the Mouse.

"Listen, Sasuke, we've got to get to the bottom of this. Enough lying on your ass, old friend. Find the mouse who gave us the fucked-up serum and those who harbor him."

Chapter Eight

"I have bad news, Kenoe."

In true Bix fashion, the Head Seeker plunged ahead and began to spill it all without hesitation.

"The guy whose digital you sent—"

"He's also the same guy I fought outside of Shinju's place. His name's Sasuke and he's obviously a friend of the family. Shinju took both our heads off."

"Yeah, well your woman is related to a badassed *yakuza* boss named Maruma Maruyama. His friends call him Max."

"You're telling me that the man who moves like a vampire but smells like, like…nothing, is *yakuza*? And his boss is Shin's brother?"

"It's worse."

Kenoe steeled himself for what he was about to hear but his head was surprisingly empty. Usually he could reason out exactly what was going on behind the scenes of whatever mystery lay before him. But the thought that Shinju might be up to no good simply didn't take root.

"We've had one of the local Seekers tailing this Max guy the past few days. According to some quietly kept Clan Li friends of his, it seems he's gotten a dose of instant vampire too. He's not out much lately and rumor has it he's been ailing. Not sure if

it's a side-effect or simply a human illness."

Kenoe tilted his head to an awkward angle, trying to work the sudden knot of tension out of his neck. "What do you mean, side-effect?"

"Wait a second, I'm putting you on speaker."

Carin's voice joined Bix's on the line.

"Hey, Key. What Bix means is that we've got a theory. Max may be suffering from whatever biotech compound he's ingested. Neither he nor the Sasuke guy gained their vampire traits by chance, nor by infusions of large quantities of vampire blood like I did. But they had to get it from someone. My guess is that it's another human."

"But how? Why?"

"Think about it," Carin continued. "After the Sidheon mess, no vampire in his right mind would go the same route that nutball did. And what was I doing when I met Bix? Trying to create an artificial means to turn myself into a vampire, or at the very least, alter my genes enough to simulate vampire traits to extend my lifespan."

"You think someone else is doing the same thing? Or perhaps picked up where you left off?"

"Sure, why not? But I can't be sure unless we acquire some specimens from the humans in question, namely Max and Sasuke, so I can run a few tests. But the bottom line is that I'm not the only brilliant gene specialist in the world. The most accomplished and most beautiful, absolutely. But certainly not the most brilliant."

A snort of laughter floated up and out of Kenoe's chest before he could stop it. Even the gravity of the situation couldn't suppress the fact that the woman was incorrigible. Carin would get along with Shinju for sure. And God help him when his woman hooked up with Tameth. The three of them would

practically rule the roost back at V.C.O.E. headquarters. God help them all.

Back to business.

"How should I proceed, Bix?"

"First off, there's no evidence that your Shinju has had any contact with Clan Li, only her brother has. Also, from what the territory leaders in Tokyo and Osaka have told me about the *yakuza's* activities in those cities right now, your girl could have an inadvertent problem on her hands if the other *yakuza* clans get wind of what her brother has done."

"Meaning?"

"Think about it, Kenoe. How do you think the other bosses will react if they find out that someone's given themselves a considerable advantage over all the others? Vampire speed, vampire strength up against humans without it?"

Damn, Bix had a point there. At best, the other crime bosses would want to get their hands on whatever Max and Sasuke had bought to increase their edge, and at worst, get rid of Max and Sasuke altogether. Or even stoop to using Shinju as a pawn to obtain the drug that would put them well out of the league of the local law enforcement officers.

The possibility Shinju's life was in danger because of her stupid brother simply wasn't an option. He had to get her the hell out of Tokyo until they could figure this out. But how? She wasn't even speaking to him right now thanks to that damned Kimora.

"Kenoe?"

"Yeah?"

"I can practically feel you reasoning this all out in your head," Bix said. And he was right. "We need a plan, and fast. First, I'm sorry to cut your vacation short, but you're now back

on duty. Second, I think you might want to bring your woman here for safekeeping, at least until we can get a better handle on what the hell is going on there."

"But how can I complete the mission you're going to give me in Tokyo if I'm not here?"

"Your mission isn't in Tokyo. Your mission is to keep Shinju from becoming a token in a *yakuza* clan war. Bring her here."

"But—"

"No buts, Seeker. That's an order. You have permission to reveal just who and what we are in order to get her cooperation."

Feeling suddenly cantankerous, he grumped, "And what if I've already—?"

"Oh please." This from Carin with a saucy chuckle. "We know you, sweet pea. You'd want to woo her as a man before revealing yourself as more than human. And you wouldn't do anything to endanger your people any more than you would endanger your woman."

Right again. Man, he loved his family.

"We've already made the arrangements. Alaan is relaying orders to the mechanics to begin pre-flight inspection on the new jet. Someone will be there to pick you up day after tomorrow. Whatever you have to do to get that woman here, do it. When that plane takes off from Haneda Airport, both you and Shinju Maruyama better be on it. As for Tokyo *yakuza* and possible leads on who's providing genetic enhancement drugs, I've already had Tameth relay orders to the Clan Li Seekers. They're all over it. They'll keep an eye on Max and Sasuke too. I'm sure your Shinju will be worried about them. Assure her they'll be fine."

Right. Considering she hadn't returned any of his phone

calls, he might just have to drag her and her temper kicking and screaming onto that jet. The woman was proving to be as ornery as a freeborn mule.

At the conclusion of the briefing, Kenoe disconnected the call. Realizing he'd paced through the whole meeting, he stopped in the middle of the living room and sank to his knees to meditate.

An image of Shinju's face intruded into his thoughts. The recollection of soft, supple skin stretched over taut muscle had his fingertips itching. Concentrating harder, he cleared his mind and relaxed as the knowledge of what he must do formed into a plan all on its own.

He spent the morning working out with his blades. Between sweating and making connections with the locals, Kenoe meditated and focused on his case.

The next morning, mental faculties firmly in place, Kenoe rose, showered, fed well and planned out his day.

Later, he hauled his suitcase out of the closet and flipped it open to reveal the only set of clothes he hadn't unpacked—his Seeker gear.

He left the apartment sporting a pair of black three-quarter shank boots and black rip-stop fatigues. His long, perfectly twisted locs were pulled into a thick ponytail at his back. And his expertly balanced katana blade, carefully smeared with Dr. Carin's nasty vampire gut-wrencher serum, was slipped into the hidden sheath beneath his custom black leather trench coat. He kissed his second favorite toy—a Taurus 24/7 OSS military pistol, a forty caliber powerhouse with stainless steel finish—and tucked it into the concealed holster underneath his right arm.

Time to go to work. First stop, Roppongi district's Seeker headquarters and Clan Li.

Later that evening, Kenoe walked down the streets lit up by the huge neon billboards and nightlife of Shibuya. A deadly Seeker openly stalked his prey—a stubborn-as-hell female. And all those with sense got the hell out of his way.

Planning to hit the stores as soon as they opened, Kimora stepped onto the porch and made her way to the small garden out back. Without warning, she was snatched off her feet and flung against the low brick wall that shielded the gardens from the street.

"Don't think you can take me on, human." The snarled words were accompanied by a blatant show of yellowed fangs. Nasty bastard. Even during her time in Lowan Hatsept-Shean's harem, every vampire and harem mate was impeccably clean, fangs included. Nothing like the rancid-breathed asshole standing over her.

"Do you believe in vampires, bitch?"

Quickly up on her feet, Kimora backed up against the wall, glad to have a solid surface behind her. Ruthlessly tamping down the terror clawing at her gut, she raised her fists and settled into a perfect boxing stance. Hell, if the bastard was going to go feral on her, there was no way he'd take her down without a few choice cuts and bruises.

"Whether you believe in us or not, you smell like you've been fucking a vampire. I can smell him seeping out of your pores. Taken a liking to a Hatsept? That silver-haired freak seen hanging around Shibuya district, I take it."

Kimora bit her lip to keep her mouth from falling open. So

the idiot thought it was Kenoe's scent on her, eh? No one except Kenoe and the team who'd taken her from Lowan's stronghold knew what, or rather who, she'd been doing in London. And if this idiot wanted to believe she'd been knocking boots with Kenoe, there was no way in hell Kimora would disabuse him of the notion.

"Rumor has it he's a badassed elite Seeker from out of town. It's making my boss nervous. If you value your pitiful human life, you'll get you and your pasty-faced vamp lover the hell out of Tokyo. We're not stupid enough to take him on. But you, well that's another story, isn't it, beautiful? And trust me..."

Kimora's gut clenched as he looked her over with a leer.

"I'd enjoy it."

Kimora wisely kept silent. As long as this guy and whatever faction he worked for believed Kenoe was here for her rather than her cousin, perhaps she could keep both of them from being "disappeared" off the face of the earth.

With a knee-buckling parting slap to reinforce his threat, the man sheathed his fangs and looked around cautiously before slinking away.

And this dimwit *was* a total rogue. No law-abiding vamp would dare reveal himself or his kind to a human. Damn. Times like this she wished she'd just gone on home to Atlanta to see her mom and gran-gran instead of coming to Tokyo.

Kimora sucked in deep, steadying breaths while commanding her head to stop reeling from the blow. In seconds she was up off her ass and securely bolted behind Shinju's door.

Well, good thing she didn't have much to re-pack.

After several hours of trying to figure out how to save both her and her relative's skins, Kimora was as jumpy as a frog on a

hotplate. Rain had begun to fall at midday. Every crack of thunder sent her skin practically running from her bones. Her heart had taken so many trips up the scale and back down, she was sure she'd gotten a week's worth of cardio done without even exercising.

It had been days since she'd burst in on Kenoe and her cousin on the verge of making love. Since then Shinju had refused to return any of his calls, even though Kimora had assured her he was honorable.

Perhaps too honorable. Kenoe was much more than a handsome-as-sin prime male, he was Council law enforcement. Hell, Kimora was surprised Kenoe hadn't waylaid her on one of her recent excursions into Shibuya's many shops and taken the first opportunity to smack her sideways.

Before meeting Kenoe and his team, Kimora had no idea there were good guys and bad guys in the world of vampires. And she'd fallen in with a lot that was as bad as you could go. As such, she was now the responsibility of the Council and had the promise of their protection should she ever have need of it—in exchange for her silence, of course. Now it looked like she might have to take them up on the offer after all.

And if anyone could protect her and Shin from the rogue that threatened her today, it was Kenoe Hatsept and the team of badasses he worked with. She hadn't seen Bix and crew around but that didn't mean they weren't.

But how the hell could she get their help without telling Shinju? Knowing Kenoe was a vampire and knowing the man was a Seeker were two different things. And revealing the identity of a Seeker was tantamount to treason in their world. So even if Shinju was banging the hell out of the gorgeous white-haired hunk, Kimora doubted her cousin knew his rank, file or serial number this early in the game.

No. Kimora had sworn to keep her knowledge of the Vampire Council of Ethics a secret—who the hell would believe her anyway?—and she'd kept, and would continue to keep, her word. Even if it meant deceiving her cousin. Besides, the less Shinju knew, the better. Revealing that she'd been accosted in the backyard by a vamp with rank breath would just send Shinju haring off after the guy. And what would that solve?

Kimora may have put on a good front to the rabid vamp who'd paid her a visit this morning, but she was a damned wreck by the time Shinju got home from school.

Poor thing dragged through the door looking like a miserable drowned rat. Kimora practically ran her down before she'd even removed her shoes.

"Hey cuz. How was work?"

"Fine," Shinju grumbled, shucking out of her rain boots and leaving them at the door. Her coat came next, followed by her book bag that hit the floor with a reverberating thunk. After a few grunts and sighs, nothing else seemed forthcoming. Yep, the girl had it bad, obviously missing her man. This particular Shinju certainly didn't wear "sullen" well.

"So, uh, what's up with summer break? I was supposed to still be in the UK around the time you went to see your mom. You still going? It's coming up soon, right?"

Of course it was. Kimora had already called Shinju's school pretending to be a parent who wanted to enroll her daughter, and was told she'd have to wait until after the month-long vacation.

"I'm still scheduled to go to your house and visit with my mom. Why, you have something else in mind?"

"Actually I was thinking perhaps we could go early? You've got some extra time off coming to you, right?"

"Sure, but why do you want to go early? Bored with Tokyo

already? I thought Kenoe would keep you company since I've kicked him to the curb."

"Kicked him to the curb? Geesh, Shinju, nobody says that anymore. Besides, I told you already that I met Kenoe through a mutual acquaintance in London. That acquaintance *happened* to be his brother, who I *happened* to be sleeping with at the time. Kenoe and I never had anything going. Besides, he doesn't even like me."

That was definitely the truth.

But she'd leave out the part where a burly Hatsept vampire named Myles had supervised her near-torture of Kenoe via the monster blowjob from hell. Holding back a sad smile, she bit the inside of her cheek—she'd been damned good at her fucked-up job. Too good. And Kenoe's almost pearlescent magnificent cock had become a mottled purple under her expert ministrations as she'd sucked and teased until just before he came, only to back off over and over again. The goal—drive him to the point where he'd tell Myles anything just to get some relief.

It had seemed wild and exciting to run with such dangerous men. Men that weren't even human, yet still managed to be the bad guys in their world. She hadn't known they were outlaws when she first visited what turned out to be a harem, but Kimora still couldn't figure out what the hell she'd been thinking to stay on with a bunch of strangers who hadn't hesitated to reveal their darker side. God, she'd come so close to harm, so close to walking right smack into the middle of self-destruction. Talk about a case of eyes-wide-shut. The sour outcome of her little foray into what she'd been led to believe was the norm in the hidden world of vampires now clung to her soul like the bitter taste of bile that coated the back of one's mouth after throwing up. Thankfully, she'd been rescued before she ever realized she needed saving.

Other than mind-blowing sex with a strange but talented Lowan Hatsept, Kimora's adventure hadn't gone well. The end result—a damned mess that spanned two continents and included a much-deserved ass-kicking by a pissed off Dr. Carin Bixler while the rest of the compound was raided by Seekers.

Well, now Kimora had a new goal, and it was simple. To get Shinju out of Tokyo no matter what. Time to put a call in.

"Hey Shinju, can I borrow your PDA phone? I'd like to look up the number to that..." But Shinju wasn't even listening to her. Simply stuck her hand in her purse, pulled out the little electronic device and thrust it at her without another word.

The second Shinju disappeared into the bedroom to change out of her wet clothes, Kimora started pushing buttons. A few seconds later came the words she needed to hear most.

"Hatsept here. Leave me a message and I'll get back to you," was spoken confidently across the phone line. Damned voicemail.

"Kenoe?" she whispered into the mouthpiece. "I had an unwelcome visitor today." After leaving some information and telling him to get his butt over to Shinju's, she squeaked a simple, "Help." Then hung up just as her worn-out-looking cousin shuffled into the kitchen to prepare dinner.

Shinju hated to admit it, but she was jonesing. Bad. Even at school she'd been so distracted her students had to call her name more than once. She'd even been summoned to the principal's office to see if she was sick and needed to go home early. But there was no way she could explain why her clothes felt too tight. Why her skin was flushed and her body so sensitive she wanted to scream. Or that she did indeed feel sick. Lovesick.

That afternoon, out of curiosity or desperation she wasn't

sure, Shinju had ducked into the ladies' room, closed her eyes as she stood behind a locked stall door and thought on Kenoe. She could have sworn she felt his echoing presence in her head. Strange things seemed to be the norm since meeting the man, so perhaps she really had heard him, felt him, though it was fleeting and faint.

Standing in the kitchen staring dazedly at the unplugged rice cooker, Shinju stiffened at the knock on the front door. Who could be calling at this hour? She doubted Sasuke was back for another kick in the balls. She looked toward the shape of her cousin lounging on the folded futon in front of the television. Hmm. Well, she didn't seem to be moving to answer the door. In fact, she looked like a frightened rabbit, which was a tough one for Kimora to pull off given her muscular bodybuilder-like physique.

"Kimmie, I'm cooking. Get the door will you?"

"It's dark out. I'm not answering that door."

"Damn it, Kimmie, what good are all those muscles of yours if you aren't willing to use 'em every now and then?"

Kimora chuckled but it certainly sounded much more strained than her typical hearty laugh. Wiping her hands on her apron, Shinju rubbed the sore muscles at the base of her spine. Bland expression firmly in place, Shinju shuffled to the door, wrapped her fingers around the doorknob and yanked.

And there on her little porch stood the most uniquely handsome man in all of Japan. Expressive and determined bluish-white eyes peered down at her just before he went down on one knee and presented her with a fresh bouquet.

"What in the world are you doing kneeling on the ground?" she asked incredulously. "And flowers too?" He was really laying it on...and she was sopping it up.

"I missed you. I couldn't stay away another day. I know you

were upset about me pounding on your friend. I apologize for making you upset," he replied in his straightforward, direct style. She noticed he did not, however, apologize for beating Sasuke to a pulp.

Then from behind his back, he produced one of her favorite treats—a giant box of chocolate-covered Pocky Sticks. But how could he have known...? Heh. Kimora. The same Kimora who hadn't even bothered to turn around to see that it was Kenoe at the door.

And the man must really want her forgiveness, considering she didn't know one single male who would kneel down on a concrete stoop in an expensive, full-length, tailored leather trench coat. Kenoe looked like a cross between GQ and Harley Davidson in a black-on-black outfit that looked tactical but so stylish she was sure the inside seams sported the "purple label". Even his purplish black, soft-soled, lace-up boots looked like danger gear, complete with embroidered designer crests and silver hardware about the laces. As much as she and Kimora loved shopping, she'd recognize those chic duds anywhere. And they looked soooo good on him.

Accepting the treats he brought, she motioned him up, twirled on her heel and headed back to the kitchen.

Stirring a pot of savory miso soup with one hand, she dumped a handful of firm tofu into the stock. Her mouth watered. But damn if it wasn't because of the man standing next to her.

And when he noticed her rubbing her back and took over the duty of stroking the tense muscles, the floor looked awful inviting for the puddle of woman she was turning into.

"Do you have a chiropractor here?"

"A what?" she moaned softly. God, his fingers felt so good pressing into the strained muscles.

"A doctor that adjusts your bones and such. A natural healer. Your tenth thoracic vertebra is out of alignment. Hold still." And those skilled fingers did something to her spine where it cracked and popped, then felt immediately better as the spasming muscles relaxed.

"So, did you come by just to adjust my spine and bring me Pocky?" she purred.

"Actually, I came by to get back in your good graces. I'm leaving tomorrow."

The tenseness that had leached away only moments before crashed into her gut.

Until he said, "I'm going home to Montana and I'd like you to come with me."

Whew. Okay, heart, stop slamming up into my throat already. Using the need to taste the soup to cover up her inability to speak, Shinju took her time, blowing and sipping the broth until she could breathe again. Setting the spoon down on the counter, she turned to face him.

"Actually, Kimmie and I were thinking about taking off for vacation early. I'm supposed to visit my mom in Atlanta for summer break. She lives with Kimmie's parents."

He moved in close and teased the dip just above her butt with a single trimmed fingernail.

"Well, can you change your plans? I'd love for you to come meet my family. Then maybe we can go to Atlanta together afterwards?"

The only words that came to mind as he continued to stroke that dip were "duh-uh-baddubba-duh, er" with the occasional intake of breath.

Having him so close, not just physically, but psychically, wreaked havoc on her ability to think straight or even pretend

to employ common sense. There was no denying the need for intimacy and companionship that had been riding her since she shooed him away. Now her need was fanned into a ravening hunger as their special connection slammed back into her consciousness. Add Kenoe's raw emotions zinging back and forth between them, and it was awfully difficult to stay detached. Well, that and the chocolate-covered Pocky Sticks.

Shinju sucked it up and reached down to the bottommost depths of her soul for her mad. It ran in the other direction.

"I'm not sure if I want to go with you."

"So you don't forgive me?"

"I accept your apology-that-wasn't-quite-an-apology."

"Then come home with me, lovely. If you don't like Montana, I promise to take you anywhere you want to go."

"You already have making up to do, so don't write a check with your mouth that you can't afford to cash."

When Kenoe's head tilted to the side, one silvery white brow raised in question, she sighed with exasperation. "I'm basically asking how in the world you can promise something like that. To fly me wherever I want?"

"The Council I work for has several private jets. If you need to get somewhere, my boss has already offered to accommodate you. He understands how important this is to me."

"Your boss?"

"Yeah, he's the head of all our, uh, law enforcement corps."

She wondered what the "uh" was about, along with its accompanying ripple of...guilt. Hmm.

"Please, Shin?"

"But what about Kimora?"

"Bring her along. You know I'm not interested in her at all. Maybe we can find some mischief to get her into and leave her

to it."

"Hey!" Kimora squawked from the couch, reminding them of her presence.

Kenoe took Shinju by the hand and urged her into the bedroom. Digging in her heels she stopped just on the other side of the threshold.

And then he was kissing her. Devastating. All-encompassing. Rough, hot and gentle at the same time. When he released her, her head bonked against the door as her hips arched into him all on their own. God she'd missed this, being touched with both mind and body by this man. She was trying oh-so-hard to hold on to her attitude, but her body simply didn't care.

With a swat, she interrupted the goal of the talented fingers trying to unsnap her pants. Kenoe chuckled and settled for easing aside the top of her T-shirt and pushing his warm tongue against the sensitive skin just above her collarbone. Sucking and tormenting the softness, his mouth coaxed and teased from that spot up along her neck to her jaw to finally capture her mouth.

A thumb zeroed in on her clit through her pants and stroked in conjunction with the movement of his mouth on hers.

"Come home with me. You can have as much of me as you can handle. Come on. Come..."

And God, did she want to come!

His strokes slowed up a bit, easing her through the frustration of not delivering the impending orgasm she craved.

In between decadent kisses, Shinju relented even as she shuddered against the door.

"Fine, you've persuaded me. I'll go."

Lips landed on hers with a quick kiss just before he crooned in her ear, licking and nipping the lobes.

"Excellent. I'll send a car for you at five-thirty tomorrow evening. We take off at seven." Then he plundered her mouth and set her afire all over again.

God, she was a damned Kenoe addict. But punk bitch, she was not.

Easing away from him, she opened the bedroom door and headed back toward her unfinished dinner.

"That was nice, for starters. I'll come to Montana with you just to give you a chance to redeem yourself. Brawling on my porch with Sasuke." She snorted. "And as for how you know my cousin, I don't even want to go there. And don't think that just because I'm getting on a plane with you tomorrow that you're entitled to any coochie." Though she'd already decided to give him some just so she could satisfy her own longing. Hated to admit it...but she needed him. Needed to be part of him as much as she needed him to be part of her.

Scrunching up her face as mean and as tight as it would go, Shinju grabbed him by the elbow and showed him to the door. How she kept the scowl painted in place when he bowed his head in respect, winked, then grinned at her, she would never know.

But one thing she was sure of, if he'd been half as miserable as she had during their brief separation, he'd paid more than his fair share for his fuck-up. There was no way she was going to tell him that, though. Well, at least not yet. The plane ride would be soon enough to show him just how much she'd forgiven him.

Damned man.

✧

Just after dinner, Max sat in his favorite chair, fighting the chills wracking his body. He didn't want his sister to worry over him so he'd gotten up, bathed and was impeccably dressed when Shinju was escorted into the dining room. He hoped she didn't notice his smile ended at his cheeks while lines of pain were etched around his eyes.

"How are you, Shin? Tea?" he asked warmly. With a tilt of his chin, Max motioned toward the perfect spread of an assortment of jasmine, lavender, green and black teas on the table. An attendant set a saucer of sweet biscuits and *mochi* filled with adzuki bean paste in front of them. It smelled heavenly, but Max knew the delicacies before him wouldn't come close to Shinju's cooking. The woman was a walking incarnation of an Iron Chef, the perfect culinary artist.

She passed on the snacks, leaned forward to plant a kiss on his forehead and joined him at the table anyway.

"How are you, bro?"

He was wretched, but said, "I'm great. Things are good. By the way, you did quite a number on Sasuke the other night. He told me all about it."

Now his smile was genuine. He'd taught her to be tough when the situation warranted it. She'd never disappointed him, even if this time she'd taken out her anger on his Second.

"I figured he would. So that means he also told you about Kenoe."

"Yes."

"And?"

"I think you should stay away from him."

"Well, I don't plan to. I'm supposed to be miffed at him for

that whole run-in with Sasuke, but still can't manage to keep my distance. Something about that man just calls to me."

Called to her? That couldn't possibly be good, given what Kenoe Hatsept was. It was taking all Max's strength to appear as if nothing was wrong, but he was fading fast. Just the possibility of his sister being hurt by the vampire was enough to piss him off. A bit of temper gave him the rush of adrenaline needed to maintain his illusion of good health.

"Damn it, Shin, you don't know anything about this man. He's not what you think."

"Oh, and you are?" she retorted. "You and I are playing the same game here, Max. You waltz around with the pretense that you're Tokyo's upstanding citizen of the year. I pretend I'm a simple, bland high school teacher. Neither of us are who we pretend to be, so drop it. Besides, I know he's a cop. And even if he wasn't, I trust him. And don't ask me to explain it because I'm not sure I can put it into words."

Yeah, but did she know he was a *vampire* cop? And he couldn't tell her such a thing. She'd simply blow him off and accuse him of trying to pull a rabbit out of the hat just to get her to dump Kenoe.

"I just came by to tell you that Kimmie and I are changing our vacation plans. Instead of going to Atlanta, we're leaving early to visit Kenoe's family in Montana. Here's the address. I'll have my PDA phone on me if you need to call."

"But Shin..."

"Don't *but Shin* me, damn it. I haven't known him long, but he's the best thing that's happened to me in a long while, and I'm going to take full advantage of it. Thanks for the tea, Max. I'll call you when I get back, okay? Maybe we can have lunch?"

She didn't wait for him to answer, but rose, kissed his cheek and practically sauntered out of the room.

Damn. His sister was involved with a Seeker. And there was nothing he could do about it. Except, perhaps, find the human who'd sold him the bug juice that was making him and Sasuke sick, and just possibly avoid a clan war and the wrath of the Vampire Council at the same time.

Chapter Nine

Bix had sent a flying palace for them. Tameth had mentioned the purchase of a new plane, but Kenoe hadn't expected a Boeing commercial-class jet. With almost five thousand square feet of play room spread over two floors, the thing had every luxury they could possibly want.

In addition to the bunk-style quarters for the crew and staff, there were three bedrooms for the passengers, one of which had a private bath and shower. There was a common area with the latest electronic gadgets, including two entertainments consoles, one for gaming and the other decked out with a theater system for the most sophisticated tastes in movie enjoyment. Fully reclining plush cocoon-shaped leather seats made turbulence a whole lot more comfortable.

The dining table seated ten guests with room to spare, and the entire space could be transformed into several cozy alcoves to allow privacy while eating. One peek in the kitchen and Kenoe knew exactly where Shinju would be spending most of her time. The place was a chef's wet dream, complete with Wüstof cutlery, granite-tiled work surfaces and stainless steel everything.

Was the vampire nation too high falutin for its britches these days? If so, it was just fine with Kenoe. Shinju deserved the best and he would keep her in high style from now 'til the

end of her days.

Kenoe showed the women where everything was. He didn't bother to hide his displeasure when Kimora settled into one of the smaller bedrooms and Shinju tracked right behind her, dropping her bags in the closet next to her cousin's luggage.

So the woman wanted to test him, eh? No worries. He'd pass her little exam with flying colors and a few points to spare.

After a shower, a nap and some much-needed meditation, Kenoe made his way to the dining room. Pearlescent light from embedded wall sconces cast a comforting glow about the room. The dining table was covered with a cream-colored cloth with matching napkins. It was all exquisite, from the table settings to the music playing softly in the background. A quick glance at his watch set a frown into motion across his forehead. Shinju should have been here at exactly eight o'clock. Only Kimora was seated, lazily munching on a variety of goodies arranged at one end of the table. Perhaps that was all for the better.

"Kimora, where's your cousin?"

"Probably in the kitchen, knowing her."

Kenoe glanced over his shoulder toward the door that led to the galley. With an expressionless face and even more bland tone, he lowered his voice and addressed his unlikely dinner guest.

"Fill me in on the rogue who threatened you the other day. I received your message but you and I obviously haven't had a chance to talk until now. Very smart of you to leave the guy's description. I called it in to V.C.O.E. headquarters. We should have something by the time we get there."

"Look, Kenoe, before we get to that, I need to talk to you about what happened in London. I don't have an excuse, but I am sorry. I was so caught up in the excitement of running with vampires, living my ultimate fantasy, I didn't consider anything

past that. Not to mention I didn't expect to ever see you again in my life."

"Your point?" Kenoe grumbled around a mouthful of some swanky hors d'oeuvres that tasted like smoked salmon and some kind of spicy peppers. Mmm, good.

"No point. I'm sorry is all. And..." She hesitated. "I'm concerned about my cousin. I don't want her hurt. Not by you or the asshole who was bold enough to step right into her backyard and threaten me."

Unable to keep his brows from knitting together, Kenoe scowled across the table. "I would never hurt Shinju. She's my mate."

"Mate? As in mate-for-life kinda mate?"

"More than that. She's my bondmate too."

"Bond...?! Hooo!"

"Keep it down, woman."

"Are you telling me she doesn't know she's the one? Doesn't know about your so-called family or the Council? Or those badassed vamps that took me out of Lowan's place? Wait a minute!" Her voice cracked as it rose. "She doesn't know *anything*? Not even that you're a vam—?"

"No, damn it, so keep your voice down. But I have to tell her before we get off this plane."

Kimora burst out laughing like Kenoe had just been caught telling the funniest, raunchiest joke ever. "Well, good luck with that, my man. I think I'll eat in my room."

With that, she unfolded her muscular frame out of her chair and snickered all the way out of the dining room and down the hall. What the hell was that about? But Kimora's parting shot reminded Kenoe of the last time Shinju had been pissed off at him. His balls tingled, bringing to mind a *way*

uncomfortable moment after the woman had been less than kind to them. In fact, the little firecracker had sent him and Sasuke to their knees. Perhaps he should have followed Kimora out of the room rather than tell Shinju he was a vampire who happened to be investigating her brother.

"Where's Kimora?"

Kenoe's neck snapped a hard right as he turned to watch Shinju enter the room unbuttoning a double-breasted white chef's coat. It had a myriad of stains down the front and looked a size too big.

"She said she wants to eat in her room."

"Huh. Okay, I'll ask the chef to take a tray. You ready to eat?"

Boy was he ever, but his stomach and his heart didn't agree on what that meal should be. In truth Kenoe didn't give a damn about food right now. Shinju looked utterly adorable with a smudge of flour across her cheek, and a few loose curls stuck to the side of her face. The smudges on her borrowed clothes told part of the story of what she'd been up to.

Obviously catching wind of his curiosity, she motioned toward the sumptuous spread on the table and said, "Well, you said your boss sent this jet for you and we're the first to travel on it, right? So I thought we could christen it, so to speak."

The image of her spread-eagle on top of the large and thankfully bolted-down table flashed into his head. Dragging his mind out of the gutter kicking and screaming, he forced himself to sit still while Shinju directed the wait staff to clear the hors d'oeuvres and bring out the main course. Shinju took a plate up to Randall in the cockpit while Kenoe sat and watched in awe as two impeccably dressed chefs brought the main course.

Even over the wonderful smells of the various dishes, he

still scented Shinju before she reentered the room. Rising, he pulled out a chair and dropped a kiss on the top of her head as she settled into it.

"Go ahead. Taste it," she urged with a big, proud smile on her face.

The woman was a wonder. The first meal she'd ever prepared for him in her neat little kitchen had made his stomach sing. This meal might just make his whole body break into a chorus of "One Singular Sensation". And hallelujah, none of it was Japanese food!

Instead his plate was piled with seafood lasagna with a sauce so savory and light, the scent alone made his mouth water. The pasta was accompanied by a simple green salad garnished with fresh green peppers and tomatoes tossed in a sweet ginger vinaigrette. The spices were unique, far from the typical basil and parsley in Italian-style cuisine. No, this was a culinary orgasm going off in his mouth. Simply delicious.

They chatted amicably but Kenoe didn't miss the occasional frown whenever he let his guard down long enough for his anxiety, though slight, to creep down the bond. Bottom line—he had no desire to see the you're-crazy-as-a-loon skepticism in her eyes when he told her what he was. God knew she wouldn't believe him.

And he was less than enthusiastic about her reaction to the fact that he, Mr. Law Enforcement, as she called him, was investigating her closest relative for something that had nothing to do with honest vamps, and everything to do with Dr. Jekyll humans.

Not to mention the possibility of her flat-out rejecting him.

Ruthlessly squashing down all concern, he filled his mind with lighter thoughts. Actually just thinking on what a fabulous dinner she'd prepared for him, what a kind and considerate

woman she was, a woman so sweet yet with an edge sharp enough to cut himself on. The perfect alpha. *His* perfect alpha.

And she'd prepared a dessert of strawberries covered with brown sugar syrup, laced with lemon zest. Oh yeah, she was a keeper. He only hoped she would feel the same when he told her...

When had she moved from her chair?

Shinju grinned and pushed his empty dishes off to the side. She held her hand out to him.

"What?"

"Up, handsome."

Wondering what she was on about, he didn't move but cocked his head to the side and waited instead.

"Naoru. Get. Up." Her tone was stern, but not bitchy. He stood and allowed himself to be positioned to her liking. Mischief danced along their developing link and tickled the nerve endings at the base of his skull.

All of a piece, Shinju pushed her desires down the bond with such force they slammed into his brain and streaked clear down to his nuts. He reached to unbutton his shirt. A playful slap to his fingers caught him so off-guard, he froze for a second.

A snarled "mine" made it crystal clear that she was the only one getting to touch tonight. Or at least for the time being. Dropping his hands to his side, his spitfire female popped open each button slowly, deliberately, then peeled the garment off his shoulders. All the while she whispered what she wanted to do to him and let those wickedly talented fingers of hers run over the exposed skin, raising chill bumps along the way.

"God, Naoru, you're so studly gorgeous."

"Studly? Is that a typical Japanese word?"

"Remember I'm not a typical Japanese female. I've got a bit of sistah in me and I just have to let her out to play every now and then." This was said as her fingernails scraped gently over the planes of his stomach and dipped into the hollows and ridges of his quaking abs. It made him tingle from the roots of his hair to his toes. Dayum!

"Amazing. I love your skin, so fair, smooth. Perfect. Like fresh cream. And that dusting of platinum silver hair on your chest. I missed that the last time I had you nearly naked. Is the hair around your cock the same beautiful shade?" she teased.

Holy shit! Kenoe balled his trembling hands into fists to keep from ripping her clothes off and taking her to the floor right then.

Instead, he said, "You're being awfully naughty, but I'm all yours, lovely, so go ahead and find out."

"I can't wait to see what your fabulous cock looks like sliding into my pussy. I missed you so much. Dreamed about you each night until I was so hot and bothered. Kinda like I am now."

"Shinju, you take too much longer to touch me and I'm going to have to do something about that. Sssss!" Her touch had moved down his chest, past his waist and down to the swelling ridge in his pants. Then she pushed him backwards until his ass hit the edge of the table.

In a blink the snap on his camo pants popped. He hissed at the sensual rasp of the fabric sliding down his thighs. When he stood there in his boxers, Shinju pushed against his chest again. Taking the hint, Kenoe hopped up on the table and waited.

With the sexiest, sauciest smile he'd ever seen on a woman, she commenced to stripping him down. First went his boots, followed by the pants that were down around his knees. Both

joined his shirt in a pile on the floor.

"The staff?" he gasped when she stepped between his legs and pushed his knees apart.

"Sent them to bed after they served dessert."

So she'd thought of everything, eh? He hoped so, because he had an urge to crawl underneath her skin and didn't think he'd survive an interruption tonight.

The tip of his rigid cock poked out from underneath the waistband of his shorts, hard against his navel. Leaning over him, she ignored the glistening head and shaped her mouth over the silk-covered pipe of his rod, breathing in and out through her mouth. His flesh warmed and cooled underneath the fabric.

"Oooh, Shin. Yeah, baby. That's good." And it got even better when a waft of cool air caressed his flaming flesh. She'd eased down his silkies and proceeded to give a full lick from the base of his rod to the tip without quite touching the sensitive glans.

Kenoe found himself coaxed off the table and maneuvered into one of the high-backed dining chairs completely naked. And his woman was fully clothed, with the exception of the pair of flats she'd toed off and kicked under the table. How the hell had she pulled that off? The thought only lasted a second as Shinju revealed the ace up her sleeve, raising her little skirt inch by inch. God, her skin seemed to go on forever. When the clothing reached the vee of her thighs, he sucked in a wild breath at the sight—no underwear—just miles of luscious caramel...including a waxed mound. The puffy lips of her sex glistened with her own juices, holding his attention. Then she pounced.

One second she was preening her commando, underwearless backside, the next she was straddling him in the chair to

plunge her hot channel down over his stiff and ready cock in one stroke.

He yelled.

God, she felt so good wrapped around him. He may have had one arm anchored around her waist while the other hand wrapped itself in the soft waves and curls of her nape, but he was far from guiding her movements. Shinju was completely in control.

She was fucking *him*. And damn it turned him on like nothing else, but her pleasure was first and foremost. After a few strokes of heaven, Kenoe shook his head to try and clear it of the haze of lust. It was his responsibility to make sure his woman was well-pleased, especially their first time together.

Time to flip the script.

Shinju found herself easily lifted as Kenoe rose from the chair, still impaling her on his ready length. Now it was her turn to experience the dining room table. And Kenoe pummeled into her, sending the nerves along her creaming channel into a dance of sparks and heat as he passed over them with each stroke. He was perfect. A thick stalk of a cock, with the perfect length to fill her up without pushing her to the point of pain.

Then she was suddenly empty.

He'd pulled out and bent over her prone body, his breath just a tease against her labial lips. His fingers caressed the cheeks of her ass that were flush with the end of the table.

"Kenoe, baby. Come back inside." Panting wildly, she pulled at his hair. The rough yet silky quality of his locs against the inside of her thighs pushed her sensory perception up a notch.

"Oooh, and what is this?" he crooned, lapping lightly at the decorated skin on her inner thigh. "A tattoo?"

"Mmmhmm." *Gasp.*

He ran the tip of his tongue over each line of the intricate graphic inked on her damp skin.

"What does it mean, lovely?"

The man wanted her to think now? God, he was crazy and definitely into seeing how far up the wall he could drive her. But if she didn't answer, he wouldn't move an inch. Somehow she simply knew he was just that stubborn.

"It means. Uh. Oooh. It's the *kanji* symbol for...oh God!"

"I didn't know God had a *kanji* symbol. Don't worry, lovely. I'll show you some mercy. You can tell me later."

Whew. Trembling with a mixture of relief and lust, Shinju spread her legs until her toes practically touched each corner of the wide dining table.

Then Kenoe rubbed his head, face and hair all over her, between her thighs, gently along the folds of her sex, over the flesh of her belly, to the swelling mounds of her breasts with their plumping peaks, then made his way back down to her sex again. It was like he wanted to bathe in her, cover himself with her scent. It was the most primal thing she'd ever experienced.

The smooth, hot glide of his tongue followed the sizzling trail left behind by his glorious hair. Finally, he settled down to the business of feasting.

"That feels so good. Yes, lick it. Just like that."

Slow, full licks set her skin on fire as he moaned his pleasure, savored her flavor. Then he buried his nose in her flesh until it pushed relentlessly against her clit as the tip of his tongue fucked in and out of her creaming slit. Who'd have thought that a man as gorgeous as this would love eating pussy so much?

His murmured "tastes so good" and "cream for me" pushed

her closer and closer to the edge. The tip of his nose was replaced with his lips as he pulled and sucked. Shinju's back bowed up and off the table as her thighs fell open, hips rolling, seeking more.

Kenoe looked up in time to watch her wrap her fingers around her breasts. She ruthlessly squeezed and plumped them, hissing and moaning with pleasure. And her pleasure gave him pleasure.

Keeping his lips plastered to the hard bundle of nerves peeking out from beneath its cowl, Kenoe slipped a single questing finger deep inside her sopping heat, pushing past the incredibly tight ring of muscle at her entrance to part the sugared walls inside her willing body.

"Aah, yes. That's so good. Naoru…" Who added another finger at the same time he delivered a sharp nip to one plump lip of her sex. Shinju yelped then gasped with an uncontrollable roll of her hips. "Oh shit. Again, please."

And he did, over and over. The bite was just enough to sting yet light enough to allow his tongue to ease it away while making her writhe.

"More."

"Not yet."

"Please, I want it."

He totally ignored her. "Shinju, you're so damned sexy. The most beautiful, luscious woman I've ever met. I want to run my hands up and over your hips, down your thighs to caress the sleek muscles there. Then I want to ease my fingers between the globes of your ass…damn, what an ass. I'm so glad you have meat on your bones. You're curvy, hippy, just the way my woman should be. Simply lovely."

His words only served to throw gas on the fire.

"And after I have my fill of touching you, tasting you, I'm going to sink into your beautiful body and fuck you until you're so far gone you either pass out cold or scream for more. Hell, perhaps both." Finally, the solid wickedness that was his cock burned the skin at her entrance, so hot her honey bubbled and brewed. Then with one smooth stroke, he was home, buried deep, branding her. The tight, rarely used muscles of her sheath quivered in an attempt to both relax and hold him tight. Pulling almost clear, he sank balls-deep again, his pace unhurried, but his strokes firm and hungry. How the hell did he do that? It was so good, so perfect. And still not enough. When his thumb reached down and brushed the sensitive bundle of nerves straining against its cowl, she yowled as her clit pulsed, climax just a hairsbreadth away. But not enough to push her over.

"Say the magic words, lovely."

"Now!" she screamed.

He increased the pressure on her clit just a touch.

"Wrong one."

Oooh, now she remembered and wanted to yell it to the sky. "Spank me!"

"Your wish is my command," he crooned. The words were followed by a gentle slap against her clit and her pussy responded instantly.

"Oh, yeah. Cream my cock, Shin. Milk me dry."

Well she could certainly accommodate him on that one.

In fact, at that moment Shinju's whole world consisted of the silken slide of the shaft of engorged muscle expertly parting the folds of her soaked pussy, sending her on a one-way trip somewhere north of the next galaxy. In short, she came apart at the seams.

And if that weren't enough, the curtain of her mind was blown back and exposed to Kenoe's raw emotions. They engulfed and drowned her even as Kenoe treaded water in the Sea of Shinju. The man was so into her, all previous thoughts of enjoying him only until their vacation was over were wiped away and replaced with a longing so fierce she shook with it.

This was not a one-time thing for him, no tap-n-go interlude. Kenoe wanted her and was determined to have her, both inside and out. The revelation floored her.

If she thought they had a connection before, now that their bodies had joined, it was as if the tie that bound them strengthened tenfold. Yet, there was something missing. Something minute, but extremely important.

"*Mmm, Shin.*" A powerful surge of his hips preceded a question. "*You are mine, aren't you?*" The bright light of his desire flickered a moment as if a shadow passed over the flame. Then it was gone as he flexed his cock inside of her and she exploded a second time. No way could she concentrate on what he meant while he moved in her body, touching her heart with thoughts of wrapping her in a cocoon of silken threads made of his very soul.

"*Oh God, yes! I'm yours, Naoru.*"

"*No matter what?*" Another stroke brought yet another mind-melting orgasm.

"*Yes, no matter what.*"

Mindless with pleasure or not, she meant every word.

Chapter Ten

Kenoe woke from a refreshing after-sex nap, rolled out of bed and eased into the private bath. He returned with a warm, moist towel. Bending to gently cleanse the tender folds between Shinju's legs, he was brought up short by her words.

"No, don't. I like the way you smell on me. I'm going to wear you for a little while, then I'll shower."

Amazing how a woman could be such a mix of sweet, shy, sexy and bold.

Kenoe left to wash up alone then roused a dozing Shinju.

"Why didn't you wait and shower with me?" she grumped sleepily.

"Because, if I get in the shower with you, lovely, neither of us will get to wash anything. Especially with you smelling so good."

"Mmm. What do I smell like?" she teased on a sleepy sigh.

"Mine." He dropped a kiss on her nose, dressed quickly, and popped into the cockpit to check in with the pilot. Bix must have felt this was of major importance to send Randall to fly him home. Randall was an elite Seeker who'd flown them on every mission Kenoe'd been on. Randall was, in a word, the best. Able to fly just about any military-grade aircraft ever made, the man seemed just as at home in this luxury private

jet.

"Hey, Randall."

"What's up, squirt?"

Kenoe chuckled. At five-foot-seven, Randall was the shortest vampire he'd ever met. Even though he had to look up at Kenoe, the man was also the oldest, most experienced and ruthless member of their team, still kicking ass at a hale two hundred fourteen years. Randall had seen and experienced far more than Kenoe—or as Alaan so lovingly called him, a Hatsept pup of a mere sixty-two years.

"Can you patch me through to Bix, buddy?"

Randall flipped a few switches and handed Kenoe a pair of over-ear headphones with a short telescoping microphone built into the earpiece.

"Bix, I've got Kenoe on the line. Hold on a second and I'll patch you through. Yep, he's sitting right here next to me on a secure line." He glanced at Kenoe and signaled the go-ahead.

"Hatsept here."

"Hey. How's it going?"

"Hell, I don't have the slightest idea how to answer that question."

"Should I take that to mean you haven't claimed the woman?"

"Bix, you know as well as I do that the bond won't form unless we both truly want it..."

"Which means you haven't told her what you are or what she is to you, right?"

Nothing but a heavy sigh ensued.

"And," Bix continued, "you probably haven't told her you're a Seeker for the Council, and the man who's brought her brother to our attention."

Kenoe's silence told it all. He grimaced into the mouthpiece. Bix was one of the only men in the world that could make him feel like a little kid who hadn't washed behind his ears well.

"Listen, I understand exactly how you feel, Kenoe. You want to protect her, and you want her to have a choice in the joining. I wanted the same for Carin. Handle this your own way, but you'd better tell her quick, or she's gonna lose it at finding herself a visitor at an estate full of vampires in the next ten hours."

"Yeah, I know."

"Hell, I didn't think anything good could come out of Kimora showing up on the scene. But at least with her there, Shinju will hopefully be a bit calmer if Kimora acknowledges your heritage without losing her mind."

"Yeah, well, Kimora spent enough time fucking my brother. She still smells like the bastard. The woman is more than qualified to back me up on busting the vampire urban legends."

"Good luck, Kenoe. We'll see you tomorrow."

"Thanks, buddy. Tell Carin and everyone I said hello."

"Speaking of Carin," Bix jumped in quickly. "You'd better prepare Kimora for a less-than-happy reunion with the woman who kicked her ass during the raid on Lowan's place. My wife's not thrilled that Kimora is coming here."

"Shit, I forgot about that. And if Carin and Kimora get into it, you can bet Shinju is going to be pissed the hell off."

"Don't worry. Just wanted to give you a heads-up. I'll see what I can do to improve Carin's mood before you all land."

Kenoe had no doubts it would include lots of moaning and panting. He chuckled into the headphones and thanked Bix for whatever he could do to eliminate any tension.

"Thanks, Bix."

"You've got it. Bix out."

"Hatsept, out."

Stuffing his emotions down into his socks, Kenoe made his way back to the master bedroom. Shinju had just stepped out of the shower and sat drying her hair at the custom-built mirrored vanity. Easing up behind her, he dropped a kiss on the back of her neck and jumped in with both feet.

"Shinju, I need to tell you something." When her spine stiffened he knew he had to tread carefully and use some wisdom with this woman. "Just a minute, I'll be right back."

He slipped out of the room and closed the door behind him. Down the hall he knocked softly on Kimora's bedroom door. When he told her what he wanted she backed up a step. Not used to having to explain his intentions to any female other than his fellow Seekers, Kenoe was ready to snap when it took a full five minutes to get the woman to come with him.

Back in their room, Shinju had quickly dressed and was sitting in a chair pretending to read one of the romance novels she fancied. He knew she was faking it when her thoughts slammed into his head, practically screaming that some tragedy was coming, or that he really didn't want her. The one that really got him was, *Oh God, he's married!*

"Shin? You all right?" Kimora asked.

"Sure. What are you two up to now?"

Kenoe walked over and took her by the hand, leading her back to the bed and into his lap. "We're not up to anything, but I thought it would be better to have your cousin here while I talk to you."

"Really."

Clearly she didn't believe him. Actually, it wasn't disbelief as much as it was fear of the unknown.

"Shinju, I want to tell you where I'm from. Who my people are."

"Why in the world would you need Kimora here for that?"

"Because, love." He took a deep breath and tightened his hold on her. "I'm...something you've never expected to exist. I'm not human."

"What the hell did you pop while you went to get Kimora? You on drugs?"

"Shin, I'm a vampire."

Immediately, her fear slammed into him like a two-ton steel demolition ball aimed at his chest. She believed him, and in the worst possible way.

"What?" she hissed through clenched teeth. Every muscle in her body tensed, ready for fight or flight.

So he said it again.

"Shin, baby, I said I'm a vampire." This time he allowed his fangs to drop into place.

Shinju struggled in his arms and he immediately let her go. She flew to the other side of the room looking for something, anything with which to protect herself.

"Shin," called Kimora. "It's all right."

"Are you fucking crazy? It's not all right," Shinju screamed, grabbing her cousin by the arm trying to haul her out the door. When Kimora didn't move, Shinju dropped her arm and took off so fast, the other woman actually stumbled.

Kimora cut him a steel-sharp glance so hard blood should have spurted from his forehead.

She snarled, "You idiot! What the hell were you thinking showing her your teeth like that?" Taking off after Shinju, she called to her fleeing cousin's back. "Shin, we're on a damned plane. Where the hell do you think you're going?"

"Away. Far. Somewhere, anywhere!"

"Shinju!" Kenoe ran to the door, yelling down the hall after her. "I'm not going to hurt you. You're my bondmate, damn it."

"Noooo!" she screamed, her voice laced with enough fury and dread to leave a trail of terror behind her as she fled.

"Kimora, we've got to get out of here."

"Shinju, will you relax already. So he's a vampire, what's the big deal?"

That worked about as well as a combination slap in the face followed by a bucket of iced water. Why wasn't Kimora freaking out too? There was only one good explanation—the woman was demented.

"Are you out of your damned mind? I don't care if we have to find a couple of parachutes and jump into the middle of the fucking Pacific, we're getting off this plane."

Just as her fingers wrapped around the knob to the cockpit door, Kimora caught up to her and pulled her into a fierce hug.

"It's okay, Shin. Honest. Calm down, it's all right."

Shinju took a deep breath, or as deep as she could between wracking sobs. Kenoe's dread of her doing something drastic slammed through her. No desire to bleed her dry, nor rip her neck to shreds. There was only care, concern. Love? The man, correction, *vam-fucking-pire,* was upset because she was afraid of him? Shinju was so stunned that Kenoe was more concerned for her well-being and absolute state of panic than he was about anything else, she didn't even jump when his hand landed gently on her shoulder and slowly turned her to face him.

Yet Kimora kept her arms wrapped around her cousin, and Shin recognized it as an attempt to reassure her that all was

145

well. Without a doubt Kimora would stand there with her strong arms encircling her until they got to Montana if that's what it took to let Shinju know she was safe. It had been this way between them all their lives. They looked after each other.

"All right, Shin?" Kimora asked as she gently stroked Shinju's hair. An air of solid calm radiated from her cousin and enveloped her until Shinju was able to breathe normally and think somewhat rationally. That was when a thought occurred.

"Kimmie? W-why aren't you wigging out? Kenoe has fangs and you're not tripping out about it. What the hell is going on?"

Kimora winked, and simply said, "Listen, Shin. There are good vamps and bad vamps, just like there are good people and bad people. Trust me, Kenoe is one of the good ones."

"But how the hell could you possibly know such a thing?" All the while her gaze darted between Kenoe's expressive, marble-pale eyes and full, sensual lips. Would he show his teeth again? She sure as hell hoped not. It made this whole drama much too real for a sistah to take!

"I'll tell you about it sometime. Right now, you two have unfinished business. And it's good business, Shin. Trust me, it's way good."

Then she slid her arms away and turned to Kenoe. With a single finger poking the man in the chest, she snapped, "Don't you scare her again, Kenoe. If you do, I won't bother trying to fight you because you're a big mean-assed Seeker. So I'll just shoot you, then tell Bix it was self-defense."

Shinju started.

Bix? Hey, she'd heard that name before. He was the head honcho Kenoe worked for.

"Wait, you know Kenoe's boss too? What the hell did you guys do in London that you know so much?"

Kimora winked, turned and was gone, assuring the flight staff peeking out from their sleeping compartments that the wild screaming and running was over and everything was fine.

Shinju flinched when she heard Kimora say in a voice that made her feel silly, "Oh Shin is fine. She was just surprised to learn that all y'all are vampires. No worries. You guys can go back to your quarters. She's all right."

One of the men stepped out of his room, bowed low over Kimora's hand, dropped a quick kiss on her knuckles, then watched her perfectly shaped, oversized ass sway until she was out of sight. Regardless of the current goings-on, Shinju had to admit that her cousin was damned good-looking. And completely okay with the situation enough that she'd brought her on a plane full of 'em? I mean, damn, everybody on the plane was a vampire?

Shinju couldn't decide whether to be pissed off or scared shitless, regardless of the soothing emotions reaching for her from Kenoe.

Yep, she was going to kill him. Death by tweezers. 'Cause she was going to pull out his eyebrows one hair at a time.

Instead of going back to the bedroom, Kenoe motioned a still-trembling Shinju to the common room, careful not to touch her. He put on some soothing classical music, then sat down in a loveseat and asked Shinju to sit in his lap.

When she balked he pressed gently.

"Please, Shin. I have to touch you, to know you're really okay."

Hell she wasn't sure she was okay. Not yet anyway. Sure, she realized that if he wanted to hurt her there'd been plenty of opportunity before now. But that didn't change the fact that her only run-in with a species that wasn't supposed to exist had

been a traumatizing event. One she'd never shared with anyone.

Instead of climbing into his lap, she sat in the chair across from him with her arms wrapped around herself, rocking back and forth, trying to keep her head together. Ugh, she had to throw up.

Kenoe spoke in a near whisper, obviously being careful not to startle her.

"Breathe, Shin, just take in a few deep breaths." After a second or two, he asked, "What happened, lovely? For someone who's not taken to believing everything she sees in the movies, what made you run from me? You know I'd never hurt you."

"As if that were the point," she grumped, hugging herself harder. Understanding nudged at her. Understanding, sadness and a smothering fear that she would run from him and never return. Looking at the man's face, you'd never know such a tempest of emotion tossed him about. Expertly schooled features gave nothing away. Cool, calm and collected was the illusion of the day.

Yet, instead of voicing his own concerns, Kenoe sought only to reassure her.

Kenoe reasoned out the true meaning of her fear as he remembered catching the scent of rogues near her home. Not once, but twice. Not to mention Kimora's run-in with some second-class vamp in Shinju's backyard recently.

"Have you had a bad experience with a vampire before, Shin?"

"It's just too awful. God knows I don't want to remember it by accident, let alone on purpose."

"Tell me, lovely."

"Naoru, I just can't." The words, thick with emotion and

fear, dribbled from trembling lips.

Kenoe rose slowly, took the few steps required to reach her, then gathered Shinju in his arms. He held her tight, determined to find the asshole responsible for reducing his woman to a terrified mass of nerves. That vamp was not only the cause of Shinju's current state of near-hysteria, but he'd broken the most important rule of vampiredom—he'd exposed their kind without need or permission.

And would never harm another living soul as soon as Kenoe caught up with the bastard.

"Shin, sweetheart. I can't help you if I don't know what happened. If you can't stand to tell me, then show me."

She looked up at him, eyes red-rimmed and thick, dark lashes wet with tears. "What do you mean, show you?"

"Just open your mind and let the thoughts flow to me, baby. Imagine an invisible string, a lifeline so to speak, that anchors your mind to mine. Then imagine yourself sending the information along it. Doesn't matter if it's thoughts or images."

He paused, then whispered along her frazzled nerve endings. *"I'll see whatever you want me to see, lovely."*

Shinju closed her eyes, reached for him, then let her thoughts tumble back to a day she so obviously wanted to forget.

She'd gone into turf held by her brother's sworn enemies. Had she ventured to this side of town simply to spite him? Of course she had. Both him and that damned Sasuke. She was grateful for all they and the Ooeto clan had done for her, but damn it, she was a grown woman now. A grown woman with a life of her own and the ability to take care of herself. They'd personally seen to that.

Stay out of Takamatsu territory? Not bloody likely. Besides, there was supposed to be a pretty cool noodle restaurant near the Tsukiji Fish Market docks.

Kenoe grinned as the images played in his head. Feisty, stubborn little witch. The smile fell from his lips when a slew of ghastly recollections burned into his memory for all time.

Shinju had caught a glimpse of a shadow down an alley. The way the person moved with an easy but determined gait reminded her of someone. Her brother. Now what the hell was Max doing down here when he'd forbidden her to come anywhere near this side of Tokyo? And given the tension between the *yakuza* clans these days, it was almost a sure thing he was being followed. Shinju's breathing hitched when another shadow dropped into position behind Max. Making up her mind to follow, she took tentative then more determined steps. If anybody was going to fuck with her brother she sure as hell would be there to have his back.

And speaking of having his back, where was Sasuke? She'd know him anywhere, and the man who'd fallen into lock step behind Max certainly wasn't Max's Second.

Glad she had on a pair of soft-soled combat boots with her dark purple outfit, Shinju took off silently after the pair moving further and further into the darkness, away from the lighted streets and closer to the dimmer throughways of the industrial ports near the canal. And further away from help. Finally, the bright streetlights and video billboards disappeared, replaced by utter darkness. Pride at having defied her brother melted away to confusion, then stark, utter fear. Her emotions fell apart, hit the ground and froze in a sheet of panic, like hot wax dripping down an icy windowpane. This situation felt four kinds of wrong as dread backed up in the bottom of her stomach, but she forced her feet to keep moving.

Max turned down what appeared to be a dead end. At the end of the street, he stepped through an unmarked door and closed it quietly behind him. Seconds later, his tail did too.

Inside the nondescript building was a catacomb of twisting and turning hallways that seemed to go on forever. She saw nothing and no one. Perhaps Max had ducked into one of the other rooms she'd passed as she moved deeper into the building? If she didn't see him soon, she'd make her way back out somehow and go to his apartment to wait. There was no way she'd continue to walk around in this place with no idea of what was in front of or behind her. In fact, it was a stupid idea to come in here in the first place.

Just as she started to turn back, Shinju stepped into a huge warehouse full of crates of all sizes and types. What the hell? Had she stumbled into the opposing clan's goody store? If so, perhaps she'd find a nice new katana to take as a prize.

Then voices sounded just ahead. Sounded a lot like Max swearing. Her stomach dropped into her knees as she sought a place to hide. Diving behind a stack of pallets piled with crates, Shinju squeezed underneath and crawled to a spot with a gap between the wooden slats. It gave her a perfect view of Max. And the man quickly closing on him was no fellow *yakuza*.

He moved faster than anyone she'd ever seen. He made no sound and was on her brother in a flash. Just as she moved to get out from under the crates, something happened that she never thought she'd see in all her days. Not only unimaginable, but impossible.

The man lifted Max, a full grown man packing plenty of dense muscle, right off the floor like he weighed nothing. Then he grabbed Max by the hair, pulled his head to an odd angle...and bit him? Yes. Bit. Him. His teeth sank right into Max's flesh like some kind of animal. No human's teeth could

puncture skin like that. Could tear out a chunk of flesh until the blood flowed like an endless stream. The man threw back his head and laughed, his face painted red. His teeth—oh my God, fangs—gleamed with her brother's lifeblood.

What should she do? If she showed herself would the man attack her too? If he could pick up Max and overpower him with such ease, what would he do to her? What to do? What to do? Adrenaline set her whole body shaking as she tried to reason it out.

But Shinju was simply frozen with terror as her brother lay dying not twenty feet from where she knelt trembling under the crates.

Blood. So much blood. It was congealing into the cement floor, flowing into the cracks. The scent reached out and wrapped around her, oozing up her nostrils, then down her throat, gagging her. Covering her mouth, Shinju held her breath, tightened her stomach muscles and forced her dry heaving to clog in her throat. Better to choke silently on her own vomit than give away her position.

The attacker's head swiveled her way. Oh no! Had he seen her? Perhaps if he had super strength and killer teeth, then maybe he had x-ray vision too. Then just as quickly as she'd stumbled onto the ghastly scene, the man took off, leaving her in the dusky warehouse with her indecision.

Another movement caught her attention. There just off to the right came another figure moving so fast it almost seemed to beam into the room out of the darkness. Hell, vampires were no longer on the list of impossible things. What other creatures walked the night among the completely unsuspecting and oblivious humans? Never mind. Shinju didn't think she wanted to know.

Several men moved in her direction, eyes searching,

missing nothing.

"Shit!" yelled one of the newcomers, pointing down at Max's twitching body, then motioning toward the direction the first murderer had fled.

"Go get him!"

"Yes, sir." One man immediately took off in hot pursuit, moving so fast he was merely a blur.

Yet Shinju still hadn't moved an inch. Maybe they were friendly? She hoped so. Max needed help. His movements were becoming less and less strong. Shinju knew that if someone didn't do something she would watch her brother die.

Another one of the men growled into the darkness. "What do we do with him? He appears to be a human."

Did that mean these guys weren't human either? Monsters like the one who'd fled?

Her question was quickly answered. The one who seemed to be in charge bared a set of sharp-looking fangs on a snarl, reached down and lifted her brother in his arms.

Oh God, no. Max couldn't possibly take another attack. She had to help him. Had to. Scooting backward and out from under the crates, Shinju ran to where her brother's blood congealed and separated on the floor. But he was gone. The whole lot of them had departed as quickly and silently as they'd come. And they'd taken Max with them.

Shinju hit the floor in a crumpled heap, and there she sat. Sat and prayed and cried until her eyes were sore and her legs numb from the cold of the concrete floor. Even when her feet felt stung by pins and needles, she'd watched the spot where Max had lain as if her wishing and hoping could bring him back.

Kenoe rocked her back and forth in the comfort of his arms as hot tears spilled down her cheeks to drip from her chin.

"It's okay, baby. It's all right. Just let it out now."

And she did. Shinju cried for her brother whose life had been drastically changed while he had no choice. For herself, because she hadn't had the courage to help him.

"What happened after that?"

Shinju wiped her nose on her sleeve and hiccupped. She looked up at Kenoe with watery red-rimmed eyes but didn't resist as he squeezed her tighter. His heart literally ached with her pain. Poor sweet baby.

"Well," she sniffed. "I hadn't expected to ever see Max again. I had no idea what happened to him after they took him away. I grieved for days, so distraught I didn't leave my house to go to work, didn't answer my phone out of fear that my mom would be on the other end of the line and I'd have to tell her that her only son was dead, but unable to explain how. A week and a half later he showed up at my house looking as hearty and hale as you please. He didn't have any fangs, so I figured he hadn't been turned into one of the fucking animals that'd harmed him."

Kenoe flinched at the venom in her voice that accompanied the word "animals" but he continued to stroke the thick, wavy coils of her hair and kissed her temple, relieved when Shinju snuggled in closer.

"What did he say happened to him?"

"Pfft. He claimed he'd been called out of town on an emergency, apologized for not calling and then sat down to dinner. He explained away the faint scratches around his throat. Chalked them up to a tumble while skiing with a client on a business trip. There was hardly a mark on him. He never offered up any more info than that, and I never asked. I never

went back to that part of town, and have watched my back when out at night."

"So you assumed that all vampires were killers?" Kenoe queried with a bit of wry humor, though in truth he understood how she could have come to such a conclusion.

"I didn't know what to think. I just figured the vampires took what they needed from Max and...and I don't know. But I do know what I saw. I had no reason to think there was any such thing as a good guy vampire. And certainly not a law enforcement bloodsucker."

"Bloodsucker?" But there was no heat to his words.

"Yeah." She pushed away and eyed him askance. "And how the hell are you a vampire without taking my blood? You do need blood, right? Can you substitute it with, like, tomato juice or something?"

Kenoe laughed, a deep, gut-busting guffaw. The little spitfire was serious, but at least she wasn't cowering from him.

Shinju listened with her whole body as Kenoe talked. She couldn't help considering the way his tangible emotions highlighted his words with something so much deeper and more profound than the inflection of his voice or body language.

She relaxed a bit after learning that Kenoe was no ordinary vampire, but was something called a Seeker for the Vampire Council of Ethics. Relief didn't begin to describe her feelings when she learned vampires couldn't be made or created like in the movies. It was simply a matter of genetic selection. His DNA was a tad bit different from hers. Talk about a biology lesson and a half.

"Shinju, I never wanted to frighten you, which is why I asked Kimora to be there when I told you who I am. You've become very important to me. You're exactly who I want in my

life."

"Speaking of life, just how long is that, by the way?"

"A very long time."

"Immortal? I don't know how I feel about that, Naoru." Puh! *Naoru.* She'd thought to mend him just to find out he wasn't even human? What a blunder.

"Not immortal. Just long-lived. And it's only because my metabolism is faster than yours. Think about it..."

Sheesh, now he had his professor hat on. She yawned in the midst of a full adrenaline crash, tired out from the emotional rollercoaster ride of her life but eager to hear more.

"Shin, are you listening?"

"Uh-huh."

"What is aging? It's basically the breakdown of organs, mostly due to the aging of cells and maintaining of toxins in the body over time. In short, as you get older and your body stops its natural regeneration, things don't work as well as they used to. But my metabolism is unique in that my cells renew faster, causing the organs to break down much slower. Basically, I can heal and eliminate toxins much more quickly because my system is more efficient. I do have to eat a lot more protein to keep my muscles healthy, among other things."

And damn what muscles they were. Was there such a thing as a fat vampire? She wondered what Kenoe's body fat percentage was. Hmm.

"Five percent," he answered proudly without missing a beat.

"Stop reading my mind, damn it! And tell me about the blood thing. Oh, and sunlight. Certainly everything on TV can't be wrong."

"Shinju, this isn't a Marvel comic book." He laughed

heartily. The humor shut down quick when he got a good look at the furious scowl on her face. Damned man. "Uh-hem, 'scuse me. Anyway, many of us are born with a sun allergy, but it's not that different from other human allergies—spend more time in it and your body learns to tolerate it. Either that or take allergy meds. The worst that'll happen to me with prolonged exposure to the sun is a light tan on top of a mild rash."

Interesting stuff. Almost made her wish she'd spent more time in biology rather than culinary arts.

"As for blood, I can't sustain sufficient amounts of hemoglobin on my own, hence the need for additional protein. The best source is blood."

"So why haven't you taken mine? My blood?"

"I'm on blood suppressants."

"Blood sup-who?"

"Suppressants. My boss's bondmate, Carin, is a genius biogeneticist. She's found a way to help us control our blood need better. It's really intended for when we're out hunting if we don't have a ready source available."

"But you're not hunting so why are you taking it?"

"Because, lovely, since I met you, just the thought of taking any blood but yours is almost unstomachable."

"Unstomachable? You know that's not a word, Naoru."

"Yeah, but it works, doesn't it?"

There was that sexy-as-hell smirk. If the nonsensical word got him to smile like that, then hell yes, it worked.

"Fine. So what's with this mate business? You said you believe I'm yours. And your biogeneticist friend, what's her name again?"

"Carin."

"Okay, you told me that Carin is human but she's mated to

a vamp? So spill."

"First, I want to commend you on your eyes not crossing while I got into the bio stuff. It's my forte, you know."

"Yeah, yeah, on with it." She stifled a yawn, then donned her poker face, needing to hear the rest of the story, yet knowing he'd tuck her into bed if he thought she was overtired, whether she wanted to hit the sack or not.

"A mature vampire male knows when he's met a woman that can satisfy him as a mate. The more time he spends with her, the more attuned he becomes to her wants and desires, and her to his, whether she's vampire or human. But for couples who are more than mates, who are bondmates, it's even deeper. It's almost like the Mr. Spock Vulcan mind meld thing from the original Star Trek."

"The Vulc… What? I just turned thirty. You know I'm too damned young to know what you're talking about." The poker face slipped and she chuckled.

"Sorry. Anyway, mating and bonding aren't the same. Taking a mate is similar to finding a person you're attracted to, falling in love and getting married. You live together, learn each other's likes and dislikes over time. But a bondmate calls to a prime male or female on all levels. And baby, you call to me, spirit, soul and body. I smell you everywhere, your skin, your hair. Your sweat before it comes up through the pores. Even my blood craves you, Shin. It's also why we hear each other's thoughts from time to time. But once we join, there will be no distance too far that I won't be able to hear you when you call."

Wow. Talk about intense. And here she was expecting a summer fling. What the hell was she going to do? She may have told Kenoe about Max's vampire run-in, but that wasn't the extent of her family secrets. If they did this bond thing, eventually she'd have to fess up to her less-than-savory family

connections. Sigh. Well, at least the man was a vampire cop and not a human one, so her brother was safe in that regard.

Kenoe's head tilted sideways as if he were listening intently to something. He was probably tuning into her thoughts. Oh crap! Time to change the subject...sort of.

"So what does this mean for me, Naoru? I mean, if I can't be turned into a vampire, certainly *something* will be different about me. I can't see doing this bond thing without repercussions."

"You can't become a vampire, but you won't age as you do now. My blood and semen have regenerative properties for humans, immediately if given in large quantities, and slowly when exposed over time. Your strength and endurance will increase. You'll heal faster and stop getting sick. So, say, twenty years from now you'll look pretty much the same as you do now. Carin calls it the Bionic Woman syndrome."

Her eyebrows flew so high, they felt like they were leaving her face.

"Oh my God! Are you kidding me? You have, what, some kind of funky super sperm or something? And if you age slower than typical humans, then how old are you, exactly?" She didn't know whether to be pissed off that they'd had hot, sweaty, jungle sex without her knowing the side effects. Or whether to be really happy that the result of making love to Kenoe would be the equivalent of getting some awesome plastic surgery done. And she still couldn't believe she wasn't totally wigging out or wailing on him or anything.

He opened his mouth to answer but she was on a roll. "I understand this mating and bonding thing. In fact it explains why I can hear you in my head, why I can practically feel you."

"It's also because your own latent psychic abilities are amplified by our connection."

"Latent abilities?" She didn't think so, but she was *so* not up to arguing the point right now.

"That's usually the way of it. If you think back, there must have been a time in your life where you seemed to sense things, know things?"

"Uh, no, not really. Other than a keen sense of self-preservation and plain old common sense."

"Hmm. I may have a fabulous cock and super sperm, but it can't create abilities in a human. It can only enhance them." His chest expanded with a deep breath, then the man tightened his arms around her as he played his final card.

"God, Shinju, you have no idea how much power you have over me. It scares the shit out of me how much I care for you. How much I want to protect you. How much I simply want you. All the time. Every minute of every day." The words seemed to catch in his throat for a moment, but he swallowed hard and pushed on. "I don't expect you to just accept this. In fact, I'm not the easiest man to live with, and I'm sure just knowing I'm not quite human will take some getting used to. But if I can't have you, I don't know what I'll do."

Her eyes glistened with unshed tears on the verge of spilling over in a torrent of emotion. But this time there was no terror or regret.

"Naoru, I-I don't know what to say."

"I understand if you need time to think about it."

"How does it work? I mean, how do we do it?"

"An exchange of blood represents the joining. But the mate bond won't form if we don't both truly want it in our hearts."

"Are you saying you've never shared blood with any other woman? If so, save it. You just explained that you need blood and you certainly don't strike me as the gay type."

"Yes, I've shared blood with other women, before I met you, of course." He backpeddled when she narrowed her eyes at him. "But it's more than just an exchange of blood. It's more like a cellular acceptance. A gifting. It's all about the intent of the heart, we have to want it. And God knows I want you more than I want my next breath. I know I don't deserve you, but be mine, Shin."

Kenoe leaned in close. The sweet musk of his earthy scent and the deep adoration he didn't bother to hide were almost her undoing. Almost.

The whole blood thing would take some getting used to, but it didn't change the fact that she trusted Kenoe. With him she was able to let her undisciplined, non-schoolteacher, raunchy side out to play...and they both liked it. On the other hand, the man was no doormat. He was a killing machine. The fact that he proclaimed to need her did spark a bit of apprehension. Handsome as sin on the outside, brooding and dangerous on the inside. Could she be tied to a man like him forever?

Amazing how the whole situation reminded her of a novel she'd just read. The heroine was so infuriating, the book had ended up flung against the nearest wall. The woman's vampire lover inadvertently turned her, not knowing that she'd been bitten twice by another really, really bad vamp. When she lay dying, he exchanged blood with her to save her life, not knowing she'd be turned. After the transformation, the goofy broad was so determined to try to continue living as a human that she scorned the man who saved both her and her brother from a really creepy vampire. And worse, she was so stubborn, refusing to accept what couldn't be changed, she'd even run out into the killing sun to prove a point. Her ridiculous behavior almost killed herself and the man who'd already saved her life twice. What an idiot representation of a supposedly intelligent female. There was the occasional glimpse of brilliance between

bouts of crying and flat-out defiance. And the chicklet kept it up for so long, if Shinju had been the hero in that damned book she would have simply said to hell with the woman.

And now that she'd had a minute to think about all of this, was she being just as silly? Would Kenoe lose patience and say to hell with her? The idea was instantly terrifying. She'd felt so connected to him. In fact, Shinju was becoming so used to his presence, the thought of being without him was, well, sobering.

"I'll think about it, Naoru. I promise."

"It's all I ask, lovely." A large hand on her cheek accompanied a gentle kiss. But gentle didn't remain the order of the evening. A flash of ravenous hunger swept in and washed away a chunk of her resistance, just enough to allow other feelings to surface and mesh with his. It was like small waves lapping at the shore, slowly sweeping the sand from underneath your feet. As you admired the beauty of the water, it slowly but surely took you out to sea. And he just kept sending those waves after her, enticing her, calling her with no shame.

Oh, how she wanted to answer. When the first hawk—she was well past the butterfly stage—took flight in her gut, her thighs automatically squeezed together in an attempt to keep the slow burn under control. Her skin went from clammy with fear to hot and flushed when *"Let me love you, touch you"* floated into her mind. Kenoe's nostrils flexed.

"I smell you. It makes me want to spread you wide and taste you. Mmm, ginger syrup."

Oh. My. God. The man was seducing her!

"Of course I am." The words caused an involuntary twitchy ache as the soft tissues filled urgently.

She took a deep breath. Big mistake. The air was filled with Kenoe. Okay, time to count. One, two, three...she forced the numbers through her mind. She had to calm down. Counting

had always worked. Four, five, six...oh, screw it.

"Okay, I thought about it."

He grinned. Shinju pinched him on the arm in retaliation. His smile widened and tipped up on one side. Damn. The fangs he wasn't bothering to hide anymore sent her imagination on a journey. Would it hurt? How much would she bleed? His fingers stroking up and down her thigh with a feather-light touch brought her back from her trip quickly.

"It takes an exchange of blood and the intent of the heart, right?" she asked.

Hmm. She liked biting and nibbling during their love play. The rougher side of sex had always appealed to her, and Kenoe fulfilled every wet dream she'd ever had since puberty. And they hadn't shared blood so there was some room to play before the bond thing happened, right? At the thought of tasting the man's blood, a little shiver worked its way across Shinju's lower belly, one part disgust, two parts burning "gimme some".

Gimme some won the battle.

"I'm not quite ready to exchange blood, but in the meantime, make love with me. Maybe we can mend each other," she whispered between hard, urgent kisses.

Her speech faltered a bit, but her intent was crystal clear when Kenoe found his back pressed against the leather of the loveseat with her lips plastered to his.

"Baby, you've already mended me in more ways than I can say. Besides, I think you could use a little TLC yourself. For now, I'll take your word that you'll consider mating and bonding with me. And I want to do this right. I want us to have the blessing of the Council."

The Council? He'd already explained that those people, Elders, he'd called them, were on their yearly trip around the world checking up on all their vampire constituents. They

wouldn't be back at the Western headquarters in the States for months. Blessing of the Council? Was he crazy? She was on fire right now.

"Oh God, I can't wait. Love me. Bite me."

Then with more speed than she thought possible, Kenoe gained his feet, hefted her over one shoulder, and sped them to the bedroom. The man barely stopped to lock the door. In seconds Shinju was stripped and sprawled on top of the big bed.

Bite her? Did she know what she was asking? Kenoe ached to do exactly what she asked but he wanted her so badly there was no way he could bite her without sinking his fangs deep. And scaring the woman this first time she gifted him with a blood sacrament wasn't quite what he had in mind.

Instead he eased into her dewy channel and kept his fangs to himself.

Her arms and legs tightened around him, urged him deeper. Her hips met his, slamming upward as much as she was able given the way she was wrapped around him. There was nothing better than a woman who let it all hang out in bed. Add the honesty of her emotions slamming into him and he was a goner.

"More. Give it to me," she panted wildly.

"My God, Shin, you totally wreck me, smash me to pieces. Undo me like...hell, I can't even describe what you do to me."

The rapid rise and fall of her chest pushed his own passion, and blood pressure, off the charts. With each pant came a small cry, with each cry came a ragged intake of breath. And each breath she took stole one of his own, yanked it out of his soul until they were a writhing mass of raw sexuality. And the words that came out of the woman's mouth—dear God, how would he

ever survive the base erotic sight, sound and feel of the body beneath him?

"Mmm, Naoru. Fuck me. Harder."

Surrounded by the sleek muscles of Shinju's contracting pussy, his cock felt wrapped in a silk fist that was determined to milk him of every drop. Kenoe's thighs cramped and contracted involuntarily from the effort of trying to keep from rutting on her like a wild animal.

And only she moved him this way, was the only female who'd ever made him want to revel in his feral side. While the need for blood was under control thanks to a healthy diet and suppression meds, Shinju still aroused the desire to nip and bite and suck.

Her neck arched beautifully and a strangled, "Ah, God," rushed past her lips. "I can feel your fangs throbbing as if they were mine. Sink them into me while you pound my pussy!"

Holy shit! The woman was so uninhibited, so free and so…nasty. Unafraid to tell him what she wanted, fearless in the taking of it. And he absolutely loved it.

The thoughts swirling in and through his head lost coherence as she approached her peak. Amazing. The wild woman meeting him stroke for stroke walked right into his head regardless of the fact that he was one of the strongest psychics in the Seeker corps and able to block just about anyone else out of his thoughts. Yet she claimed to have no psychic ability at all?

"Naoru, more. Please… Bite me."

Aw hell, he couldn't resist. Not when she begged so earnestly.

As his cock strode home, he lowered his head and sank his fangs deep into the tender tissue just above her left nipple.

And she lost it.

"Yes! Oh God, suck me!"

He was practically gobbling her up as it was. With each draw on the supple flesh his woman went more and more buck wild. Yet nothing could have prepared him for the utter rush of that first taste of her blood. It was nothing like drinking from a donor. This was more like a bottled thunderstorm that flashed a magnetic current clear to the back of his eyeballs. And so sweet, the taste rivaled the juicy ripeness of a summer apricot.

The pulsing walls of her slick channel caressed then gripped his shaft as he began to move wildly, unable to help slamming into her. Shinju met each thrust with a fierce swivel of her hips until finally falling apart, she yelled his name.

Kenoe's voice hoarsely echoed hers. He joined her in flying loose at the seams in orgasm.

Ah, what a soulful mix of sweat and satisfaction. One he vowed to experience often. The moment they landed in Montana in a couple of hours wouldn't be soon enough.

Chapter Eleven

Kenoe stuck his head out of the guest bathroom door the second the two women waltzed into his apartment as if they owned it. Carin called out as she sat down at the kitchen table. "Hi Key. Oh, that coffee smells good." And as quickly as she sat down, she was back up on her feet raiding his cupboard. Mug in hand, she poured herself a steaming cup. "Want some, Tam?"

"No, thanks. I promised Alaan I'd cut down on the caffeine. I drank so much on the last mission it kept me up all night and the next morning I was shaking like a damned crack addict. I'll have a slice of that cake on the table, though."

Fussing as he wiped the shaving cream from his jaw, Kenoe stepped out of the spare bathroom with nothing but a damp towel slung low on his hips.

"Will you guys knock, please? I have a mate now. You can't just come barging in here whenever you feel like it. What if Shinju and I had been busy?"

Carin and Tameth looked at each other, then burst out laughing.

"What? What's so funny?"

"You're just so cute when you're all flustered and carrying on. Not to mention you look like a total jungle stud in that towel. And you might have all the other Seekers afraid of you,

but we know you're a total sweetie." Carin grabbed him by the ear and gave it an affectionate tug. And Kenoe, to his horror, blushed like a kid.

Tameth chimed in. "And we'll try to remember that you're a mated vamp now." She pecked him on his freshly shaven jaw, sending the temperature of his face soaring again. Damned women.

"All right, all right." Kenoe waved away the fingers pinching his cheeks and the two pairs of lips making little kissy sounds at him. Easing away from his tormentors, he got himself a mug, filled it with hot, rich coffee, then reached into the fridge for some O-positive. "So what are you guys doing here so early?"

"And what are you doing with that bagged blood? I thought you and Shinju—"

Kenoe waved Carin's question away and mumbled, "We're working on it."

"Speaking of Shinju, we came to borrow her awhile. Oh, this is so good." Tameth moaned around a slice of coconut cake Shinju had baked the night before. "God that woman is a wonder in the kitchen."

Rounding on his company, he pointed an index finger at the two of them. "Damn, when do I get to borrow her myself? Every time I turn around you guys are sneaking my woman away."

Tameth only grinned and said, "Yeah, but you're the one who gets to sleep with her all night. We only get to see her—"

"For all the rest of the time," he snapped.

"What can we say? We like her." Tameth held her hand out for another piece of cake which Carin was already slicing.

"You come in here without knocking, you drink my coffee, eat my food and steal my woman," he grumped with no real

heat. After all, he was getting what he wanted—real friends for Shinju. He was thankful these two ladies had kept Shinju company the entire week she'd been a guest at the estate. At least she wasn't alone while he worked on new compounds with the research teams headed by Dr. Lyons and Dr. Carin, or helped coordinate details for some of the missions for the other Seeker teams. But Kenoe wasn't on duty right this minute and these two were spoiling his plans for some early morning loving.

Just then Shinju came out of the bedroom looking like sex on wheels. Her full breasts filled out the stretchy material of a blood red T-shirt. Her legs were shrouded by a pair of white and silver embroidered harem pants that floated around her ankles as she walked. The material was so sheer, Kenoe could see straight through it to the black skintight leggings she wore underneath, giving him a perfect view of the shape of her ass. Strange, the black combat boots should have looked completely out of place, but somehow she made it all work.

"My God, girlfriend, you're going to make Kenoe blow a gasket stepping out of the bedroom looking like that," Carin jested as she walked over and delivered a friendly hug. "Ready to go?"

"Yep. See you later, Naoru," Shinju said with a sweet kiss to his lips.

Kenoe wrapped his fingers around her wrist as she made to turn away. Carin was right—the sight of her in that get-up sent his blood pressure soaring, or rather diving...right into his groin. He was glad she'd settled right in since arriving at the estate, but this quickie kiss stuff just so she could run off and play wasn't happening.

"Oh no you don't. If I don't get to see you all day I'm certainly going to get more than a little peck and a wave."

He swept her into a kiss so blatantly hot, not only did it

leave his cock throbbing, but when he looked down at Shinju she appeared stunned and out of sorts. Their two guests examined their toes and grinned while easing toward the door.

The silence was broken by Shinju's erratic breathing and Kenoe's lusty moan as he brushed his lips across hers once more.

Tameth finally spoke into the still air. "Uh-hem. Sorry to interrupt the necking, but Key, you're wanted in the communications center. I have a feeling you'll be a while, so we'll bring Shin down to meet up with you after lunch. If we're a bit early we'll give her a tour of the place until you're done."

"So why don't either of *you* have to be there?" Kenoe queried. One snow white brow inched up as he crossed his arms over his chest and waited.

In unison they said, "I'm off duty today." Then turned to each other and said, "Jinx!"

"And what about Kimora? Is she coming with us this morning?" Shinju asked, now out of the stupor Kenoe wished he had more time to cultivate.

Carin didn't bother to hide the less-than-pleasant curl of her lip at the mention of Kimora's name. Shinju, to her credit, just chuckled and shook her head. Carin and Kimora were supposedly observing some sort of truce. Kenoe would have to ask Bix about it again. So far, every time he'd tried to get the big, dark Head Seeker to explain how he'd talked his wife into not beating Kimora to a pulp—again—for her part in Kenoe's sexual torture, Bix just shook his head with a wry grin and swore that Kenoe didn't want to know what he'd gone through to get Carin's cooperation.

When they'd first landed and stepped off the jet, Kimora's eyes had gone wide as dinner plates at the none-too-relaxed sight of a glowering Carin standing on the tarmac. But to

Kenoe's surprise, Carin had forced a toothy grin, extended her hand to Kimora and growled, "I know the first time we met wasn't under the best circumstances, but welcome to V.C.O.E. Western territory headquarters. Perhaps you can come and visit me and Bix's home, a short chopper ride from here, while you're visiting. Happy to have you." Kimora's mouth had fallen open, right before she wrapped Carin in a fierce, but sincere hug, babbling about how she was so glad there were no hard feelings and such.

Sure, Shinju had questioned him, but he'd been, and would remain, too embarrassed to be completely honest. Thankfully, Bix had taken the reins and simply told Shinju that they'd been on a mission in London and helped Kimora with a situation. Bix said no more. And thankfully, Shinju hadn't asked again. But the woman wasn't stupid. She knew that whatever had happened hadn't been pleasant. Yet she'd also made it clear that since they were all here together and everything was fine between her and Kenoe, the matter of whether Carin and Kimora liked each other simply wasn't serious enough to pursue.

"Kimora's having breakfast with one of the Beta Seekers who flew in a few days ago for training."

"Really? Where, in the great hall?" Shinju asked Carin.

"No," Carin mumbled, gaze rolling up to the ceiling. "In her apartment."

"How do you know?" Kenoe pressed, then wondered why he'd even bothered to ask the question. This was Kimora they were talking about. In spite of his previous experience with Kimora, she really wasn't half bad. Though outgoing and outspoken, the woman was fun to be around, including her snarky sense of humor. Then there was her fit and toned body, muscular and ultra-defined. Yep, Kimora was a beautiful

woman who reveled in her sensuality. To sum her up in two words—sex personified.

Boldly, Carin answered, "Well, we walked by her rooms to invite her to hang out with us, and by the sounds coming through the door they were already busy in the living room."

Kenoe rolled his eyes, and Shinju covered her mouth to stifle a giggle.

"Way more info than I wanted to know." Kenoe turned on his bare heel and strode into the bedroom to change. Sigh. Nothing like being back on duty.

"I still can't believe Kenoe doesn't know you can do this," Carin huffed from her position off to the side of the combat floor. They'd been sparring for at least an hour and all three women were winded, having worked each other hard. Carin had just left the sparring mat for a much needed swig of chilled, watered-down apple juice while Tameth and Shinju finished up their bout.

Tameth blocked one of Shinju's well-aimed spinning back kicks, then countered with a solid punch that Shinju deftly ducked before landing a hit to Tameth's solar plexus.

Tameth grunted and came back at her. Shinju was no match for either of them, but for a human, damn if she couldn't hold her own pretty well.

Carin winced as Shin went flying over Tameth's hip to land flat on her back with a thud. With Tam's knee in her chest, Shinju grunted and signaled a yield.

Tameth happily complied, rolled off of her opponent and lay sprawled next to her. The two women lay side by side panting and giggling like old friends.

"So, Shinju," Carin said, handing them each a glass of pseudo-juice. "What's the deal with you keeping your ninja-like

skills to yourself?"

"Aack! What's in this?" Shinju sputtered.

"It's apple juice, mineral water and some vitamins. I should have warned you. Carin has managed to doctor up just about everything we eat around here." Tameth chuckled as Carin cut a snarky glance her way.

"Drink it. It's good for you," Carin mumbled, downed hers with a grimace, then burst out laughing. "God, I know it's awful, but I swear it'll help all of us recover faster after putting in such a vigorous workout. Bleeeck!" She collected the cups, handed each of her companions a clean, fluffy towel then sat down on the huge mat next to them. "Okay, Shin, spill it."

"Spill? No, I-I can't."

"Girl, please," Carin said with a nonchalant wave of her hand. "You fight like a damned machine, but won't tell us why you can share this side of yourself with us, but not with your mate?"

"I know it sounds stupid. And we're not quite mated yet, by the way."

"Why not?" Tameth pressed, earning a scowl from Carin.

A strong empath, Carin easily sensed Shinju's turmoil as it meshed with a need to confide in someone. "You can trust us, Shin. Loyalty is deeply ingrained in vampires, and while I'm not one, I'd protect any and all of them with my life because we're all family. Something I'd missed until Bix found me."

"I know. And I appreciate it. I've never really had friends."

"Yeah, tell us about it," the two women said in unison. "Jinx!"

"Well, my brother and his, uh, men, taught me how to fight from the time I was little."

"Really? How old is your brother and what in the world

does 'his men' mean?" Carin questioned easily.

Shinju dropped her head and wiped the sweat from the back of her neck.

"My brother's name is Max. He's a good fifteen years older than me. He's been hanging around with some pretty tough fellows since he was a teen. Now he runs the outfit and they work for him."

Carin's eyes narrowed as Shinju's emotions flared off the charts. She was obviously loving and protective of her brother, but a frantic fear played just around the edges. Time to change the subject. There was plenty of time to get the rest of this intriguing story.

"Your mom lives down in Atlanta, right? What made her leave Japan?" Carin wondered aloud. And there went Shinju's feelings again, soaring for the high-beamed ceilings of the workout room. And not in a good way.

"My dad died years ago. My mom just didn't care for Japan without my dad, and she didn't want to be a burden to Max. He pretty much stepped in and looked after me and mom doesn't particularly care for his line of work."

"Which is?" Tameth asked.

"Well, considering you're a Seeker I'm not sure I can tell you."

"Why not? You've already shown us your mad ninja skills." Tameth laughed, poking Shinju playfully in the side. "You're as good with your hands and feet as you are with a blade. So, what's the big deal about telling Kenoe?"

"Promise not to say anything?"

"As long as your bro isn't killing people I think we can keep your secrets, though you really shouldn't have any secrets from your mate, Shin."

"Yeah, I know, but I just can't tell Naoru right now."

"What does that mean, by the way? That name?" Carin queried, her head tilted to the side as she continued to work through the emotions pouring off of her new friend and soon-to-be sister.

"Naoru? It means 'to be mended'. A perfect description for my man, don't you think?"

"Absolutely!"

"Jinx!"

"You two are a hoot. Anyway, Max is a clan boss, the *kumicho* of the Ooeto clan. I can't believe I'm doing this. I've never told anyone. And I mean *anyone*, outside of my family."

Tameth's neck tilted hard to the left. "Sweet pea, *you* are Kenoe's, which means we *are* your family. And do you mean clan boss as in *yakuza*? Organized crime?"

"Now you see why I can't tell Naoru? My brother is a criminal, though he plays nicely enough with the Japanese law dogs and the other clans. But Kenoe makes a living putting criminals away. I can't tell him I'm related to one, educated by one, and trained to kill a man by one."

"But what your brother does is no reflection on you, Shin." Carin sensed her words were beginning to sink in. Perhaps the woman would reconsider her decision to keep her family history under wraps. She certainly hoped so. It would really hurt Kenoe to learn Shinju was willing to tell her and Tameth what she wasn't willing to tell him.

"We all have our skeletons, hon, but considering the strong possibility that Kenoe is your bondmate, this could come back to bite you later. I'm sure he's explained the difference between mating and bonding. There's not much you can hide from a bonded mate. And if you and Kenoe do take the final steps to make this thing between you permanent, I would hate to see

something as silly as what your brother does for a living become a wedge between you. Besides, your brother has taken care of you, loved you. He can't be all bad."

"Yeah, Shin. You know Carin is right," Tameth added.

With that, Carin and Tameth embraced a sulking, long-faced Shinju and dragged her to the locker room.

Quickly showered and changed, the ladies had a light lunch together, with Shinju grimacing at Tameth's chilled, blood-laced cranberry juice.

"I love my Bix and all," Carin teased around bites of roasted turkey and old-fashioned cornbread dressing. "But I don't think I'll ever have a taste for blood in anything."

"Sure," Tameth teased back. "That's what you say now. But I bet the blood that fills Bix's cock is something you'll always crave."

Shinju sat there with her mouth open as Carin squealed in outraged amusement. "Oh, you are such a damned hussy!"

"Damned straight! And it takes a hussy to know a hussy, 'cause I'm hooked on Alaan's blood, cock, and everything else!"

Shinju laughed so hard she practically choked on her macaroni and cheese, but she was glad the meal was such a lighthearted affair. Their easy camaraderie brought her spirits back up after the deep conversation they'd had on the workout mat.

The communications center in the middle of the estate was a good twenty-minute walk from the main house. They passed the horse stables and made their way up a rise that allowed a nice view of the golf course off in the distance. Wow, these vamps knew how to live. And Shinju was happy to be among them. Who'd believe that the first real friends she'd had in too many years to count weren't quite human, and oh so cool.

She knew that she and Kenoe were going to have to sit down and have a heart-to-heart about Max. Perhaps sooner rather than later. Besides, the morning she'd stepped off the plane and met all of Kenoe's family, friends and peers, she'd been welcomed with open arms. Kenoe had denied her nothing, let her go where she pleased and do what she wanted, even though she wasn't one of them. He'd been clear about the fact that his kind had survived through the ages only because they'd managed to keep their existence a major secret from the world. Yet he trusted her not to betray him.

Certainly she could trust him with Max's secret. Trust him not to judge her over it. Mind made up, her step felt just a little bit lighter and her smile more easy.

Still giggling at a bawdy joke Tameth had told, Shinju followed her and Carin through a set of secured steel double doors and into an elevator that surprisingly took them down several floors instead of up. On the way she learned more about how the dynamics of vampire clans and families worked. Hell, it was enough to make her head spin.

Of the ten clans of the vampire nation, the Seratis were considered the most bad-assed while the Hatsepts were considered just plain old bad. They were harem keepers, for cripes sake! She'd definitely have to talk to Kenoe about his tendencies in that regard. Then there was the whole matriarchy thing that only applied to Clan Serati. For example, when Carin was taken in as the adopted daughter of Alaana Serati, the Matriarch of Clan Serati and Alaan's mother, Alaan became Carin's brother and Carin immediately gained a higher social status than any Serati male. But then there were the Seekers, a law unto themselves. Shinju shook her head to clear out the buzz of all the information being dumped into it.

One thing was inexplicably clear—the two couples, Bix and Carin, Alaan and Tameth, worked closely with Kenoe on official Council business, but when off-duty the team was just as close as any family could be. They worked, played and loved with a zest for life that Shinju envied until she realized that they well and truly considered her to be one of them.

"Wow, this is some set-up you've got here," Shinju said on a low whistle.

"State of the art, military-grade everything," Carin replied. "I don't get to come in here often, but it never ceases to amaze me how swanky everything is. I bet this get-up has the CIA beat by a long shot."

Down a wide hallway they entered a large room with huge screens embedded into the walls. News channels played on some of them while satellite images and surveillance cameras streamed information across others.

They kept walking until they were deep in the middle of the place, something Tameth called the "Seeker's private domain". Shinju wasn't sure what she was talking about until she looked around. Every man—Tameth was the only female—sported a long leather trench coat similar to Kenoe's. Carin called it their Matrix outfit. Each one was just a bit different, but all were expertly tailored, cut to the same length and sported various nooks and crannies where weapons were tucked.

They were all armed to the teeth, yet their expressions were friendly as if this was a normal occurrence. Well, she guessed it *was* normal. After all, their job was to look after every single soul on this compound and be ready to hop a plane to get to wherever they were needed to either protect or mete out justice to their kind.

"Where do you think Kenoe is?"

"He should be in the briefing room." Tameth motioned

toward a wall of windows a bit further down another wide hall.

Carin gave her a quick hug and a wave. "I can't go in there, even if the windows are clear. Besides, I need to see Dr. Lyons down the hall then get back to the lab, so Tameth will take you the rest of the way. I'll see you guys at dinner."

Shin hugged her back and planted a little peck on the side of her face. "Thanks for everything. I really appreciate everything you said. Not to mention, you're a really bad girl...and I like it."

"Yeah—" Carin smiled, "—and you're just as bad. Don't worry, word will get out and we'll be running this place. See you later."

Shinju waved back and turned to follow Tameth.

"What did Carin mean that she can't go in even when the glass is clear?"

"It's built like the kind of rooms you see at the Pentagon. When the panes are white the room is soundproof and practically impenetrable. When they're clear, like regular windows, then there's nothing top secret going on. Either way, only a full Seeker or Iudex Judge can enter the room, so we'll just wait outside."

With that they turned the corner and Shinju came to a screeching halt. Her lungs burned, her eyes watered, but she couldn't move. The words she heard through the open glass door had her rooted to the spot.

"So we should be able to wrap up the investigation on Max Maruyama in how long? Days? Weeks?" Bix had asked the question. And to her utter shock, Kenoe answered.

"Give me another couple of weeks. Keeping Shinju away from there while all this goes down is at the top of my priority list. Her safety comes first. After the scheduled con-call with the territory leader in Shibuya district, I'll have a better idea

whether I can let her go back home or not. In the meantime, Seeker Tof-Li have both Sasuke and Max under surveillance. If the rogue that accosted Kimora gets anywhere near them, we'll have him."

Of all the nerve! *Let* her go home? Since when did she need anyone's permission to do a damned thing? And what rogue that accosted Kimora? What the hell was going on here?

"And if they don't take the bait?" This question from Alaan, the refrigerator-sized Mr. Angel of Light with the ocean-deep voice. Tameth's husband.

Bait? They were using her brother as bait? Oh just wait until she got her hands on Kenoe. Bastard.

"We'd better pray they do. Max is the only lead we've got to whoever provided the gene poison to them."

Poison? Max had been poisoned?

She shook Tameth's hand off her shoulder and barged right into the middle of their little undercover vampire powwow.

"You fucking bastard! You're using my brother in one of your cases? And worse, the fact that you knew he was my brother and you didn't say anything. You're willing to hang him out to dry? And poison! You warped sons of bitches."

The shock that rippled across her link with Kenoe bored into her heart. A heart that dripped icy venom. She would never forgive him.

"I'm outta here. Literally." Rounding on Tameth she snarled, "Did you know about this?"

"I'm not on this case, Shinju. I didn't have all the details." Tameth glared daggers at Kenoe, Bix and crew. "However, I was aware of some of the things going on with the rogue factions in Japan."

"I see." Shinju's words sounded flat even to her own ears.

Considering the anger boiling hot in her stomach, she wondered how she was keeping her voice so even. "I'm going to the airport if I have to walk from here. All I need is my purse and my passport. Please send the rest of my stuff to me in Tokyo. It was nice meeting you, Tameth. Goodbye."

Retreating she heard Tameth growl, "How could you guys be so stupid talking about this stuff with the door open? You knew we were coming. Idiots."

Stretching her stride as long as she could without actually running, Shinju got the hell out of there fast. If she stayed one second longer, Kenoe would find out just how good she was at shaving balls without a razor.

Chest heaving from the sprint through the rolling hills of buffalo grass, Shinju kept going, zigzagging through several groves of trees until she found herself at the top of another rise.

After storming out of the secret Seekers' room, her intent had been to go back to Kenoe's apartment, get her handbag and head to the private airstrip. But once clear of the communications center she'd taken what she'd hoped was a shortcut back to the main mansion, and ended up lost.

She stopped running at a small building, not realizing it was a gazebo until she was practically on top of it. Ducking through the opening, she was happy to find several benches embedded into the solid walls of fragrant cedar and flopped down onto one. Leaning her head back to rest against a solid wall, she glanced up and sighed. A clear jewel blue sky looked back down at her. It was so peaceful here. Enough to begin to calm down and collect her thoughts.

God, how could she have been so stupid to fall so hard and so completely for Kenoe? She'd known from the beginning that he was a cop. A gorgeous cop who could no doubt have any

woman he wanted, human or not. What good was she to a man like him, other than to lead him to her brother?

And here she was, concerned he would wig out at her association with criminals when he was already hunting said bad guys. Sheesh. Could she possibly feel like more of a dolt? Not bloody likely.

Tears ran unchecked down her cheeks even as a trail of white, fluffy clouds slid past the bright sun and blocked out the light. Just the way the news of Kenoe's current assignment had flipped off the light of her heart. A heart that was currently breaking into a million pieces, like spun sugar thrown against a wall.

Kenoe found her two hours later in the gazebo overlooking Smith Lake. The only reason he hadn't chased her down sooner was because he knew exactly where she was from the second she stormed out of the communications center. She hadn't gone to the airstrip and for that he was grateful. He really wasn't in the mood to drag her back to their apartments while they were both in such a volatile state—but if push came to shove, drag her he would.

He stopped just outside the gazebo and felt her out for a moment. To his surprise the woman wasn't even bothering to rein in her feelings or shield them from him. Instead, they cascaded off her in a steady stream of pain. The ready retort about her running off alone and unprotected died in his throat. Right now his woman was hurting. She needed some understanding and loving. But damn if it wasn't killing him to keep his temper in check and not lay her over his knee and light up her perfectly shaped ass for running off. Even on their well-protected property, he wouldn't trust her safety to chance.

He stepped over the threshold and simply told it like it was.

"Shin, I never meant to hurt you. What I have with you has nothing to do with my job or your brother."

"Right." The snark was unmistakable. "My brother is probably the only reason you're hanging out with me. It wouldn't be the first time some sneaky-assed man tried to use me to get to Max."

"Look woman, don't piss me off more than I already am. You put yourself at risk out here running around alone. Vampires aren't the only wildlife in these mountains, damn it. And you're only saying that because you're mad and want to lash out at me. Fine, I understand that. But don't make the mistake of thinking that because I'm easy with you that I'm some fucking pushover, Shinju."

Trying to keep his anger in hand, he turned his back on her and ruthlessly squashed his temper down. "You know damned well that what we have is deeper than any investigation of your fucking brother. You feel it, and don't you dare lie and say you don't."

"But why didn't you say anything? Why lead me on?"

"This is the last time I'm going to say this, woman. I did *not* lead you on. I was insanely attracted to you before I even knew you had a brother."

"Sure. Any other secrets?"

"Absolutely." Like the fact that he'd slept with Tameth, had done a complete background check on Shinju and knew she was an expert with a blade and a gun. Along with any-and-everything about Max Maruyama. "But it's all job stuff, happened before I met you or serves no purpose in furthering our relationship." Which was all true.

"Still," she persisted with a stubborn tilt to her chin and a tightlipped frown.

"Bottom line is I couldn't tell you. Shinju, I'm a Seeker.

Even as my woman, there are some things I just can't share with you."

"Oh yeah? I bet Big Blondie Alaan and Bix tell their—"

"No they don't. They can't. Except Alaan and Tameth's case is different given that they're both Seekers and often work the same cases. Even Carin still gets miffed when she isn't let in on the intel about Bix's missions, unless she's on the case herself. I may be a Seeker, but I have no reason to flat-out lie to you."

His explanation seemed to smooth her ruffled feathers a bit. But only a bit.

"Come here, lovely, let me remind you of what we really have."

Kenoe threw the link open and in seconds Shinju's eyes glazed over. Succulent lips parted on a gasp. Her bottom lip trembled once, twice, until her teeth locked onto it to keep it still. Yet, no amount of self-control could keep her from inhaling sharply with a sensuous, though muffled, whimper.

"Stop jumping into my head, you nasty bastard. Not fair." But the heat of anger was quickly being replaced by another heat. And he aimed to push the temp gauge higher until she melted.

"Who says I play fair, woman? And yes, I'm a nasty bastard, but *your* bastard, it would seem." He pushed against her mind harder, held nothing back. She hadn't come to him like he asked, but her head met wood as she leaned against the wall of the gazebo. Fine, he would make the first, or rather second, move.

Kenoe walked over to her but stopped just out of reach. Instead he stood and watched her wage a battle against the desire she felt for him. And lose.

"Oh, dear God," Shinju gasped. "I won't allow you to use me," she hissed, fighting against his sensual onslaught.

"I've never had any intention of using you. I'm sorry you had to hear what you did. But I do not apologize for doing my job. Besides, what you didn't hear was that we're trying to protect your brother from the unintentional shit storm he's walked into the middle of."

"The what?" she gasped.

"No, not now. I promise to fill you in later as much as I can. Now, you need some tender lovin' care and I intend to give it to you."

"No, I—"

"Close your eyes," he commanded.

She resisted, or tried to. Then her lids slid shut and what was displayed against them was almost more vivid than real life. Behind her eyelids was a vision of her very naked self sitting on one of the benches embedded in the gazebo's wall. Kenoe knelt in front of her, leaning forward over her cunt with his face buried in her flesh like a dog in his bowl. One leg was pulled over his shoulder, the other thrown wide and held there as he feasted.

Her resolve crumbled and fell like a house of cards caught in a windstorm.

"Yes, that's it, lovely. Feel how I want to touch you."

Unable to help herself, Shinju's hands eased up her body in a hard, rough caress in a simulation of what Kenoe was doing to her in her head. When her fingers reached her breasts she squeezed and pulled on them until the breath caught in her throat. One hand traveled lower to the vee at the crotch of her pants. Pressing hard, needing relief, she worried the swelling lips of her sex through the flowing fabric, sending her back arching and hips into a slow grind.

Shinju opened her eyes just as Kenoe grinned, his fangs gleaming dully in the shade of the building. The sight still took

some getting used to, but the little shiver-wince that typically wiggled around at the base of her spine at the sight of his elongated canines was swallowed up by a tremor of need.

But she had to stand her ground. Or at least go down fighting. Right?

"It's going to...oh, yes. Take more than...than... Ah! Sex for me to forgive you."

"Yeah, but it's a start."

With her senses already on overload, another raunchy mental push sent her careening into oblivion, complete with limp limbs and a goofy smile.

God, the man was talented at rocking her world. And he hadn't even touched her.

Chapter Twelve

Oh come on! Who could be banging on the door at this time of night, er, morning? Shinju rolled over with a huff, but her miffed grunts were nothing compared to Kenoe's snarl as he kicked his way furiously out of the covers and stomped to the bedroom door stark naked. Her gaze remained plastered to his sculpted, muscular back until he disappeared from sight.

And she wanted him again even though they'd just made love—she had to garner some energy to lift her head and look at the clock on Kenoe's side of the bed—okay, two hours ago. Damn the man had a fine ass, even at four o'clock in the morning. Wow. All those miles of pale skin and hair should have been a major turn-off. But God, he worked it so well with a face and physique so handsomely perfect that everything about him made Shinju all hot and bothered.

The way his muscles flexed and danced as he moved, like thick ropes overlaid with the fairest flesh. She grinned. Kenoe had a bit of a tan now since she'd had him teaching her how to ride horses and fish under the strong Montana summer sun.

The languorous smile fell from her face and hit the floor when Kenoe flew back into the bedroom. Shinju sat up, eyes wide as apprehension streaked from the nerves at the base of her skull clear down to her feet. Something was wrong, she could feel it. Or, in truth, she could feel *Kenoe* feeling it.

"Naoru, what is it?" Jumping from the tangle of covers, she instinctively dove for the pile of clothes she always kept bundled next to the bed out of habit, ready to don at the first sign of trouble.

He motioned toward the living room as he jumped into a pair of sweats. Shinju was right behind him as he once again left the room. Her feet ground to a halt. Bix, Tameth, Carin and Alaan all stood waiting, and none of them looked happy to be there.

"What?" Shinju demanded. Alarm pounded at her temple in agitated waves when no one answered. "What is it?"

Cutting a glance toward her mate, she froze at the cold glint in his eye. His focus was on the Head Seeker as if what was coming was all Bix's fault. But the emotions streaming from him held stark and utter fear coupled with no small amount of anger. What the hell was going on?

"Shinju, you will come with me." Bix's authority rang quietly through her.

"Naoru?" But he wouldn't look at her, wouldn't say a word. Instead he turned and disappeared into the bedroom again, leaving her standing where she was. She thought he wasn't going to come back at all when he suddenly appeared dressed in his badass leather trench coat, black stretch tee and tactical pants. His soft-soled combat boots made no sound as he tracked to the apartment door and out into the hall, both stance and frigid body language screaming "pissed off". Shinju just managed to get her gaping mouth closed when Carin and Tameth came to her side, each taking one of her hands in a comforting gesture.

They led her down to the first floor and into a palatial round room she hadn't been in before. Kenoe was already there, pacing like a hungry predator in front of a huge raised dais big

enough for a Broadway production.

At the top of the dais was an ornately carved half-moon shaped table that looked fit for royalty. This must be where the Council convened when they were in residence.

Bix walked to the dais, climbed the stairs and pushed a button in the center of a swanky-looking console set into the polished wood. Two seconds later the lights dimmed and a large LCD screen dropped out of the ceiling followed by a dial tone that resounded around the room. Every face present was granite hard and completely unreadable as the Seekers stood at ease. She would have actually been impressed if not for the underlying tension filling the space. That, combined with the arctic chill rolling off of Kenoe, set her nerves on edge.

The screen lit up but remained blank. Alaan's deep voice broke through the silence.

"Shinju, this is an urgent matter or we would never involve you or any non-Seeker."

Both he and Bix cut a glance toward Carin, who waved them off with a huffed, "Oh please". Bix narrowed his gaze. Carin rolled her eyes, but didn't say another word.

"Not long ago, our men in Tokyo intercepted a wireless communication from your brother's phone. We thought we should get to the person making the call."

Anxiety clawed at her gut. "And?" she pushed.

Bix turned toward the screen and spoke quickly. "Caller, are you there?"

A familiar face filled the screen and Shinju just knew she was going to throw up as the blood drained from her face.

"Sasuke?"

"Shin, I wish I didn't have to interrupt your holiday, but I need you to come home right away."

"Why? What's happened?" Immediately Kenoe was at her side, hauling her against his steady frame with one strong arm. He obviously had a clue of what was coming. Sasuke nodded his head in greeting with a simple, "Kenoe, glad you are there with her."

"Well, *her* would like to know what the hell is going on," Shinju demanded, trying to keep the edge out of her voice. It proved impossible.

"It's Max. He collapsed on the street."

"What? Where is he now, Sasuke?"

"I have him bundled up on the living room couch for now. Luckily we were just outside his apartment building. I called the ambulance. They're on the way. You have to get here, Shin-chan. It doesn't look good."

"But he looked just fine when I left—"

"He was faking it. He's been ill for some time now. He didn't want you to know."

"Oh my God. I'm coming Sasuke. As soon as I can, I promise..."

Kenoe's firm reassuring grip steadied her on her feet. Then he stepped forward and took over as Carin and Tameth moved away from their mates and replaced Kenoe as her anchor. Each woman took a hand and held tight.

"Don't worry, Shinju. We'll all go with you, okay?" Tameth reassured with a whisper. Shinju felt herself nod as her thoughts jumped from one to another, but wouldn't settle or slow long enough for her to piece a sentence together.

"Look Sasuke, Dr. Carin and I are the most qualified to figure out exactly what's happening to you and Max. We have some ideas but need to examine both of you right away. Max needs care, but at the same time, we can't afford to allow

human doctors to get their hands on him. Go to the hospital with Max. Stay by his side and don't let him out of your sight. If they want to give him oxygen and something for the pain, fine. But don't let them run any blood tests. Come up with a reason. Say it's against your religion or something. Anything. Understand?" Kenoe instructed.

Sasuke nodded, then doubled over. A wracking phlegm-riddled cough rattled his chest hard enough to dislodge a lung.

Shinju's hands flew up to cover her mouth as blood trickled from one corner of Sasuke's. Shock didn't begin to describe the terror she felt at seeing the man turn such an unexpected shade of purplish gray.

"Oh, no. Sasuke." The words were barely a whisper, but it was all she could manage to squeeze out.

Kenoe practically yanked her off her feet and into his arms, his hands firm against her back, but his touch gentle and reassuring. And he was pissed clear down to his black buffed boots. With her head tucked beneath his chin, she heard him say, "We're coming, Sasuke. Just hang tight until we get there. Since the ambulance is on the way, even if we'd called in our guys five minutes ago, they wouldn't beat that ambulance to Max's place. We'll have them redirect to the hospital and take Max to a secure facility equipped to handle this kind of thing."

"I understand. I will take care of it. The ambulance is here. But once we're at the hospital how will I know the people who come to get Max are the ones you sent? Word has it there are others who would like to get their hands on him."

Shinju couldn't believe it. Sasuke deferred to Kenoe as if it were the most natural thing in the world. He hadn't even asked her opinion at all and this was *her* brother they were talking about. And to her surprise, she was glad her man had a real pair of balls.

"We're aware of the others. We also know of Max's connection to Clan Li. Both you and Max are in danger, but not from our law-abiding kind. The men who come will be dressed like me, Seekers. Second, they'll call me or Bix the second they arrive and we will verify via video phone that they are who they say they are."

A man with slanted slate blue eyes and dark, bone-straight hair pulled back into a ponytail appeared on the conference screen.

"This is Slade from Clan Li," Kenoe continued. "He will be with his partner, Alex from Clan Akicit. Both report directly to the Head Seeker, Jon Bixler or the Second, Alaan Serati, just as I do. If someone shows up claiming to be there for Max, but they aren't with Slade and Alex, shoot them in the head and get the hell out of dodge. Wheel Max out on a fucking gurney if you have to."

"Kenoe!" Shinju shrieked in alarm.

He glanced down at her, his expression furious yet contained. "This is life or death, lovely. Playtime is over. Now, go pack. We've got a plane to catch."

Chapter Thirteen

"He'll be all right, baby. I know he will. Clan Li will protect him from rogue vampires and rival human clans alike. Please don't cry. It just breaks my heart to see those tears. I can't stand it," Kenoe crooned against the shell of Shinju's ear.

He pressed gentle but firm strokes across the spot on her lower back that always seemed to ache at the end of the day. They'd been in the air for hours and due to land any minute, and he had no idea what would happen once they touched down.

Shinju's eyes were puffy, her face swollen. And after he'd given her the details of what they believed was going on with her brother, her temper was on edge.

The love and concern for her only sibling overflowed her soul and almost brought Kenoe to his knees. The internal struggle she tried to keep to herself leaked out of her pores. He could practically hear the gears grinding out one question after another in her head. What to do? Return to Tokyo and stay to take care of Max, or go back to Montana with Kenoe? Take Max and flee, simply disappear? Go to the police?

At least they didn't have to worry about Kimora, who should be safely in Atlanta now accompanied by the Beta she'd been screwing. The vamp had considered himself lucky when Bix asked him to be Kimora's security detail while posing as her

latest fling. Especially since it wasn't too far from the truth.

Kenoe sighed and wished he could help his woman. Just knowing that a female like Shinju, so strong and loyal, could care so deeply for someone to the point of worrying herself sick caused a fat lump to lodge behind his Adam's apple. And it wasn't just concern for her brother, Sasuke, and her cousin, but for Kenoe also. What had he ever done to deserve such a ballsy, honorable woman? Hell, he'd spent the first half of his life learning how to take lives, and the second half perfecting what he'd learned during the first half. Yet this female wanted nothing more than to give to him, not take. To make him whole, rather than strip him of his pride. To love him instead of using the power she had over him against him.

And if she decided she was better off without him, a vampire—worse a vamp whose job was to slice others to ribbons—in her life, then so be it. It was all about her and what she needed.

God, what would he do without her?

The answer? Let her go her own way and spend the rest of his days in mourning. Because life without Shinju would become an event no longer worthy of his notice.

Tameth brooded as she pored over the mission's checklist for the hundredth time since they'd taken off from the States. It felt like something had been overlooked, but for the life of her, she couldn't figure it out. Bix and Carin's children, accompanied by their nanny and five "uncle" bodyguards, were on their way to meet Alaan's parents and would finish up the Council's yearly tour with them. The Council apartments in Tokyo had been prepared for them. Alex and Slade had checked in and confirmed that Max was settled and sedated at the V.C.O.E. medical facility in Roppongi district. There were two

Clan Li Seekers standing watch over him at all times. Carin was in contact with the medical staff and they'd already set up everything she'd asked for. Kenoe had literally rocked Shinju to sleep after she'd gotten so upset Carin had to give her a sedative while on the plane. Thankfully the woman was still asleep, tucked into one of the other cars speeding toward their lodgings near the medical campus. Still, Tameth was uneasy about this whole business. They were missing something. Not to mention, her best guy friend was currently miserable because Shinju was miserable.

"Hey, you doing okay?" Alaan's deep, soothing voice was laced with concern.

Tameth looked up and let a tired smile grace her lips. Her husband had tossed their luggage into the trunk and settled into the small back seat next to her. Amazing how much smaller cars were here on this island versus the roomy Japanese Lexus SUVs they usually rode in back home.

She answered quietly, not wanting Bix or Carin to overhear the conversation from the front seat. They were probably just as wound up as she was.

"Yeah, I'm okay. It's just that I've never seen Kenoe this upset. I mean, even during the Lowan hunt he was focused and determined, but never upset."

"You know what it's like to be concerned for a mate."

"I know," she sighed. "But I'm still worried about him. About them." She shifted in the seat and turned to face Alaan square on, knowing her dark brows were drawn down into an urgent frown. "I mean, did you know that he doesn't take Shinju's blood? He still uses the bagged stuff."

"So do I."

"But not every day. Not when we're home."

"Perhaps he wants to wait until they can be joined

according to tradition," Alaan reasoned.

"Oh come on, Alaan. Bix and Carin's was the first traditional joining in umpteen years. And the only reason you and I were taken before the Council was because you're the Matriarch's only son."

"Tameth, why are you getting into their business?"

"Kenoe has been my best friend for years. He means a lot to me. And while I think Shinju is perfect for him, I can't help be concerned about him considering all he's been through in his life. I want him to be happy. I don't want him to have to go through any unnecessary drama behind all this."

"It's his life, Tam. And his job. And he knows how to do both damned well."

"Well at least Max is resting comfortably at the V.C.O.E. urgent care facility. I'm sure Shinju will want to be there when he wakes up."

"Kenoe will take care of it. And knowing how we prime males are about our women, he won't let her anywhere near that place until she's had some rest."

"Yeah, but "

"And if you have time to worry about how Kenoe handles his woman, then I obviously need to give you something else to think about."

Oooh, she knew what was next. After all, this man of hers took her happiness quite seriously.

Alaan's oh-so-skilled lips coaxed and teased hers into compliance. Tameth felt the burden of Kenoe's troubles slide off her shoulders along with her leather trench coat. Her man's fingers skimmed down her arms, leaving the fine hairs on her skin waving in the non-existent wind. One large hand stroked lovingly over a burgeoning nipple while the other eased along

the lines of her stomach, playing catch with the butterflies gathering there.

Alaan whispered against her ear, his breath warm against the lobe. "You know beautiful, we haven't been bonded long, but I truly intend to make up for all the lost time I wasted while not pursuing you."

She knew he referred to the years of self-imposed celibacy while he mourned a woman they'd all thought had been killed in a rogue attack some six year earlier. And Tameth had spent what felt like forever working with Alaan, hunting bad guys side-by-side with him while quietly wanting, needing him. Just like she needed him now.

The telltale sign of his arousal nudged against her thigh as he gently repositioned her. Alaan kicked things up a notch, gently twisting and tugging her nipple, knowing she loved that little edge of pleasure-pain in their sex play. The hand between her thighs stroked relentlessly against the seam of her black leather pants. Her hips wiggled even as her legs spread wide all on their own to give him better access.

"And now tell me what you're thinking about, baby."

"You are such a bad man," she gasped, then bit her lip to keep from crying out.

"I'm waiting, Tameth."

"I-I'm thinking about the way your lips feel when you suck my nipples. When you bite them," she whispered.

"Mmm, I can see that," he groaned quietly. Then his head lowered. Sharp teeth nipped through her T-shirt. He pressed his lips together over the sensitive bud and clamped down. She held back a shriek. God, it felt so good.

"What else are you thinking about?"

She was panting now, half out of her mind.

"And I plan to send the other half to join the first. Now, tell me." The words were rasped right into her head.

"I'm thinking about your fingers buried in my pussy, finding that spot only you know about."

But it wasn't going to happen in the backseat of an SUV. Thankfully, Kenoe and Shinju were in another car with Randall. But hell, Bix and Carin were driving *this* one, well within earshot. Not to mention Tameth wore a tight pair of leather pants plastered to her legs.

"I'm talented, remember?"

Alaan licked a path up her neck. As he suckled the sensitive spot just below her ear, Tameth felt her belt sliding off, followed by a puff of cool air against her heated flesh as her zipper eased down.

"How's this for getting your mind on your own man where it belongs?"

Coming up for air just long enough to raise a fuss, she hissed as him. "*Alaan, stop. Carin and Bix are in the front seat.*" And what was it about Alaan and his tendency to get her bare-assed naked in the back seat of a vehicle?

The big blond god simply ignored her and kept right on working at his goal. In seconds her legs were free of the constricting material of her pants...and Bix turned the music on and up. Loud. Even still, Tameth heard Carin's laughter over the JPop tune now blaring out of the speakers. They were so busted.

And Alaan didn't give a shit.

"*Damn, woman, you smell so good. And you're all wet and hot for me. If I can't sink my cock into you, at least let me get a taste.*"

Taste? Was he mad? One, he was too damned big to fit

down low enough in the seat to get between her legs. And two, there was no way she'd be able to keep quiet once his mouth met her pussy. He was just too good at getting her off.

"Then I'll have to settle for a touch…"

As soon as his thoughts settled in her mind the man proceeded to stroke her to madness. A precise thumb strummed her swollen clit as two fingers sank into her sopping core. A flick of his wrist brought the tips up against the little spot deep inside her channel that sent her senses off the map.

Alaan covered her mouth with his, slid her a bit of wicked tongue and swallowed Tameth's cries as they rang out in tune with the booming radio.

Dan couldn't believe his good fortune. Not only would Max Maruyama soon be dead and gone, but Dr. Carinian Derrickson was on her way to Japan. She'd probably be with the two gargantuans who'd jacked him up the night she'd almost been killed. But that could be easily remedied. His last acts before he left the country would be spectacular—he'd tie up the loose ends and take advantage of the opportunity to get his arms around the one woman he'd always held in the highest esteem.

Carin had been a natural bodybuilder back then. Now she was probably mega strong since she'd no doubt ingested large quantities of vampire blood over the years. No worries. One good dose of the new modified serum he'd been working on and she'd be docile as a lamb. No more vampire speed. No more vampire strength. Just warm, beautiful woman. And with her at his side, perhaps they could figure out what caused the deadly side effects of the compound he'd developed. If anyone could get the formulation right, it was Dr. Carinian Derrickson.

And once she saw how good they were together, there was no doubt she'd remain by his side. Yes, Dan was a much better man than he'd been before the Sidheon pooch screw three years ago.

After the two vampires from hell accosted him, Dan had gotten the hell out of dodge quick. But he'd heard the whole ordeal from the rogue community and the story was practically legend now.

Dan wasn't as stupid or irrational as Sidheon. No way would he flat-out try to take the woman. It was suicide. This called for a more subtle approach using more expendable *associates*.

Chapter Fourteen

Shinju looked down at her brother. She'd been in this very spot since arriving at the V.C.O.E. hospital early this morning. Max hadn't stirred once. She knew he was asleep, but he just looked so still, his skin a sickly yellow rather than the golden brown that was the norm.

"Shinju, please. You'll be no good to Max if you wear yourself to a nub."

Someone must have given Max a sponge bath while she napped in the chair next to his bed. His short cropped wavy hair was still a bit damp, glistening under the soft lamplight.

"Shinju?"

"I'm not leaving his side, Tameth, so just drop it already." She knew it was irrational, but she simply hated everyone right now. Was it Kenoe's fault that Max was up to his proverbial ass in trouble due to some funky vampire illness? Was it anyone's fault her brother had basically done this to himself? No. But it didn't change the fact that she was in a total funk and on the brink of losing it. What would she do if she lost Max? The thought was too painful to even contemplate.

"Well if you're determined to stay here without resting, you can at least eat something. Kenoe may not show it, but he's going bonkers worrying about you."

"Yeah, I know."

"You know, but do you care? Or are you more concerned with getting back at him for not revealing classified information?"

"Look, I expect you to take his side since you've known him longer than me, but—"

"Hold it right there. Knowing him longer doesn't mean a damned thing in this case, Shinju. That man would take a bullet for you. You have a connection with Kenoe that none of the rest of us do. I know you're more than aware how tormented and awful he feels about all of this. And you enjoy making him feel that way? You're okay with the fact that he's miserable?"

Ow. The words cut to the quick.

"I like you, Shinju, but don't mistake my kindness for weakness. It's never okay to deliberately hurt someone. Ever." Tameth's voice dropped to a menacing snarl. "Keep it up and I'll have to kick your ass. Then Kenoe, who's been my best friend for years, will try to put me down to protect you, which means Alaan will jump into the fray. Want to tear up my family, not to mention the best elite force of Seekers the vampire nation has ever seen? Keep fucking with Kenoe over your selfish revenge."

With that, Tameth turned on the heel of her SWAT issue boots and strode from the hospital room.

A few moments later a voice invaded her head. A voice she loved to hear, but she wasn't sure how to get past her anger enough to let him know she still loved it. Tameth was right, she was being foolishly distant with Kenoe for something that was beyond his control. She was pushing away the one person she felt truly connected to. And it was wrong. Not to mention, she still held a few of her own secrets close, like the fact she could probably get pretty close to taking him one-on-one, blade-to-blade. Sigh.

"Are you all right? I just felt your emotions spike."

Kenoe.

"Yes, I'm fine. Thanks."

"I know you don't want to talk to me right now, lovely, but we need you out here. Carin is on her way down from the labs with the final results of the prognosis she and I worked up on Max."

Releasing her brother's much-too-cool hand, Shinju was out of the chair in two shakes, bolted through the door. The fact that all of her new friends, Kenoe's family, filled the room didn't stop her from hurtling into Kenoe's waiting arms. Just the place she needed and wanted to be. She pushed against his chest, but not enough to break free. Besides, she would only escape his embrace if he decided to let her. He was so gentle, so sweet and giving. But it didn't make him a weakling by any stretch.

Enfolding her, Kenoe buried his nose in her hair and inhaled deeply. The pain coursing through the man speared Shinju right in the heart. And suddenly she couldn't stand to be apart from him another minute. Instead of trying to escape, she wrapped her arms around his broad back and held tight.

"Kenoe, I'm so sorry. I was wrong to take out my anger and frustration on you. I'm just so afraid of what will happen to my brother. Please, I—"

"It's all right, lovely."

This time she did push away, looked up, and then wished she hadn't. The usual lively sparkle of his glacial gaze was muted with pain. Dark, puffy circles made his eyes look haunted and drab. The blue-white irises were dull and ringed with bloodshot tissue. He looked, in a word, awful. Tired. Worn out. And it was all her fault.

"No, it's not all right, Naoru. Someone reminded me that it's never okay to purposely hurt someone. Period. And I'm sorry I shut you out. I'm just not used to having a companion. Just

give me some time to work things out, okay?"

He dropped a kiss on her forehead and she sank back into his embrace, sighing with relief and trepidation as his arms came around her back. Strong hands stroked the length of her spine in comforting circular caresses. The tears she'd forced to remain bottled up inside since laying eyes on her brother this morning pushed against the cork of her soul and burst forth.

By the time Carin joined them, Shinju was sobbing her eyes out, interrupted by the occasional wracking cough and loud slurpy sniff as she tried to bury her head in Kenoe's chest.

"Come on lovely, let's sit down."

Kenoe led her to a big comfy chair and settled her in his lap. Oh God, this must be bad. The whole team was here, and then some. Carin sat down in the chair across from her with her super-duper-alpha vamp, Bix, behind her with a big supporting hand on her shoulder. Tameth and Alaan stood holding hands off to one side of the door, while Randall took up a stance on the other side. The door crept open and Shinju froze.

"You!"

In walked one of the stars of her nightmares.

"You're the asshole that took my brother out of that warehouse that night! What did you do to him?"

"Shinju, calm down," Carin said sharply. The sympathetic expression on her face took some of the sting out of her order. "Bix?"

The big, dark vampire stood forward.

"Shinju, this is Yuu Tof-Li, one of my Seekers as well as a territory leader in Northern Japan. He's Clan Li."

"But my brother, the night he was attacked four years ago.

I saw this man!"

The newcomer stepped forward and said, "And I saved his life. Max and I have been friends, though quiet ones, ever since."

"You...you saved him?"

"Well, it does make sense, doesn't it? He'd just had his throat practically torn out, yet the next time you saw him he was just fine. But I swear, whatever is wrong with him now, I did not do it. I would never hurt Max. He's a true friend."

It was true, Max had acted as if nothing at all had happened after she'd seen him bleeding out with her own eyes. But she had another question to ask. "What happened to that bastard who attacked him?"

"He was put down like the rabid dog he was," Bix responded. "Attacks on anyone are against our laws, but moving against a human is the worst crime a vampire can commit. The rogue's name was Darius Zhang, formerly number seventeen on the V.C.O.E. Most Wanted list. I didn't know the man he'd attacked was your brother, but Seeker Tof-Li reported the incident as well as the capture of Zhang."

"But you said he was put down," Shinju challenged.

"And he was. Once the Council was briefed on the capture of the scum, I gave the order to execute."

Carin stood and began to pace. Bix remained close by, always at her back.

"Shinju, we asked Yuu to be here because he's as much a part of your brother's life as you are a part of ours. I've run a number of tests with Kenoe's help and we've come up with a scenario of what's going on with Max's body."

Kenoe clarified. "Basically, whatever concoction was given to him and Sasuke has permanently damaged their DNA. The

only thing that has strong enough regenerative properties down to the molecular level is another source of DNA. A serum, synthetic antidote, or genetically altered material won't do them any good. It's got to be something from a natural source. Basically, blood. Vampire blood."

"What!"

"There's nothing we can do for them, Shinju. Without a partial transfusion, they'll both die," Carin said. "I'm sure it's how Yuu healed your brother before, so we at least know he can tolerate it."

Bix added, "And we're still not sure of the source of whatever was given to them. Someone cooked up a drug with some nasty side effects. Max and his Second are probably not the only ones who bought it, but we don't know who the dealer is yet. We need Max and Sasuke alive to help us, if they're willing."

Just then, Sasuke walked in, hunched over like a man three times his age.

Shinju jumped out of Kenoe's lap and ran to him.

"Sasuke! Where have you been? We flew in last night and got here first thing this morning. I'm glad to finally see you."

"Me too, little sis."

Then the hacking started, followed by shivering so severe Shinju wondered if the man was having a seizure.

"Bix," Carin yelled, "restrain him, quickly. Yuu, get the med techs in here right now!" And Carin was immediately on Sasuke, pressing a cloth into his mouth to keep him from biting his tongue clean off. Then she spoke calmly to him, so close they were practically nose to nose.

All Shinju could do was watch and pray.

"Sasuke, stay with me. Stay with me, all right?" Carin

called quietly. Her voice lowered to a more soothing timbre as Sasuke's shaking subsided.

"D-Daniel...Daniel M-Moss." Sasuke's final words before he passed out cold on the floor. The medical personnel had come in and were already gently picking up Sasuke's trembling form. Shinju tried to go with them when they lifted his limp body onto a gurney.

"No. Stay here. I've got to help get him stabilized. I'll come for you when you can see him." Then Carin turned to her husband, her lips pressed so tightly together an ashen gray line appeared around them. "Bix, did you hear him? Did you hear what he said?"

"I heard him, all right." If the snarl alone hadn't given a clue that Bix was livid, the fangs Shinju had never seen bared made it clear enough.

Shinju looked around the room. Tameth and Alaan both wore stone faces, only Alaan's fangs were bared too. The man clenched his fists and tried to control what was clearly a case of rage. Carin looked like she'd seen a ghost, while Kenoe and Bix could have spit nails. Even Alex and Slade, who'd come in right behind Sasuke, were cursing a blue streak.

"What the hell is going on?" Shinju demanded. She sure seemed to be asking that question a lot since meeting these long-toothed people.

Kenoe answered as the room began to clear.

"Daniel Moss. We used to call him Dan the Mouse. He worked with Carin back in San Diego. He sold her out to Aleth Sidheon three years ago, almost got her killed. He's also the man who subsequently, through a sheer act of cowardice, saved her life."

Alaan growled, "Yeah, with a little persuasion from me and Bix."

"And now it looks like he's trying to pick up where I left off in my gene research. Only he's killing people," Carin spat. Her face a veritable storm cloud, she turned and followed hard on the heels of the med techs already rushing down the corridors with an unconscious Sasuke.

The second the private waiting room door of Max's suite snapped shut, Kenoe was bombarded with his woman's anguish. Her first thought was to clam up again, shut him out and deal with her problems on her own. But where had that gotten her in the past, other than miserable and lonely? The grief, almost soul-deep, leaked out of her. All her life she'd avoided getting close to anyone to protect her family's reputation. When the realization sank in that she didn't, *really* didn't have to shoulder life on her own anymore, the feeling was so foreign the woman couldn't quite figure out what to do with it.

So she just held on to Kenoe a bit tighter, fisting her hands in his shirt to keep from falling off the edge of her tolerance. And he was determined to stay exactly where he was and hold her all day long if that's what it took.

But past that, what were they to do? Both were torn—Kenoe for Shinju, and Shinju for her brother and Sasuke. After a few moments of tender, yet emotionally shredded silence, in true Shinju fashion she looked up at Kenoe, tightened up her raggedy composure and got straight to the point.

"So what do we do?"

Kenoe kept silent a moment, trying to process the jumble of emotions streaking around his woman. Yes, Max and Sasuke were her family, and now his to protect as well, but right now his role was to simply be there. And Kenoe absolutely would not make this decision for her...unless she either asked him to or

put herself in danger.

"What do you want to do, lovely?" He wasn't trying to avoid providing a solution, but he instinctively understood what Shinju needed from him—support. Nothing more. Nothing less.

"Was that a trick question? No, I take that back. I'm sorry," she sighed. "Truthfully, I want to save my brother, but I'm not thrilled with giving him a vampire blood transfusion to do it."

Kenoe didn't say a word, but waited for her to continue poring through the barrage of concerns swirling about her brain and, consequently, down through their strengthening bond.

"I know he can't be turned and that the effects will wear off over time," she whispered.

"True. A large enough infusion of blood will jumpstart the healing process and begin to repair his DNA. It'll wear off as his own blood supply replenishes itself. He won't relapse, nor retain vampire speed, strength or any of our other traits."

Indecision and panic pushed through her thin shell of calm. The woman knew she didn't have a whole lot of time to ponder this. Two men lay dying and the decision to save them was hers.

No pressure, Kenoe snorted to himself.

"I think I'll go get a cup of coffee and maybe a snack. Nothing helps a female think like caffeine and pastries. Bring you something?"

"You sure you don't want me to go with you?"

"No, no, I'll be fine. I just need a minute alone." Kenoe caught a flicker of something sharp and impulsive, but it was quickly hidden again under a veil of cool detachment. What the hell was this? Whatever it was seemed different from when she'd given him the cold shoulder and cold everything else the last time she was upset with him. The more he looked into her

eyes the more she started to squirm, like an ant under a magnifying glass. Hmm.

Eyeing her askance, Kenoe chuckled at her blush and decided to leave her be.

"Go on, lovely. I'll be here when you get back, all right?"

She nodded, wrapped her arms around his waist in a tight, shuddering hug and headed for the door.

"Shin?"

"Uh-huh?" But she wouldn't look at him.

"Don't leave the compound. If you need to get off the grounds for a while, call to me. Use your cell or your mind, either is fine. We're not quite bonded, but anywhere in this building is close enough for me to hear you."

"Yeah, all right," she huffed, but there was very little heat behind her snarky agreement. She seemed to be in some kind of limbo, unable to decide whether she should be upset, determined, mad or hysterical. Damn. Poor baby. Poor bull-headed, stubborn-as-hell, determined-to-get-into-trouble baby.

Kenoe sighed and waited about five minutes. Then he tapped the wireless earpiece hidden beneath his locs.

"Slade, you on her?"

"Yep. Keeping my distance, but I've got her."

"What the hell? Tam, you see that?"

Tameth's head swiveled around and followed Carin's line of sight. Exceptional vision revealed the slightest movement of a shadow along the tree-lined path near the fence across the way. That path led to a grotto that couldn't quite be seen from here, and on the other side of the thick stand of trees was a locked gate that was supposed to be guarded twenty-four seven.

"What the hell is she doing? Kenoe's gonna kill her."

"Yeah? Well who does she remind you of, Tam?"

Tameth rolled her eyes but couldn't help but answer honestly…sort of.

"She does *not* remind me of either of us." Tameth replied blandly.

"Riiiight," Carin drawled. "What about that little excursion to Sausalito after we got back from the London mission?"

"You can't count that," Tameth huffed. "We are both Serati females and can do as we please. I was not even on duty and had no need to report in. Besides, I was well prepared to look after both of us."

"Yeah, but you didn't have permission to take Stealth One. Which you, uh, sort of failed to mention at the time."

"Oh shut up. You got a nice pair of designer pumps out of that shopping spree, didn't you?"

"Sure did. And Bix on my ass. Hell, I was almost looking forward to him getting sent off on a mission somewhere just so I could go take a pee by myself!"

"Drama queen."

"Me! And who complained after Alaan actually gave her a spanking then revoked her pilot's license for three months?"

"Nobody I know," Tameth lied boldly. Carin laughed out loud, then clamped her lips shut. She didn't want to bring any unnecessary attention to them right now. Considering they'd gotten into plenty of trouble together by wiggling out from under Seeker radar, the last thing they needed was anyone running off to find their husbands.

The shadow eased closer to the grotto entrance then darted out of sight into the trees.

"Come on, we'd better save her ass before Kenoe turns it another color, like blazing red." Carin wrapped her fingers

around Tameth's upper arm and tugged, almost surprised when Tameth didn't put up a fuss.

Tameth shrugged. "What can I say? I like her. She's good for Kenoe."

"Yeah, but I have a feeling she won't be good for his nerves."

Shinju knew she was being followed. At first she didn't really care, actually eager to engage someone, anyone, just to work off some steam. But when her mind recalled exactly who, or rather what, was embroiled in her current life's situation, she could have strangled herself. Max had been playing both sides of the fence with the vampires—friends with Clan Li on one hand, and doing deals with a human, rogue-associated, vamp drug dealer on the other. And the odds that the person tailing her was a little old Japanese lady in need of directions to the nearest fish market were slim to none.

Stupid, stupid, stupid!

Why in the world hadn't she stayed at the hospital where it was at least assured that the vamps walking the halls were good guys? But nooooo, she just had to go walk it off, had to get away from everyone so she could think about things. When would she learn that getting away from everyone was exactly what she needed to *stop* doing? She had Kenoe now, along with all of his family and friends who'd already accepted her into the fold.

Oh well. Nothing to be done for it.

What she really needed right now was a weapon. Again, her mind shot back to the medical facility. Why? Because she happened to have a six-foot, muscle-packed, white-haired, katana-toting, deadly weapon that loved everything about her. A weapon who would give and do anything for her—Kenoe

Hatsept. And where was he? Waiting for her to return to her brother's hospital suite ready to give the doctors a decision about the blood transfusion. Not to mention the fact that she was supposed to be getting herself sated on hot coffee and perhaps a baker's dozen of brownies.

Shinju held back the urge to slap herself in the head, then without looking back she took off at a dead run and ducked around the next corner into an alley. Chest heaving more from the burst of adrenaline than the short sprint, Shinju was faced with the possibility of her own mortality. If these were rogue vampires stalking her, without a full bond with Kenoe and the advantage of sharing his blood, she would be no match for them. Stronger and faster, they'd gut her in no time.

God, she didn't want to die. All she'd needed was some time to get used to the whole vampire boyfriend thing. After spending a bit of that with Kenoe and company, Shinju wanted nothing more than to bond with him and get on with their no-doubt exciting lives. But here she was all alone in an alley about to face God-knows-what. Was she too far for him to hear her if she called? Only one way to find out.

Her right foot lashed out at the first pursuer to speed around the corner as she yelled for Kenoe with all her psychically non-talented might.

The exact second Shinju landed in trouble, her call rang inside him like a large bell. Seconds later, Slade called.

"This is bad, man. She's being tailed by two rogues. One of them fits the description of the idiot who jacked Kimora in Shinju's backyard. They're closing in fast. Whoa! Carin and Tameth are right behind them."

It took everything in him not to bellow into the receiver. After a couple of deep breaths that didn't calm him at all, he

snapped, "Get there now, Slade. I'm on my way."

Kenoe shot out of his chair and voice dialed Bix and Alaan while bolting for the nearest exit. Relief warred with terror and flat-out rage. Slade, Tameth and Carin, all skilled fighters, would be on the scene to help Shinju. Didn't change the fact that the woman had no business roaming around Roppongi district alone. Especially with her new knowledge that the ballpark in which the human race played was teeming with fanged people who wouldn't hesitate to do her harm.

He followed Slade's GPS transmission toward Shinju's exact position. Kenoe prayed his pretematural speed would get him there before it was too late.

The scene Kenoe rushed in on would have been somewhat satisfying if Shinju hadn't been covered in blood, both hers and her attackers'. The air was full of the scent of rogue, rotten to the core and unmistakably rancid. The smell mixed with Slade's and all three women's.

Slade was injured and crawling with the last of his strength to get to and cover Shinju's body with his own. Bowie knife still drawn, Carin was trying to push Slade back enough to examine Shinju. Tameth stood guard at the alley entrance.

With an aggravated tap on his earpiece Kenoe called in the cavalry.

"Hatsept here. Clean up, fast. Sending GPS coordinates. One Seeker injured. Four rogues down." Not just the two Slade originally reported as tailing her. Squashing his rage, he spoke through gritted teeth and reported, "And one human also down. Dr. Carin is already on the scene."

Thank God.

Shinju lay flat on her back twitching weirdly. A strange yellow foam bubbled up out of her mouth and dribbled down

her chin.

Two steps had him at her side.

"Is it okay to move her? Anything broken, severed? How can I help? What can I do?"

"Kenoe," Carin snapped. "Get hold of yourself. Her vital signs are weakening, but none of her injuries are life threatening. Something else is going on here."

Easing Shinju off the cold, hard pavement and carefully into his arms, Kenoe saw Carin was right, as usual. A quick inventory revealed no serious wounds at all. A few cuts and scrapes along her arms and legs, a cut under her eye and a goose egg over her brow. One injury, a deep sluggishly bleeding slash from her left ear down to her collarbone made it appear the dogs had aimed to kill but simply missed by sheer luck.

None of it explained the woman's deep level of unconsciousness or the frothing liquid pouring past her lips. What the hell had they done to her?

Slade filled in some of the blanks. "They were waiting for her."

Kenoe looked up and briefly met the gaze of his fellow Seeker. Slade had managed to push himself up against the wall to sit up. His eyes were bright, unclouded. And pissed off.

"I followed them around the corner expecting two bad guys. Instead there were five. One got away. Outnumbered, the women were already kicking ass and holding their own pretty good. Even without a weapon, Shinju was in the thick of it. Next thing I know she screams like you wouldn't believe. I turned in time to see one of them stick her in the neck with something. She fell to the ground and started flopping around. I was running to her. That's when one of the bastards got me in the back."

"So how are they down if you were already out of the fight?"

Kenoe wondered aloud. But he never took his eyes off the now convulsing body of his woman, her skin so unusually pale, clammy and blood slick. Where the hell was the clean-up crew, damn it?

"I said one of 'em got me in the back. Never said I was down," Slade grunted with a wry, tight smile as he sat up a bit straighter, one hand holding his ribs. "I sliced 'em, *then* I hit the pavement." Slade's chuckle became a hack, then he spat a wad of mucous-laden blood off to the side.

Tameth strode over, reached down to help Slade up then turned to a sulking Kenoe. God, he never sulked. This was new. Couldn't look past the fact that his best friend thankfully had been there for Shin when he hadn't.

"Come on, Key. The ambulance is here."

Tameth paused and cocked her head sideways. The fat braid down her back was mussed as it flopped from side to side.

"Kenoe, I know that look. This is not your fault."

Easing to his feet, he moved to one of the unmarked ambulances that had just backed into the alley. Trying not to jostle Shinju's battered little body, he kept his eyes front and his gait smooth.

"Thanks for being in the right place at the right time, Tam. I should have been with her."

"But it would have been worse if you hadn't put Slade on her. You knew she was going to sneak off. I'd fault you if you knew it, but did nothing about it."

"I knew she would pull something. It's in her nature to work things out on her own. But I should have been the one tailing her. It's my responsibility."

"Yes, but it was *her* choice." Tameth said gently, firmly.

Carin had already climbed into the ambulance and was

busily, and rather loudly, batting away the hands of the attendants.

"Damn it, I'm not the one who's hurt. Stop groping me already!"

But her hair was plastered against the side of her face with a clotting bloody gash, and more of the red stuff was sprayed down the front of her shirt.

The hands kept reaching for her.

"Shinju is the one who needs your attention. Now quit it or I'll put something in your food to give you a flaming poo!" Then she looked up and locked eyes with Kenoe. Confusion, concern, it was all there in her expressive eyes as she motioned for him to move faster.

Before he handed his lovely mate over to the ambulance techs, he cut Tameth a glance and said, "What a fucking mess, Tam. First Max and Sasuke, and now Shinju. I mean, what are the odds that my woman and her only family in all of Japan would be laid up in the hospital at the same time because of the same shit?"

A low, miserable groan from behind them caught Tameth's attention. But Slade was there first. The vamps they'd knocked out all had been cut in one place or another. They were now semi-conscious and barfing like dogs. Good. All hail Dr. Carin's barfinator serum smeared on the edge of their blades. A nondescript van pulled into the alley just as the ambulances pulled away.

Bix and Alaan jumped out, followed by Alex and several Clan Li Iudex Judges. Yep, interrogation was going to be fun.

Chapter Fifteen

Back at the medical facility, Kenoe sat in a chair next to Shinju's bed and fought to keep his sanity in check. It was the strangest thing not to have her presence, no matter how faint, tucked in that little corner of his mind. He hadn't realized until now that he'd gotten used to her being there already.

And when she woke up he was going to skin her alive. Damned woman.

A soft tap sounded. He glanced through the huge window of the hospital room and toward the entrance on the other side of an oversized sitting room. He saw exactly who he needed staring back at him through the pane of glass set into the solid wood of the door.

Before Carin and one of the resident doctors stepped over the threshold, Kenoe knew what he was going to do. He'd known hours ago, the second Shinju's subtle scent began to change.

The little vid phone vibrated against his thigh just as Carin reached his side.

"Hatsept here."

"It's Alaan. How you holding up, pipsqueak?"

He'd punch the next person who asked him how he was doing, simply because he didn't know what to say. He was so

angry over the whole situation it was difficult to think about, let alone describe how he was handling it. He could have lost his woman today. God, living this way would turn his silver hair gray long before its time. And if the woman wasn't willing to let him do what he was born to do, protect his people and his mate, then what the hell was the point? He'd made a decision in his head to let the feisty bit of female go, but his heart couldn't stomach the notion.

Between the guilt and the rage, he'd clenched his jaw so tight his head pounded with each beat of his heart. This was insane—vampires didn't get headaches.

"I'm hanging, Alaan," he finally answered. "How's Slade and Tameth?"

"Slade was admitted, stitched up and will be released in the morning. A little sleep and he'll be good as new. But Alex and Tameth, who's gonna get her ass paddled later, have been questioning the prisoners who can manage to string more than two words together between blowing chunks."

"What?"

"Yeah. Tam held the antidote to the blade serum in front of their faces, then refused to administer it until they talked. They all started talking and puking at once."

"And?"

"Briefing in three hours."

"I may be indisposed."

"No worries. I have a feeling I know where you'll be. If you're up to it, we'll come to you. Work?"

"Yep. Works." He clicked the phone shut, sat back in the chair and blew out a frustrated sigh.

"Key?" He looked up into Carin's soulful brown eyes. Her hair was freshly washed and pulled away from her face. The cut

along her temple had a few butterfly stitches on it and looked sort of purple about the edges. Other than that, she appeared fine. More than he could say for Shinju.

"How are you holding up, sweet pea?" she asked quietly.

Instead of answering the woman's question, he posed one of his own.

"What's wrong with her?"

"Whatever they gave her is attacking her immune system. Almost like some kind of super dose of the stuff that made Max, Sasuke and God knows how many others sick. But it's working too fast. Her cells can't keep up. Would you like to go over the blood work? You've already got clearance to the labs."

A biochemist at heart, Kenoe would have normally jumped at the chance to help Carin solve a biological mystery. However, leaving Shinju's side just wasn't an option.

Declining her offer with a single shake of his head, Kenoe got down to the point. "How much time?" he blurted, bracing himself for the answer.

"Three days. Four at the most."

Shit, he was barely keeping his temper in check. The pain at hearing Shinju only had a few days before her light would be extinguished from this earth forever sent him hurtling toward the end of his tolerance. Pushing out of the chair, he promptly walked over to the wall farthest from the still woman lying in the bed, and put his fist through it.

Slowly, he turned back to Carin.

"I can't decide for Max and Sasuke, but this woman is my mate. Regardless of how this came about, in the end I am responsible for her well-being. Give her my blood, Carin. As much as you think she needs, as often as she needs it."

Nodding, she walked over to where he stood near the

ruined wall and patted him on the shoulder. "I had a feeling you'd want to do this. I've already ordered the equipment to be brought in. Why don't you go scrub up? Meet me back here in fifteen minutes and we'll get her taken care of. Okay?"

"Sure," he answered without looking up.

"Carin?"

"Yeah, sweet pea?"

"How's her brother?"

The good doctor's hesitation should have been enough of a warning, yet it didn't soften the blow.

Finally she whispered, "Kenoe, I'm so sorry. Dr. Robins put him into a medically induced coma as soon as he got word that Shinju was hurt. He's trying to slow down the organ deterioration, knowing Shin couldn't make the decision about the transfusion right away. He thought it was the best way to give Max a chance until Shinju is coherent."

Max was in a coma because Shinju couldn't give permission for a blood transfusion when she needed one herself? Another hard shot to the gut. For the next several moments, Kenoe waded through the possible solutions until his brain buzzed from the effort. If he gave the okay for Max's procedure on Shinju's behalf, would Shinju feel betrayed because he'd taken the choice from her? If Max died, would she ever forgive him for *not* making the call when she was unable to do so herself?

God, it was too much for any vampire.

"Nothing like a catch twenty-two," he grumbled, headed for the surgery center to change into scrubs and wash up.

Three hours later, Kenoe bolted upright in bed. What the hell? A strong and capable hand landed in the middle of his

chest and pushed him back down to the pillows.

"Whoa there, Hoss, stay where you are. You need the rest," Bix ordered. Carin, with her hand firmly in her husband's, nodded her head in agreement.

"What the fuck? What am I doing here?" Butt naked, the soft pillow top of the air mattress cushioned Kenoe's body. This was no hospital bed. He was back in the condo he'd shared with Shinju at the V.C.O.E. high-rise in Roppongi—the condo they'd spent all of one night in since arriving in Tokyo.

Alaan, with a dozing Tameth in his lap, gently roused his mate and rose from a cushy-looking chair across the large bedroom. The couple exchanged their seat for a spot near the edge of the bed as they both moved in closer. Kenoe relaxed, comforted by the presence of his friends, his family.

"How you holding up, pipsqueak?" Alaan asked while Tameth nodded her head on a yawn, obviously wondering the same thing.

"I feel pretty good. A bit sluggish." The whole muzzy-brained thing left him just short of annoyed until Bix explained.

"After Carin took your blood, I ordered her to slip you a sedative. No, don't say anything. You would have never agreed that you needed the rest and you never would have left the medical facility. And I need you ready for what comes next."

Kenoe listened carefully. As pissed off as he was, he still had enough sense not to mouth off to the Head Seeker. It took biting his bottom lip until a bead of moisture eased down his chin, but he held his tongue.

"And don't worry," Bix assured. "Shinju has two guards in the room and two outside. Serati Seekers, females, flew in with my permission as a favor to Tameth."

Holy shit. Now *that* was saying something. Clan Serati females were warriors to the bone, bad as hell and would give

any vamp a run for his money. They were such a handful, Bix didn't dare station too many of them in one place. Hell, they'd be running things before the week was out. Tameth was the only one in all of the Western territories in the States, and on the elite team of Seekers. The rest were spread all over the globe. Thank heaven.

"Bix, are you nuts? Four Serati female Seekers in one place? At the same time? Carin, you should have left me under the sedative a little while longer. God, I hope Shinju stays asleep. They'll corrupt her for sure," he snarked.

Tameth shot Kenoe an "I dare you to say another word" glare. Kenoe couldn't hold back a chuckle. And it had the desired effect. A bit of the tension broke and soon the room was filled with companionable laughter.

Carin disappeared out of Kenoe's bedroom for a second and returned with a glass of something purple. But they'd all learned that just because it looked like juice didn't mean it was, especially coming from Carin. And he wasn't disappointed.

"God, what is this? It tastes like ass!"

"Drink it, Kenoe. The sooner the better. It'll cut your replenishing time down from twenty-four hours to twelve hours so you can give Shin some more blood."

"Yes, ma'am." He took a sip. "Ugh. That's just nasty." He downed it in four big gulps then directed his attention to Bix. "So, what do I need to be rested for?"

Bix spoke quietly, his voice laced with venom and steel. "Hunting season. The rogues were after Carin."

"What!" Carin whirled his way with a genuinely perplexed shriek. "What the hell are you talking about, Bix?"

"Friends of Dan's, obviously. We don't yet have all the details. And even after we do, you won't be in that briefing. I'll fill you in afterward."

"You son of a—"

Bix cut her off. "Watch it, woman. Both you and Tameth—"

"Hey, don't put me in this," Tameth piped in from her perch on Alaan's lap.

"—are both lucky that neither of you are confined to the building after that stunt you pulled," Bix finished, without missing a beat.

"Whoa! We kicked ass and you're upset about it?" Carin asked incredulously. The toe of her serviceable leather shoe tapped on the hardwood floor.

Tameth smartly kept her mouth shut.

Exactly twelve hours later, Kenoe walked into the medical facility right as rain and ready to give Shinju another round of blood. Afterward, he drank some of Dr. Carin's nasty purple stuff and sat by the bed watching Shinju sleep.

God, her eyelids weighed a ton. Sensing Kenoe in the room, Shinju managed to push them open and immediately sought the beauty of his barely blue eyes. Her sleepy gaze met his relieved one. A slight stir of his body, more a mere rippling of muscle, belied the nature of the predator just below the surface of the skin. And for the first time in a while, Shinju was forced to remember and acknowledge just how dangerous her man was.

He was a hunter, and a damned good one. Ruthless, cunning and powerful. Yet with her, he was such a gentle soul. So sweet.

"Sweet, eh? Just wait until you're well, woman."

If she hadn't understood his meaning right then, the warning was crystal clear when a second later all the love and

relief in his heart folded under a pool of anger at her recklessness. In one big dose, it all lodged squarely in her brain. She was in big trouble.

Kenoe's first spoken words were barely a growl, each syllable pushed between white, very sharp teeth.

"Good evening, lovely. How are you feeling?"

Shinju wasn't quite sure how to answer that question. Hmm. She certainly didn't feel as awful as she should. Closing her eyes again, a quick inventory of skin and muscle told her that whatever had happened, she'd healed hella fast. And there was no doubt she'd been injured because she remembered the vibration of every blow, both delivered and received.

"Let me think about it for a minute," she croaked, then relaxed into the pillows without another word.

"Well?" he pressed gently, his voice all liquid deceptive comfort.

"I'm still thinking," she croaked. "How about some water?"

A cool cup was pressed to her mouth. God, it felt so good touching her lips and trickling down her parched throat. "Mmm, that's nice." Lifting her hand to hold the water, she said, "I'll just keep sipping. In the meantime you can tell me how I got here and what's going on." As an afterthought, given the volatile temper she sensed in the man, she added a syrupy sweet, "If you don't mind, of course."

Kenoe arched a single silvery brow, conveying his knowledge of her attempt to wiggle out of trouble, but he went along with it. For the moment.

After a quick explanation of the ambush and how she'd come to be in the V.C.O.E. med facility as a patient rather than a visitor, Shinju gave thanks to every God she could think of for some serious grace. Living to see another day—more importantly, to see Kenoe—was a big deal now that she was

done with being bullheaded about it all.

"How's Max?"

"Shin, I don't know how to break this to you gently so I'm just going to say it. He's in a drug-induced coma. The doctors are trying to slow the failure of his internal organs. He's fading fast."

"You didn't give the transfusion?"

"It wasn't my decision to make." He lowered his thick platinum lashes for a split second before an expressionless, hard-as-stone mask was plastered across his features. She felt him attempt to erect a barrier, a wall, in his mind. But it wasn't quite working. Interesting.

"Okay, what exactly *didn't* you say just now, Kenoe?" she asked after another sip of water.

"It is not my place to decide the direction of Max's care. However, it is my place to direct yours. For now." Unapologetic. Stoic. Firm.

Shinju froze like a deer in the headlights. "Oh my God, you gave me your blood." Was she relieved? Dumb question—alive and relieved seemed to go hand in hand. What did he mean by "for now"? And what about the bondmate business since they'd shared blood?

"Don't worry, lovely. One-sided bonds do not form."

"Oh, right. Because I wasn't conscious to make the pledge?" she reasoned aloud.

"I'd like to think that's why it didn't form."

That was the dumbest thing he could have fixed that gorgeous mouth to say. It wasn't Kenoe's fault she walked out of the medical facility and got jumped by five monsters. In fact, he'd respected her wishes to the extreme where her brother was concerned.

There was no way she'd admit it just now, but Shinju knew she would have been pissed if Kenoe had gone ahead and done whatever he wanted in regard to Max, no matter what kind of shape she was in. Just the fact he understood how important it was for her to make the decision pushed the walls of her heart open just that much wider.

But she felt him pulling away from her. Distancing himself.

So, the man thought she didn't want a solid, unbreakable bond with him? Oh she wanted one all right, not just because he'd saved her life, but because she couldn't imagine being with anyone but Kenoe Hatsept and all his overbearing, pain-in-the-ass ways for the rest of her days. Even if worse came to worst, she had Kenoe now. A man who managed to dip down into the deepest well of her soul and was satisfied with her being just the way she was. He wasn't asking her to pretend to be someone else. This man accepted her quiet, rowdy or raunchy moods, yet was nowhere near a doormat that she could walk over and later come to resent. No, this was a man's man. Beautiful? Absolutely. Wimpy? Not even close. Just the right mix of alpha and beta. Just the right mix for her.

Funny how near brushes with death helped one figure out what was really important in life. With that part of her future decided, she snorted and moved on to the next thing.

Max and Sasuke needed vampire blood to survive. The fact that she felt pretty darned good after what Kenoe had described as a couple of tense days in the hospital, there really was no reason to delay. The choice was clear as day.

"It's just a partial transfusion, right? Just like what I had?"

At Kenoe's simple nod, she said, "Give Max the blood."

"And Sasuke?" he queried, with a little tilt of his gorgeous head. Her heart rate kicked up and the bottom of her feet began to sweat. Strange, here she was laid up on a hospital bed and

all she could think of was Kenoe naked.

"Geesh, what a 'ho," she mumbled to herself.

"Excuse me?"

"Uh...oh nothing. Sasuke has no next of kin. So, on behalf of my brother, his closest friend, I'm okaying a transfusion for Sasuke as well."

Before she could finish the sentence, Kenoe was already moving toward the door sending the nearest woman to find Dr. Carin.

"Carin will be on her way shortly to take care of things. I'll come visit you after a while."

He opened the door, his wide back retreating. He was leaving? And this didn't feel like a "why don't you rest" departure. It was too heartfelt. Too...permanent. The bottom of Shinju's stomach hit the floor.

"Kenoe?" she yelled. No pride, no concern for who else might hear. "Where are you going?"

Without turning, he said, "If I can't protect you, I don't deserve to keep you." Sigh. "I'll send Dr. Carin in now that you're awake."

"Don't you dare leave me, damn it."

Kenoe whipped around so fast his locs wrapped around his head and hit him in the face. Before he could ask a question, Shinju wasn't sure if she was doing it right, but she threw open the connection between them and let all her love and regret pour through, along with her need and desire to be with him as a lover, a wife. If he would have her.

"Please don't leave me," she pleaded softly as she bit the inside of her cheek to keep from crying.

The softening of his expression was like a balm to her soul. And from now on she would...wait. There were women guarding

her? Shinju lifted her head and looked a little closer. Not only were they guarding her, but they were both inside and outside of the room. And these were some pretty dangerous looking chicks, decked out in Seeker garb like Tameth's and Kenoe's.

"Uh, Kenoe," she demurred, or at least tried to sound like it. "Introduce me to my caretakers, would you?" 'Cause she had some questions for them. Very serious questions.

Kenoe glanced toward the door, then pinned Shinju with a glare before turning back to the female Seekers in a double-take. All four of them watched him with professionalism and a bit of saucy challenge, gauging his reaction to her request.

Shinju laughed at his disgruntled expression. Big mistake.

"If you can laugh at me like that, then you can certainly take a bit of punishment for the stupid endeavor that landed you here."

Uh oh. Voice and pitch were too smooth, too controlled. And that flash of fang? Shinju choked on her water as anticipation wiggled its way up from her toes to dance on her belly. The man's snarl certainly didn't match the lasciviousness massaging their developing bond. Dayum!

Jaw clenched and tense, he jerked his head toward the door.

"You two, please wait outside," he demanded. The women calmly but immediately complied, and took their time easing out the door. They may be Clan Serati, but Kenoe outranked them as long as they were on duty.

The second they cleared the threshold, Kenoe dropped the blinds on the pane of glass that allowed people to look in from the private sitting room.

"And now let's see how you really feel," he taunted.

Several minutes later Shinju lay on her back with the flaps

of her hospital gown laid open, baring her skin. Kenoe had shown her each spot on her body where a wound had already healed. Now she lay gasping like a winded, out-of-shape...something or other. She couldn't think straight long enough to figure out which animal she resembled. But whatever it was, it was wild, untamed and obviously in heat.

Kenoe had her playing a wicked game of "catch-me" where she tried to get hold of his tongue, lips, hands, or anything else as he teased her mercilessly. The man nipped and lapped every exposed piece of flesh from her forehead down to her belly button until her heart threatened to slam out of her chest.

In between each lick, he pushed his thoughts into her head.

"What would I do if I could never touch you anymore? You will never, ever, place yourself in danger like that again." The order was followed by the heat of oh-so-talented fingers, the light, erotic scrape of manicured fingernails and the mouth from heaven...or hell. She couldn't decide which.

"Wouldn't you miss this?" he asked, then proceeded to wring the answer out of her.

Sweating profusely, trying to keep his face smashed against her humming breasts, Shinju cried out as he eased away. His long locs slid down her skin. The soft but rough sensation sent her senses whirling even higher. How the hell was it even possible to feel more than she already did? It was insane, but all she wanted was more.

"I thought you said I should be resting. If you're not going to put me out of my misery then at least let me go to sleep." Right, as if she could sleep now. God, she was on the verge of begging him to strip off the rest of her gown and dive between her legs. Good thing someone had given her a bath while she'd been unconscious. Nothing worse than a funky coochie.

"You are resting. I'm doing all the work," he protested with a fanged grin. "And just so you know, while you were sedated to allow the blood to work, I gave you a bath. You are hard to handle even when you're asleep."

He tongued her bellybutton again.

"Asshole tease," she gasped. But couldn't stop moaning, panting, pleading.

"Damned straight." Kenoe planted little kisses from one side of her face to the other while she once again chased his mouth with her own.

There was a quiet knock on the door just before it eased open.

"Oh thank you, God, for sending someone to save me!"

Kenoe's chuckle echoed in her mind as he eased her gown closed and pulled the covers up to her chin.

Whew! Shinju was grateful to be rescued by Dr. Carin and another physician. They walked in all scrubbed up and ready to go with a donor for Max and Sasuke—Yuu Tof-Li.

Chapter Sixteen

Shinju was released from the med center after a few more days of precautionary observation. Both Max and Sasuke were on the mend and recovering nicely. The Serati Seekers remained with them and would accompany them home to Max's house when they were released. Word had it the women had a soft spot for the two bachelors. Meanwhile, Yuu Tof-Li went with Bix and the entire elite team on a little hunting expedition in southern Japan.

On the flight back to V.C.O.E. headquarters in Montana, Shinju had grumbled and complained.

"That's so not fair they went while I was still in the med facility. Why not wait until I was completely well so I could go too?" Shinju had protested. All she'd earned was a snort from Carin who hadn't been allowed on the "official" mission either.

Once back at the sprawling estate, Shinju was grateful that Carin was nice enough to spend time with her whenever she wasn't working up in her labs. In fact she'd met her match when it came to gorging on popcorn and action flicks, and practicing hand-to-hand combat. The woman wasn't much for a blade though.

Carin had laughed when Shinju offered to teach her how to use the katana. "I figure if they get that close, I'll just shoot 'em."

The company kept her mind off of how much she missed Kenoe. One incident almost sent Shinju into full depression.

Late one night after falling asleep in Bix and Carin's living room, Shinju woke to find her friend sitting at the kitchen table staring down at the polished wood surface with a dazed look on her face, grinning. Shin lay on the couch watching for a moment, expecting Carin to simply snap out of whatever she was thinking about, get up and head to bed.

After about ten minutes, the woman hadn't moved, but the smile was bigger and her skin appeared somewhat flushed. Was she ill? No, probably not. She certainly wouldn't be showing that many teeth with such a happy expression if she didn't feel well.

Shinju rose slowly, careful not to startle the other woman, and moved toward the breakfast area.

"Carin?" she called softly. No answer. "Carin, you all right?"

After a second or two, the good doctor blinked rapidly and swiveled her gaze toward Shinju, goofy display of teeth still in place.

Okaaay? This is weird.

A big contented sigh filled Carin's chest, then came out a satisfied whoosh.

"Hey, Shin. What's up?"

"Uh, I was going to ask you the same question."

"Oh, nothing much. I was just talking to Bix."

Huh? Talking to Bix? Shinju looked around but didn't see or hear anyone. Not to mention Jon Bixler was a big-n-tall, dark-haired, distinctive-looking man. Definitely hard to miss.

"Carin, should I call Dr. Lyons or someone?"

"Girlfriend, I'm not sick. I was talking to my man."

"But, uh..." Shinju said warily, still looking around the

huge apartment. Maybe he was in the bathroom and they were speaking psychically? If that was the case then Kenoe must be back in their apartment waiting for her! She needed to go.

"Shin, are you telling me you haven't talked to Kenoe since he left to go hunting?" Carin's expression morphed from dreamy to incredulous.

"Of course, I have. He calls me on my cell every evening."

"Cell?" Carin chuckled. Shinju didn't see what was so damned funny. She was miserable without Kenoe's presence, little more than a dim light in the corner of her mind rather than the vivid companion who accompanied her when he was close by.

"Shinju, I thought you and Kenoe had mated and bonded already?"

"What does that have to do with it?" She hadn't meant to snap but this was a subject she *so* didn't want to talk about right now. Not when uncharacteristic tears were so close to the surface at the thought of Kenoe in possible danger so far away. Before Kenoe had gone to hunt Dan the Mouse, she hadn't mentioned completing the bond and he hadn't asked. Could that be why he was barely a blip on her radar? She closed her eyes in regret at having avoided the subject of bonding.

"When a vampire mates, the couple shares a certain connection. Wait, Kenoe explained this part to you, right?"

"Yeah. We can speak when Kenoe is close by. But you said you were talking to Bix, who happens to be with Kenoe halfway around the world. That doesn't seem to qualify as close by."

"Duh." Carin sighed. "Back to the point. When you find a bondmate and accept the bond, the connection is profound, much deeper than a mating. Bix and I are bondmates and I can talk to him as clearly as I'm talking to you no matter where he is. The only thing we've found that can keep us from

communicating is a special neuron-inhibitor that acts as—"

"Whoa, whoa, whoa! First off, it makes my eyeballs cross when you and Kenoe launch into the biotech stuff. And second, you mean that once you made a commitment to the bond you could talk to Bix anywhere?"

At Carin's nod, a hole formed in Shinju's stomach, turned into a lead ball and fell out the bottom. She'd been the one putting off the whole bond thing. And, patient as he was, Kenoe hadn't pressed her about it. And what had been her reason for avoiding the whole magical business when she wanted nothing more than Kenoe anyway? There were plenty of grounds before. Now, she couldn't think of a single one. What if something happened to him? She wouldn't know where he was or what was going on. Stupid, stupid, stupid!

She went back to her cocoon on the couch and slipped into a fitful sleep filled with all kinds of gory possibilities involving Kenoe.

The next day, the members of the Council who planned to spend the rest of the summer there at the V.C.O.E. estate showed up in one fell swoop. Shinju found herself walking on eggshells except around Carin and Bix's children. Everyone was cordial and welcoming, but she was still finding her place as part of this vast household.

As for the children, Alaina was a three-year-old "old lady", a mini-brainiac version of her mother with her father's dark good looks. The child was, in a word, sharp as a blade and had a real knack for talking her way out of trouble. What three-year-old had a vocabulary that included the word "peptides"? And little Russian Bixler was the fattest, happiest baby Shinju had ever met. He wasn't much for sleeping when he should, but at barely a year old, the kid could put away steak and eggs for breakfast if Carin let him have it. Not to mention he was into everything,

almost walking like a pro and had several teeth already. Must be the vampire genes.

Both of them were too cute for words and occasionally playing with them gave Shinju an outlet for her teaching skills and kept her mind off of other things, like missing a certain Hatsept.

If she let them, the events of the past months sent her into a tailspin funk. First, discovering the man of her dreams was a vampire, then her brother and his Second had dabbled with their own genes by doing business with a human that trafficked vampire drugs, then almost getting herself killed by sheer stubbornness, and seeing both herself and her brother brought back from the brink of death only to watch Kenoe waltz off to take down rogues as if he were going to a Sunday tea. Not to mention leaving her behind when she definitely had a dog in this fight.

Then there was going to bed alone at night in a suite of apartments bigger than her whole house in Japan. Sleeping alone was something she'd been doing since she was a toddler, but now it felt downright lonely and *wrong* without that damned debonair and dangerous white-haired vamp of hers. The man had been correct—they called to each other, spirit, soul and body.

At least Max's secret didn't have to *be* a secret any longer. Kenoe knew all about, and accepted, her family. As long as Max stayed clear of vampire criminals, he was safe from V.C.O.E. law enforcement.

However, there was one thing Shinju still hadn't shared with Kenoe—her knowledge of the butt-kicking arts. She wasn't deliberately hiding it, but somehow after all they'd recently been through, it just didn't seem as important as it had before. Now, something else consumed her thoughts, something she

absolutely must find a way to accomplish. And that something was number two on her list of things to do. Number one was jump Kenoe and keep him ensconced in their apartments for at least three days after he returned.

In the meantime, the daily occurrence of breakfast was something to look forward to with Carin, and Carin's adopted mother, Alaana Serati, the Matriarch of Clan Serati. The history of vampires and their contributions to various societies and cultures down through the ages was quite interesting. Though learning that some of the people around her had been teenagers during the French and Indian Wars was a bit disconcerting. And the stories Ms. Alaana's bodyguard and second bondmate, Jaidyn, told about the Musketeers? Forget about it!

The extraction team under Bix's command had started on Japan's southern island and worked its way all over the country in pursuit of the first human on the V.C.O.E. Most Wanted list in centuries. So far, their contact, Raiden Vigee-Lamb, had gotten them within a hair's breadth of Dan the Mouse. But no cigar. The journey had brought them back to Tokyo.

Moving into position, they prepared to raid yet another nondescript warehouse.

Today, Kenoe ran point with Yuu. Tameth and Slade took flank with Raiden between them. Alaan and Bix brought up the rear. A second wave of four Beta Seekers and Iudex Judges waited for Kenoe's signal from a few blocks away. Two identical teams, tucked around the corner in an alley on the south side of the huge facility, mirrored their strategy.

The plan: Take out any faction-affiliated players between the entrance and the center of the building where Dan's lab was

reported to be. When all was clear, the Betas and Judges would join them. All four teams would meet up in the middle and take stock from there.

Kenoe tapped his earpiece. "Okay, team two, we're moving into the alley. Breach perimeter of the building in five minutes. See you inside."

At Kenoe's signal the Seekers, all bristling with weapons and stoking smoldering attitudes, moved as a single, cohesive unit toward the lair of their prey.

Kenoe kept a barely leashed snarl behind his lips as Raiden played escort, quietly directing them toward the hidden entrance to an underground warehouse. Raiden. *Pufft.* This was the owner of the scent he'd caught more than once near Shinju's home, but he was not the same vamp who'd accosted her cousin. The bastard was lucky. The only thing that kept him breathing was the fact that Bix had brokered a deal between this rogue and the Council. But it still wouldn't have stopped Kenoe from stomping a mud hole in his rabid ass if he'd been the one who'd waltzed onto Shinju's property with the sole goal of terrorizing Kimora.

All was shrouded in shadow. Kenoe moved carefully and made no sound as he stepped around greasy puddles and wads of trash. The walls seemed to press in on him. Smothering. Repressive. Good thing he wasn't claustrophobic.

Strange how dank and dreary this part of town was, considering it was barely midafternoon and nowhere near sundown.

An involuntary shiver worked its way up Kenoe's shins and lodged behind his kneecaps. This all seemed so familiar. Damn. He couldn't grasp it. Then suddenly it clicked into place—he'd been here before...in Shinju's memories. It was where Max had been attacked by a rogue and subsequently saved by Yuu Tof-

Li.

Kenoe crept up on the two outlaws guarding the entrance to the building. He curled up his lip—one of them had a scent like fermented cabbage. God, there was nothing like the stench of a vampire gone bad.

Before Yuu could plug the guy with his weapon of choice, Raiden screeched to a halt and dug in his heels.

"This is where I leave you, gentlemen," he said quietly to Kenoe before turning to Bix. "I'll be no good to you if I'm seen." Yeah, yeah, yeah, they'd already been down this road. The man didn't have to keep reminding them every time he took them to the starting point of a raid. "I'll check in with you in two days, Bixler. If Dan is not here, we'll set up the next stakeout at another likely location. I should have some additional intel by our next communication."

Both Kenoe and Bix nodded briskly, grunted and watched the man retreat, not moving an inch until his scent faded from their nostrils. Kenoe knew his commanding officer was thinking the same thing as himself—Raiden had played a big part in closing the gap between the V.C.O.E. and Dan, but the rogue helped them out of self-preservation and not out of any sense of honor or justice. Both Shinju and Carin had been targets of this man's boss, and Raiden was instrumental in Dan knowing where the women were and how to get to them. Kenoe just couldn't bring himself to be grateful for Raiden's presence or his help knowing the vamp would sell them out if given a big enough profit margin.

Kenoe cast a quick glance at Yuu, and the other man immediately matched his pace step for step as they met their first targets. Amazing. Six elite Seekers brought death on swift wings, yet the vamps were completely oblivious. In fact, they continued to talk about what they planned to do after they got

off their shift right up to the moment that Kenoe put a ten-second sleeper hold on one, and Yuu simply cold cocked the other, knocking him out with one punch. Piled next to the door they'd been guarding, the two rogues made an interesting heap of garbage.

Another tap on the earpiece. "Send two from Beta team one to secure the guards. You have one minute. Hatsept out."

Once inside, Kenoe braced himself against the onslaught of emotion brought by the memory of the pain and fear Shinju had shared with him about her visit inside this place. Pushing the thoughts away, he picked up the pace as he recalled the twists and turns his mate had taken to get to the center of the building. So far, it all looked just as she'd remembered. Thanks to Shinju, Kenoe knew exactly where to go.

A few flights down and through a narrow maze of hallways, they approached an unmarked door. The hair on the back of Kenoe's neck started dancing wildly.

Without slowing his pace, he tapped his earpiece again. "Be on guard," he whispered into his com unit. "I know how to get to the room Raiden claimed is Dan's lab, but I expect to meet some resistance."

"Why? We haven't seen anyone so far," Yuu replied.

"If Dan has been smart enough to stay one step ahead of us to this point, he's smart enough to surround his inner labs with more skilled outlaws than the ones guarding the door." This from Alaan, clearly in stalker mode, gun raised, eyes alert, body loose and ready to engage the enemy. "I hope he does have someone down here. I'm itching to plant my foot knee-deep in someone's ass." The growl in the bass of Alaan's voice made Kenoe glad that the man was on his side.

The quiet *thwipp* of a fired modified pistol broke the eerie silence as a slew of snarling vampire no-goods poured in

around them. Following the sound of the shot, Kenoe's gaze slammed into Bix's as the first casualty met the cement floor, courtesy of the Head Seeker himself.

Kenoe rolled his eyes. "Damn it, Bix! Didn't you just remind us all to take the guys alive if we could help it?"

"Yeah, well, I couldn't help it." Then Bix's dark, menacing expression morphed as he looked past Kenoe. He motioned over Kenoe's head and snapped, "Watch your back, Seeker."

That was enough of a warning for them all.

The entire team formed a small circle, backs to one another. Tameth, Bix and Kenoe all whipped their katanas from the sheaths hidden in the seams of their trench coats, while Alaan and Yuu dipped into their holsters and instantly held a gun in each hand, one full of bio barf bullets, the other loaded with silver hollow points.

In tandem, all three bio-smeared blades made contact with rogue vampires. Within seconds, the recipients of the stinging cuts hit the floor, retching like sick puppies. All over their comrades' shoes.

The distraction was perfect. Kenoe almost grinned when the approaching bad guys seemed to have trouble deciding whether to help their fallen friends, fight the growling Seekers in front of them or turn tail and run.

By the time they decided, Bix and Alaan had already taken out four more of the enemy between them. Yuu had taken down two of his own. Kenoe shot a buzz-cut vamp in the knee, sliced another across the chest and, thinking of Shinju, kicked yet another in the balls. And if anyone was taking count, Tameth had outdone them all.

In all, they took down sixteen rogues in less than ten minutes. Not bad, though none of them would have been surprised if the rogues claimed they'd been outnumbered.

"Hatsept here. Send in the Betas for clean-up and the Judges for sentencing. We've got a good crowd in here. Moving on. None of these guys are going anywhere. Hatsept out."

"Yo, guys!" Tameth called. "Over here."

"So, whatcha got there, Tam?" Kenoe teased as he sauntered her way, playing with his blade and showing a good bit of fang.

A vamp lay quivering at the woman's feet. His hair was a rare platinum blond in a riot of curls all over his head. Though a bit on the shorter side, he was stocky, wide-chested, muscular and obviously a fighter. In fact, he could have been the Mini-Me version of Alaan. With a hand clamped over his mouth, the vamp blanched to a strange shade of grayish-green. A deep cut bleeding through the sleeve of his shirt told enough of the story. And the uncontrollable heaving told the rest.

Striding over, Alaan picked the stocky vamp up by the collar and snarled into his face. "Look asshole, we've been instructed to take as many of you alive as possible. So in that, you're lucky. However, there's nothing in my orders that says I have to be nice about it. You have two fucking seconds to show us where Dan conducts his research or I'll turn you over to a Serati Seeker." The man paled when Alaan added, "A female Clan Serati Seeker." The rogue's mouth fell open. Alaan continued, "Who happens to have the cure for what ails ya." Then Alaan swung the scum around to face Tameth. A steamed and mightily pissed off Tameth bouncing a small bottle of clear liquid in her palm—the antidote. And the woman looked none too inclined to give it to him even if he did cooperate.

Again, self-preservation and lack of loyalty won the day. Between dry heaves, Big Blondie blabbered like his life depended on it...because it did.

After getting what they needed, Tameth reluctantly gave the

man an oral dose of the antidote. When he could manage to stay on his feet, Blondie led them further into the building to a room that wasn't on the original schematic.

Alaan once again took the rogue by the shirt. "This better be on the level or I'll let her carve your ass into little bitty pieces. Got me?"

The man nodded so swiftly, surely his brain was bouncing around his skull with the jarring motion.

With weapons drawn, they rushed into the room and came to a halt.

Kenoe glanced back at his teammates. "Looks like nobody's home but the rats. Or rather, the rats' leavings."

"We'll see," Bix growled. "How are the Beta Seekers doing in the other room?"

"Let me check." After a few seconds, Kenoe replied, "They've handed the perps over to the Iudex Judges. The vans are already in the alley loading them up. Orders?"

"Have any of the Betas not on escort duty join us. At least there's something here this time. Let's see what we can find, boys and girls." While Kenoe would have rather had Dan's neck between his hands, there was no mistaking Bix's take on the matter. This was, after all, the first time in weeks they'd managed to get close enough to Dan where the man hadn't had time to fully clean up after himself. The room was a goldmine.

The second the Betas arrived, Bix gave them instructions and they all set about tearing the place apart.

Loose papers, notebooks and boxes, both empty and occupied, were strewn throughout. Boxes of vials labeled as viable serum, skin and blood samples, small crates with master serums and various prototypes. Even several pieces of equipment had been left behind. Everything they needed to reverse engineer Dan's process for manufacturing the drugs he

peddled.

The only thing not in that damned warehouse was Dan himself.

Three hours later a call came from across the room near a far door that would take them up out of the maze of hallways and out to the street. "Head Seeker, we think you should see this."

Kenoe rode Bix's heels as he strode over to one of the Beta Seekers waving a small piece of paper. He read over his commanding officer's shoulders then cussed a blue streak.

"Fuck!" Kenoe fumed and Bix echoed his sentiment.

It was a copy of an application for a work visa for Dan. In fucking India. Well, at least they had a clue where he'd gone.

Alaan joined them, took one look at the document and clenched his jaw so tight Kenoe could have sworn he heard the man's teeth crack.

"You know what this means, right?" Alaan asked Bix.

"Yeah, I know what it means," he replied on a sigh. "I don't like it, but it makes our next steps easier to plan."

"What do you mean?" Kenoe queried. "We headin' to India?"

Bix turned eyes on him and said, "Nope. Doesn't make sense to follow what would obviously be a cold lead by the time we got there. It's a big-assed country. And just because Dan got a work visa in one part of the country doesn't mean he won't disappear into another. Better to let the territory leaders of the vampire clans over there pick up Dan's trail. The Seekers protecting the place are just as capable of delivering the man to V.C.O.E. custody as anyone else. I'll relay orders to that quarter after I hear from Raiden in a couple of days."

Kenoe was both relieved and pissed off when Bix tapped his earpiece and radiocd to the plane. "Perform the pre-flight check.

Nothing more we can do here. We're going home."

Damn.

Barely awake, Shinju cracked open an eye and noticed the curtains had been pulled back. Warmth eased over naked skin as the first light of the new day lazily streamed through the sliding glass doors leading to the master balcony. Shinju smiled sleepily, knowing those curtains had been shut tight when she'd gone to bed. Which could only mean one yummy, overdue thing.

"*Good morning, lovely,*" floated into her semi-conscious mind.

Mmm, she knew that voice. Smooth, just shy of deep, and invitingly sultry. Knew that when she looked up, the owner of said voice, who her mind and body ached for, would no longer whisper from a little corner of her mind. No dream. He was real, solid and scant inches from her body.

"Kenoe."

Shinju reached up and connected with the firm, warm flesh of his chest. Underneath the skin, the muscles rippled, tightened, then relaxed under her touch. His locs teased her shoulders and arms, giving the illusion of a thousand tiny little caressing fingers.

She wrapped her arms around his neck and squeezed for all she was worth. The sense of relief at his return eased the weight of worry that had taken up residence in her chest. It was amazing to discover that even homesickness for Japan and Max didn't touch the anxiety she'd forced down while Kenoe hunted far from home.

Then his lips were on hers, his hands explored from collarbone to knees. They both exhilarated and soothed the burning need that had built over the days and weeks he'd been away. He didn't say a word. Didn't need to. She felt the barely leashed hunger beating at him, through him until it surrounded her, fed the craving that gnawed at her own soul.

In mere moments the kisses and caresses turned wild and rough. Mmm, there was that growly thing he did just before his fangs came out to play.

Kenoe's sexy moans sent Shinju's temperature soaring. A mix of goose bumps and sweat erupted all over her body as she twisted and writhed. Body heat soared and the plump lips of her sex swelled and ached. His hard, scalding length eased back and forth, sliding along the sensitive bundle of nerves of her clit while he nipped and taunted her nipples.

God she wanted him to suck on them until he inhaled her. Wanted him to slide deep. Wanted him so bad it bordered on desperate.

"Kenoe, I missed you. Missed this," she panted, tilting her neck a bit more to give him better access to the spot he was sucking. She'd probably have a hickey later.

"Do you want me, lovely?"

Was he kidding? Want him? Was there a single word in English for can't-breathe-without-you-please-fuck-me-like-an-animal?

He chuckled, obviously having plucked her thoughts from the air.

"Not hard to do, Shin. You're projecting like a fire beacon."

"Then put out my fire!"

"Open for me, lovely. Open wide." The fat, plump tip of his cock pulsed as it eased into the heated passage of her pussy.

One large hand went to her hip, the other anchored underneath her shoulder.

Then her man went wild. And she met him stroke for stroke, shouting her joy to the mountains just across the valley and anyone else who cared to listen.

For a split second, Shinju wondered if similar conversations were occurring in other parts of the mansion.

Carin's eyes were plastered to the play of well-developed muscle all along Bix's chest and back, watching droplets of water slide beneath the damp towel draped over his hips. He'd come in before dawn, hopped in the shower and eased silently into their bedroom.

She'd clicked on the nightstand lamp just as he reached his side of the bed. He turned in surprise and the towel fell away. She sighed in appreciation of the view.

"What are you still doing up? It's almost dawn."

"I felt you come in." She tossed the covers back on his side and he climbed in. Her heart rate shot off the charts. God, the man simply got to her.

Clearing her throat, she clenched her hands at her sides to keep them to herself. This was a ritual of sorts between them now—he came in, gave her a quick rundown of the mission, then they fucked like bunnies. She was trying *really* hard not to skip to step three.

"Dan got away."

"That was *so* not what I wanted to hear," Carin said.

"Before we came home we managed to secure the aid of an insider who's switched allegiance. Smart rogue. He realizes that sooner or later we'll catch up to Dan now that we know what he's about. He'd rather work for us than end up in vampire jail

or executed. God, I can't believe Dan and his minions have managed to fly under the radar for three years straight."

"Why not? He's working with rogues. Can you think of a single vampire bad guy that would purposely bring himself to a Seeker's attention unless he was turning himself in?"

"You always were a smart woman." Bix scooted close and nuzzled her ear.

"Yeah, your better half." Carin giggled, welcoming the arms coming around her.

"So now what?" she whispered on the leading edge of a contented sigh.

"We're already gathering intel for the next mission to take him down. He's the first human on the V.C.O.E. Most Wanted list in centuries. Should make for an interesting project."

"For both of us," she breathed, nipping the strong tendons of his throat.

Bix pushed back, settled his weight on his hands and tilted his head in question. Even if Carin hadn't been so skilled at picking up his emotions she would have caught on anyway. The man was already thinking there was no way she was going on that mission.

"With a human blatantly in the middle of vampire affairs, not counting Shinju and myself of course, that means I'll have to make some changes in the formulations I'm working on. They're all engineered for the metabolisms of vampire bad guys."

"I think I can help you with that...for a price."

"Oh, really?" she snorted.

"Dan cleared out quick. I've got all kinds of goodies from our raid on his makeshift lab. And some of them will no doubt look familiar."

She sat up in the bed so fast it sent him flying onto his back in a near sprawl. Sometimes she forgot some of the benefits of being mated to a vampire—enhanced strength, doncha know. "You're kidding! It's my stuff from Idac, isn't it? Son of a bitch! Just wait! I'm gonna kick—"

"Carin!"

"What?"

"Woman, put that energy of yours to better use. It's time for step three."

With that she went willingly back into his arms to forget about Dan the Mouse for one more day. Well, maybe two.

Chapter Seventeen

At breakfast with Alaana and Carin, Shinju learned that her official audience with the Head Seeker had been granted. It would take place in two hours in one of the hardwood-floored sparring rooms. She was grateful the man hadn't asked what she wanted and simply trusted it was important.

When she arrived, the room was empty. Standing there alone, she did a few deep breathing exercises to calm her nerves. She needed to perform shortly and while she was never completely calm in the middle of such things, it wouldn't do for her to be a basket case either.

A few minutes later Bix walked in, followed by his Second, Alaan, then Tameth. All were decked out in Seeker gear and armed to the teeth. Everything seemed normal.

Then to her surprise, Kenoe walked into the room behind his fellow Seekers. Immediately his head tilted sideways in question.

Bix stopped in front of her, braced his legs apart and folded his arms over his huge chest. The outline of sculpted muscle was visible through the stretchy fitted sports tee. The mantle of power this man wielded was cloaked around him and he carried it with grace and ease. This wasn't the Bix who joked with them when off duty, or backed his wife into a corner and kissed her silly when he thought no one was looking. This was a seasoned

warrior standing in his office as the chief enforcer of his people.

She looked from Bix to Kenoe and back again. Alaan and Tameth were no surprise—Alaan went everywhere Bix went, and Tameth was next in rank. But why in the world had she expected Bix to keep Kenoe out of this? Shinju wasn't stupid enough to ask, but her body language gave her away.

"I may be high up on the V.C.O.E. food chain," Bix stated clearly. "But Kenoe overrules me, the Council and anyone else when it comes to matters of your safety. And I have a feeling he may want the opportunity to do just that."

"Shin?" Kenoe sent the query quietly into her head. She sent back reassurance that nothing was wrong. In fact, if this went as expected, she didn't think her life could get any more perfect.

Without further ado, Bix signaled the start of the meeting. "So, Shinju, what can I do for you?"

Shinju locked her knees and blurted the words out. "I want to be a Seeker."

Bix and Alaan both looked at Kenoe, who'd promptly gone ashen. She didn't think she'd ever seen him that, or any other, shade of gray.

"I can already fight. Max saw to it that I was trained in the arts of war, including hand-to-hand combat and blade training since I was old enough to hold a katana."

Terror, palpable and vivid, flashed through to her, so strong she almost flinched.

"What? Shinju, a Seeker? Are you crazy?" Kenoe protested. Loudly. His arctic focus on Bix, he lowered his voice to what would have sounded polite except for the dangerous snarl accompanying the words.

"Sir, with all due respect, I do not agree with your even

considering drafting Shinju into the corps."

"Draft?" With the smirk from hell plastered firmly across his mouth, Bix said, "It wasn't my idea." His gaze swung a hard left and landed on Shinju.

"Shinju Deni Maruyama," Kenoe snapped. Hmm, never a good sign when your lover used your whole name in a sentence. "Who the hell put you up to this? Tameth? Carin?"

Okay, now *that* pissed her off.

"What, I can't come up with a great idea on my own?"

Kenoe's jaw clenched and for the first time since he'd run from the debauched harem of his half-brother decades ago, he saw red. Opaque, almost stifling, anger-laced red.

The mere thought of his woman, his *human* woman, even *thinking* about accompanying a group of hardened vampires on a rogue hunt sent his blood streaking inward. A heart attack was surely imminent. The next thing Kenoe knew, he was in her face and not at all sure how he'd gotten there from across the room. Her request was so outrageous, he simply didn't care about propriety.

"Don't even think about twisting my words, woman. And it's not a great idea, damn it! It's stupid and dangerous!"

"Back. The. Hell. Up. And stop yelling at me."

"Yelling? You're lucky that's all I'm doing!" He wanted to grab her by the shoulders and shake her until she saw either stars or common sense. Instead, he clawed his way toward some semblance of self-control and met her snarl with one of his own. Kenoe didn't miss the fact that everyone else had backed up a few steps.

"Look, Shin, you are not hunting rogues, period. If you think I'll permit such a thing you are out of your fucking mind! It's too dangerous *and* you're a human. Not even an enhanced

one, like Carin, because you won't bond with me or take my goddamned blood!" Who cared if the final word had come out a roof-shaking bellow?

"Kenoe Hatsept, are you cussing at me?"

"Look, woman—"

"You think I can't protect myself because I'm just a plain ole human? Well, prepare to defend yourself!"

Kenoe knew Tameth could have easily stopped Shinju from getting to the blade tucked into the modified sheath that ran along the spine of her trench coat, but his fellow Seeker didn't even flinch when Shinju went for it. Instead, her lips morphed into a proud parent-type grin. Figured.

Three-foot blade in hand, Shinju dropped into a wide horse stance.

"Shin, what the hell are you thinking?" Kenoe snapped.

"I said," she gritted out, "prepare to defend yourself."

With that, the sting from hell streaked across Kenoe's chest as the blade in Shinju's hand left a thin trail of blood across his pecs. Damned woman had ruined his shirt. It now hung limply from his body with a gaping diagonal slash across the middle.

"Woman, are you out of your fucking mind? Oh, wait. I already know the answer to that one."

She didn't bother to reply, but came at him again, this time her intent clear when her gaze dropped for a split second to a spot just a hair below his waist.

At the last second, Kenoe slipped his own katana out of its back holster and blocked a ruthless slice headed for his groin.

"Damn it, if you ever want to be a mother, watch where you point that thing!"

"Talk is cheap, Seeker. Surely a mere human couldn't do you any harm. So bring it."

He laughed and all it did was fire her up more. But there was no help for it. He knew exactly what she was up to. And he must be just as crazy because he felt a feral smile spread across his lips. The sight of her preparing to skewer him turned him on like nothing else.

So the woman was not only a wildcat in the sack...she was a wildcat, period. And a skilled one, he thought as he lowered his katana to block a slice headed for his ankle. He'd expected her to be good given her quietly kept background, which she obviously thought he didn't know about.

A flux of fierce determination slammed into his consciousness. Shinju's determination. Why the need to fight him so hard? Why not just let him wrap her up in his love and keep her happy, safe and content for the rest of her days? Suddenly it became clear as polished glass. Bottom line—Shinju needed this. Needed to avenge her brother and be the one to take care of *him* for a change.

It was something he could relate to all too well, having spent most of his early years with nothing on his mind but revenge. His single minded dedication to becoming a Seeker was for the sole purpose of dispatching his own brother. And he'd been so consumed, it had almost cost him his soul. He couldn't let that happen to Shinju. Yet how could he deny her the opportunity to seek what he so thoroughly understood?

Then another thought occurred to him—she'd made her choice. To train as a Seeker, Shinju had to make a commitment to remain among his kind and live as one of them. Live...with him? Permanently, as in bonded?

"Yes, blockhead. Took you long enough," she hissed into his brain. But that hiss carried with it a dose of love and a dash of humor. *"Now, let's see if you can kick my ass. You win, you make dinner. No McDonald's."*

That could certainly be arranged. *"Snarky-assed woman."*

Taking her measure, Kenoe blocked each kendo cut, each slash. She was good, very good. Her half and full cuts were made with perfect form. Nothing less than he expected. Yet he had the advantage of height, reach and vampire speed. And he sure as hell would use them.

A silent chuckle was pulled out of him when he felt along the bond, looking for any weakness, any dent in her defenses. He encountered a wall of irritation that quickly gave way to flat-out refusal to lose.

He pushed through it and sent a tune of arousal streaking into her thoughts. Kenoe's keen nose easily picked her scent out from the others in the room. Salty sweat mixed with the unique smell of the sweet nectar gathering between her legs. With every other clash of their blades, Kenoe sent an imaginary stroke along her inner thigh, up the curve of her ass and down her spine. God it was killing him to concentrate on so many things at once—one, bombarding her with naked, frantic images of what he had in store for her once he got her out of here; two, keeping his head on his shoulders as she tried to slice-n-dice him; and three, commanding his unruly cock to stop screaming and wait to claim her.

So instead of working it out on his own, every thought that had just flashed into his brain now flashed into hers, including the throb of need through his now marble-hard erection.

"And the balls being squashed by these damned pants when they'd rather have your tongue tickling that sensitive little spot just on the underside."

Shinju gasped and almost tripped over her own feet.

Kenoe turned on the natural speed and strength borne of a vampire and pressed her hard while she was distracted. The next thing he knew, a collective "aah" sounded from those

present as he sent Shinju's katana skidding across the floor toward the other side of the room. Instantly, Kenoe's blade was at the pulse point of her throat.

"Hey, that's not fair!" She was panting now, and not all from exertion.

"Yeah, but I don't play fair. And neither do the rogues you want to hunt."

With his hand full of her silky waves, she was forced to swallow something she'd seldom tasted in her life—defeat. The woman yielded, and not a second too soon. If he didn't get her out of there he would strip her on the spot and take her on the floor.

The second Bix nodded in acknowledgement of his triumph, Kenoe dropped his blade where he stood, tossed a shrieking Shinju over his shoulder and disappeared through the door.

The adrenaline from their blade encounter still pumped through their bodies as Kenoe took the stairs three at a time. Once inside their apartment, the man slammed the door and stripped faster than any male alive. Before Shinju could let out a good squawk, she found herself with her nose inches from the living room carpet, newborn naked and ass up over the thighs of an equally bare Kenoe.

It was like the man had made her drink a hot mug of "Instant Horny". He couldn't kiss her enough, touch her enough, caress the hidden places of her mind enough. Scratching at the carpet, she let out a breathy moan.

His fingers were everywhere. Not a single stretch of skin escaped attention. Trimmed nails scraped lightly over her sensitized body, leaving goose bumps in their wake.

"Want me?" he asked.

"Dumb question," she replied with a gasp. Squirming caused the silky smooth ridge of flesh between his legs to massage and tease her breasts. His cock was so hard and hot it practically scalded her. So she squirmed some more.

It felt so good. But good wasn't nearly enough.

"God, Kenoe. You're depriving me of cock."

He lowered his head, rubbed his face back and forth across her shoulders, then dragged his locs down her back while inhaling the scent of her skin.

Shinju shuddered.

"Say the magic words."

"Make me," she challenged with a growl.

"Oh lovely, I've already made you." His fingers dipped lower and found her wet and ready.

God, he was so right. She was a damned cock addict thanks to this chic, handsome vampire.

"Now, the words, Shin."

"Spank me."

And he did. His large hand came down on her ass which automatically pushed back at him, seeking more, needing that slight edge of rough play she'd always desired in a lover. Sure, the psychologists said that any woman who put up with being struck by a man needed counseling. Then she must need a lifetime's worth, because the controlled contact of skin on skin, with that little touch of sting, sent her pussy up in flames.

Maybe those psychologists who swore this kind of foreplay was a bad thing needed to experience a good spanking once in a while?

In between the firm pats, one hand massaged the individual bones of her spine while the other pressed past her creaming slit and teased her clit with a light tap and a circular

caress or two.

"Oh God, yes!"

Kenoe shifted, positioned her flaming body exactly the way he wanted then slid home in one firm thrust.

Yes, this was what she craved, what she needed—jungle sex with Kenoe, the one man who touched her inside and out, accompanied by a rosy ass, a stuffed pussy and carpet burns. Hell yes!

He couldn't get close enough, couldn't get deep enough. The words that tumbled from her kiss-swollen lips were his undoing.

"Kenoe, I want you. Deeper. More."

So he slammed his hips forward. When Shinju pressed her hand into his chest to gain his attention, his head cocked to the side in curiosity and concern.

"That's not what I meant. Bond with me. Join with me."

Still buried in her welcoming body, Kenoe went completely still.

"Shinju, are you sure? If you need more time, I—"

"Right here. Right now. I need you in a way I can't explain. It's too profound, too deep. Too much. Please, Kenoe. I'm so ready for this." Her sweat-slick fingers touched the side of his face and smoothed an errant loc back behind his ear. And the love she had for him shone in her eyes, echoed into him with every beat of her heart. "But let me taste you first, because once you bite me I'm going to explode." Her voice was strained, barely a whisper. Her hot pussy flexed and pulsed around him, and he realized she was trying oh-so-hard not to come.

Keeping himself buried deep, he rolled them over until she was on top. Then with a quick nip, a decent flow of his life force

oozed up out of the skin at the fold between forearm and elbow. She leaned forward and the soft globes of her breasts burned into his chest when full, sensual lips wrapped around the wound and pulled hard. Kenoe held his breath and hoped his head didn't pop off his body. Holy shit! It was the first time she'd taken him this way of her own accord. It was damned sexy and so erotic it was all he could do to stay in his skin.

And she just kept going, sucking and pulling at the flesh, sending him higher and higher. Like the Energizer Bunny, the woman was insatiable. If she didn't stop soon, he'd literally see stars.

Then again it was so damned good perhaps he was due for a close-up with the sun.

"Stop, Shin. It feels so good, I can't take anymore."

When she looked up, the glazed expression told him she was right there with him. With a single swipe of her tongue across her bottom lip, not a single drop of blood escaped.

"My turn," he drawled.

Lifting just enough to get a mouthful of breast, he bit down, suckling her nipple and the sweet nectar of her blood as he shuttled his cock in and out of her sopping wet folds.

One deep stroke, then two. His heart beat so fast he was surprised it hadn't just given up trying to pump blood through his body.

Three strokes, four. Her gasps became screams as she held his head to her breast and begged him to take more of her.

Five. Oh God!

Six. Fuck!

The disgust she'd expected to experience when Kenoe bit into the fleshy part of his arm and pressed it to her lips had

never materialized. It simply couldn't compete against the craving beating at her through the connection she shared with him. He wanted this, wanted this tie with her more than... God, there just weren't words.

But nothing in the known universe could have prepared her for the power-driven, wildly wicked flare of lust and love that rocketed through every cell of her body at that first taste of his life source.

Tears gathered beneath her closed lids when he was suddenly *so* there, filling her mind, her heart, her very soul.

Shinju's womb spasmed as the honeyed walls of her sex clamped down on his cock. They exploded together as the final, fragile tendrils of their bond strengthened and wrapped around their hearts to knit them together. Forever.

Chapter Eighteen

One year later

"Shinju Maruyama, please step forward."

Shinju stepped out from the small crowd of graduates and approached the Council dais. She was the last one to receive her commendations. Decked out in black urban camo pants and matching tactical shirt, shoulder harness complete with titanium coated Taurus SP-99 handgun, and a special blade sheath that extended down her back, she climbed the stairs and stopped in front of Bix, biting her lip to keep from grinning.

She'd done it! She'd made Seeker with full rank and recognition, and in record time too. Her status might be near the bottom of the rung for a full Seeker, but she was still well on her way considering she'd outperformed, and now outranked, her fellow classmates, who'd graduated to the Beta Seeker ranks.

Alaana Serati, the Matriarch of Clan Serati, approached. Shinju's knees began a funky little buzz just below the caps. Then Kenoe bounded to the forefront of her mind. With a sigh of relief, she accepted her mate's surge of pride and strength as it filled and fortified her.

"Usually the Head Seeker makes these presentations, but I asked if I could do this one. Shinju, you are a very special young lady and I am so very proud of you," said Alaana. Barely

taller than Shinju, this woman was as sweet as she was formidable. Alaan's mother had platinum curls and jewel blue eyes, just like her son. And she was so beautiful it was hard to believe that she was one of the oldest females in the room. Not to mention she was the Elder for the Western Territories on top of being responsible for the only matriarchic Clan in the vampire nation with the baddest female warriors on the planet. Including her daughter-in-law, Tameth, and her adopted daughter, Carin.

"You have done something that has not been accomplished in a very long time. As a human, you have not only completed but excelled in your chosen profession as a Seeker for the Vampire Council of Ethics."

A loud, raucous cheer echoed through the room. God, these people were a rowdy bunch. And it was right up her alley.

"All of your classmates and peers speak highly of your skills and tenacity. And you've also improved a thing or two in the culinary department as well."

A chuckle spread through the crowd, along with an occasional muffled "Thank God!"

"I am so proud to present to you the denotation of your rank. Congratulations, Shinju."

The applause was deafening as Bix stepped over to the Council's table, picked up a sleek garment, and spread the black custom leather trench coat of a Seeker over her shoulders. She looked up then blinked back tears as she caught her brother and Sasuke dabbing their eyes on the sly. On the other hand, Carin and Tameth were doing a fair job of soaking tissues as well.

Is everybody in the place bawling? she wondered with a loud sniff and watery smile.

She slipped her arms through the sleeves and preened,

noting that her coat matched Kenoe's in every way, with the exception of being cut for her height. With a bow to the Council she turned to leave the dais.

"Hold, Shinju, remain where you are. We're not quite finished yet." Alaana's voice was still friendly, but a hint of steel had crept into the words. Certainly she couldn't be in trouble already, seeing as she'd just received her position.

Alaana nodded to Bix, and he went to stand on the floor with all the other Seekers, Beta Seekers, Iudex Judges and vampire clan members.

With something akin to trepidation swimming around in her gut, out of the corner of her eye Shinju watched her man break ranks and approach the platform. He stopped just short of the bottom step and stood watching her like a predator eyeing a meal. What was it that made her want to flee…right to their bed? Was it the fire and ice in his gaze as it raked her over from head to toe or the gleaming fangs just visible from his one-sided grin? Yeah, she knew that look all right—something was up. Damned man. She'd get him later.

Alaana motioned to the crowd at large and all went quiet.

"It is my honor to claim yet another daughter as my own. Shinju, will you accept a place in the Matriarchy of Clan Serati as an adopted daughter of the Clan Elders and sister to every Serati female?"

The entire throng went completely still. It was so quiet you could have heard a pin drop on the thick plush carpet.

Oh. My. God! Now *this* she was not expecting. Shinju was going to be Clan Serati? Which meant Kenoe would be both Hatsept and Serati since he was mated to her.

The only sound was Alaan's deep voice as he grumbled into the silence. "Aw hell, not another one." Of course Tameth and Carin shot him a glance sharp enough to cut steel.

With a nod and a hug from Alaana Serati, Shinju Maruyama, a little schoolteacher from Shibuya district in Tokyo was now a Serati female who suddenly had a higher social standing than every natural and adopted male in her new Clan.

Including the most dangerously sexy man she'd ever known. And that man stood watching from below, yet all that flowed through to her was fierce pride and a deep, abiding love.

Alaana was speaking again, but Shinju was so caught up in the sizzling look Kenoe passed her way she almost missed what the Elder was saying.

"Kenoe Hatsept, please come forward. This is long overdue."

Strong, long legs carried him up the stairs. What came next was perplexing and equally unexpected. Shinju wasn't sure what to do with her feelings when her man not only bowed to Alaana—well, respect to Alaana made sense—but he lowered his head in deference to Shinju.

Amazing. This man who'd accepted her as she was, regardless of what he knew of her and her family. A man who'd taught her that she deserved to be happy, deserved to be loved. Who'd spent his life protecting humans and vampires alike from those who would hunt them. Yet he bowed to her? Talk about a humbling experience.

Then he moved closer. And closer still.

"Last order of business, you two." Alaana interrupted what was sure to have been a toe-hair-singeing kiss.

"Shinju, as is the right of each member of our Clans, you're now entitled to take the name of your new family. We are aware that you two had a private joining ceremony, yet we wish to add our blessing to your mating and bonding. So without further ado, Shinju Serati-Maruyama, daughter of Clan Serati and Seeker for the Vampire Council of Ethics, we wish to acknowledge the finding of your mate and bondmate, Seeker

Kenoe Hatsept, son of Clan Hatsept and now son of Clan Serati."

A gasp of shock echoed around the room, including one from both Shinju and Kenoe. Shinju bit her lip again to keep a grin from spreading across her lips. After all, she'd put this off far too long. It didn't matter that everyone knew they were mated. Kenoe deserved a woman who'd make a public commitment to him, and not just quietly share his life, his bed. Shinju was so ready to be that woman even though he'd pretended to be content with the private joining, careful not to pressure her into going before the Council to seek their blessing.

The Elders seated around the exquisite, ornate carved half-moon table stood. Every eye was plastered on her and Kenoe as Alaana spoke.

"Do the Elders of Clans Serati, Vigee, Li and Sewell recognize the mating of Seeker Serati-Maruyama and Seeker Hatsept?" Alaana continued with the traditional questioning of the Council Elders. All ten answered in the affirmative and Shinju felt herself get more and more giddy as the ceremony proceeded until she was practically cackling in her mind.

"Seeker Shinju Serati-Maruyama and Seeker Kenoe Hatsept, we the Elders of the vampire clans, representatives of the Vampire Council of Ethics, recognize not only your mating but your bonding as well. We wish you goodly success. Shinju, you may now claim your bondmate."

Oh hell. As the higher ranking female, it was up to her to claim Kenoe by "blessing" him with her blood. What was she supposed to do, considering she didn't quite have the apparatus to draw any? Relief flooded through her when Tameth eased forward and slipped her a small Swiss Army knife. Nothing fancy, but it would work.

The sleeve of her new trench coat was pushed up, followed by her long-sleeved tee until both bundled beneath her underarm. Next came the sting of the pocketknife as she nicked her forearm just deep enough for the blood to flow.

Kenoe didn't hesitate to latch on, wrapping his beautiful lips around the wound, laving it. Licking it. God, how could something so earthy and elemental be so damned sexy at the same time? And with each draw on her flesh, the temperature of her body ratcheted up a notch until she was so hot all she wanted was for him to strip her bare and ride her into oblivion.

Now it was her turn. Kenoe nipped the tip of his middle finger. The symbolism wasn't lost on Shinju and she unashamedly sucked the digit into her mouth and drew it in deeply.

This time when she took Kenoe's blood, the bond they'd formed alone in their apartments instantly strengthened. It slipped from under the skin, down into the sinew and muscle, through the nerve endings and into her very blood. This was beyond profound, beyond deep. Beyond soul-stirring. And she'd denied Kenoe this for so long? A wispy cloud of sadness settled over her, obscuring the gaiety of the moment, now that she realized what both she and her man had been missing because of her ambivalence of consummating the bond with the blessing of the Council.

Committing to the bond, just the two of them, had been fine for her. But now that she realized the power that came along with the Council blessing, Kenoe was more than good enough to receive such a gift.

"Kenoe, I'm so sorry," she sobbed against his chest. "You wanted our joining to be special. I thought it was. I just didn't understand, didn't know it would be like this. I avoided this for so long, had no idea what I was keeping from you. This is so

much more, and I deprived you of such a depth of feeling—"

She was rambling but just couldn't help it. She felt so selfish that the regret just poured out of her.

"There was no way you could have truly known what it would feel like to receive the blessing of the Council. It's not a requirement, just a little something extra. This is old, innate magic. Don't cry, lovely. You know what it does to me. Besides, this is a happy time for us. Let's enjoy it, all right?"

As Kenoe wrapped her in his embrace, any sadness was replaced with joy and quite a bit of carnal buzz for two reasons: the stream of happiness flowing from Kenoe stripped away the gloom, and his burgeoning hard-on pressed into her belly.

Now that always got her attention.

Her husband and bondmate before the Clans, he stepped back and said to the crowd at large, "I am proud to be mated to such a strong Serati female."

"But it doesn't change anything that happens between us once we close the apartment door behind us, Kenoe. You're still the man."

He cut her a heated glance and flashed that near-orgasm-inducing smile of his.

"And you're still my freak?"

"Damned right," she sighed into his mouth as he dipped low for a kiss and swept her literally off her feet. Again.

About the Author

Born into a musically eclectic family, TJ's first love is music. She enjoys singing, even outside of the shower. So, where does this writing stuff come in? It actually began with reading. TJ is an avid reader and you'll find her with her head buried in a book every day of the week, whether it's her own creation or something snagged at the bookstore.

What about ideas? Working for an interesting organization allows her to interact with even more interesting customers. With an imagination expanded beyond belief after the birth of her two (now teenaged) children, spinning life's experiences into tales is a blast! And now that books have caught up to technology, TJ's eBook reader is shown no mercy, forced to entertain her at all hours of the day or night. Even in the dark!

Her favorite compositions are multicultural romances in various genres, some naughty, none nice. She currently lives out West with her two children, and enjoys working as a technical resource with a company that provides analytical solutions to lifesciences companies.

To learn more about TJ Michaels, please visit www.tjmichaels.com. Send an email to TJ@tjmichaels.com, subscribe to her newsletter, *TJ On A Tangent*, to join in the fun with other readers and authors, as well as TJ.

One woman's mission to bring down a sexy elemental shifter turns into a battle of wills...and hearts.

Into the Mist
© 2008 Maya Banks
Falcon Mercenary Group, Book 1.

Hostage recovery specialist Eli Chance has a secret. He was born a shifter. A freak of nature.

While on a mission, Eli's men and their mercenary guide are exposed to a powerful chemical agent, and suddenly his secret has become easier to hide. Now he's not the only one with the gift. But for his men, this "gift" is becoming more and more of a curse.

Tyana Berezovsky's brother Damiano was the guide for Eli's team and was the worst affected by the chemical. As he grows increasingly unstable, Tyana fears she's going to lose him to the beast he is becoming.

Tyana will do whatever it takes to help him, even if it means using her body to go after the one man she thinks holds all the blame—and possibly the cure. Eli Chance.

Warning: Violence, blood, guns, knives, ass kicking, people who do mean things, bad people dying, explicit sex and smart mouths.

Available now in ebook and print from Samhain Publishing.

For two Seekers of justice, hunting rogues is dangerous business. But not as dangerous as their yearning for each other.

Serati's Flame
© *2007 T.J. Michaels*
Vampire Council of Ethics, Book 2

There's a rogue on the loose, and the Vampire Council of Ethics has just the man for the job. Alaan Serati, along with his team of elite fighters, is a Seeker for the V.C.O.E. The lethal vampire law enforcement assassin is also the most eligible bachelor of Clan Serati. His job: Take out the rogue vampire who killed his mate years ago. But working with a fellow Seeker quickly becomes a pain in his backside. How is he supposed to accomplish the mission if he can't keep his mind or his hands off of his fellow officer?

For more years than she wants to remember, Tameth Serati-Cole has worked almost every day, side by side, with the gruff and gorgeous Alaan. It's been hell considering the special bond between them, something rarely developed between mates. But Alaan doesn't really want her. He's still pining away for the woman taken from him years ago. So when he declares his need to bond with her, this lady Seeker ain't biting…even if she's wanted to since the day they met.

Available now in ebook and print from Samhain Publishing.

GET IT NOW

MyBookStoreAndMore.com

GREAT EBOOKS, GREAT DEALS . . . AND MORE!

Don't wait to run to the bookstore down the street, or waste time shopping online at one of the "big boys." Now, all your favorite Samhain authors are all in one place—at MyBookStoreAndMore.com. Stop by today and discover great deals on Samhain—and a whole lot more!

WWW.SAMHAINPUBLISHING.COM

GREAT CHEAP FUN

Discover eBooks!

THE FASTEST WAY TO GET THE HOTTEST NAMES

Get your favorite authors on your favorite reader, long before they're out in print! Ebooks from Samhain go wherever you go, and work with whatever you carry—Palm, PDF, Mobi, and more.

Samhain Publishing Ltd

WWW.SAMHAINPUBLISHING.COM

Printed in the United States
145741LV00003B/67/P